DAWN

ELEANOR H. PORTER

1ST WORLD
LIBRARY
Literary Society

Dawn

Eleanor H. Porter

© 1st World Library, 2008
PO Box 2211
Fairfield, IA 52556
www.1stworldlibrary.com
First Edition

LCCN: 2007935377

Softcover ISBN: 978-1-4218-9326-6
Hardcover ISBN: 978-1-4218-9426-3
eBook ISBN: 978-1-4218-9226-9

Purchase *"Dawn"*
as a traditional bound book at:
www.1stWorldLibrary.com/purchase.asp?ISBN=978-1-4218-9326-6

1st World Library Literary Society

Giving Back to the World

"If you want to work on the core problem, it's early school literacy."

- James Barksdale, former CEO of Netscape

"No skill is more crucial to the future of a child, or to a democratic and prosperous society, than literacy."

- Los Angeles Times

"Literacy... means far more than learning how to read and write... The aim is to transmit... knowledge and promote social participation."

- UNESCO

"Literacy is not a luxury, it is a right and a responsibility. If our world is to meet the challenges of the twenty-first century we must harness the energy and creativity of all our citizens."

- President Bill Clinton

"Parents should be encouraged to read to their children, and teachers should be equipped with all available techniques for teaching literacy, so the varying needs and capacities of individual kids can be taken into account."

- Hugh Mackay

To My Friend

MRS. JAMES D. PARKER

CONTENTS

CHAPTER I

THE GREAT TERROR

It was on his fourteenth birthday that Keith Burton discovered the Great Terror, though he did not know it by that name until some days afterward. He knew only, to his surprise and distress, that the "Treasure Island," given to him by his father for a birthday present, was printed in type so blurred and poor that he could scarcely read it.

He said nothing, of course. In fact he shut the book very hastily, with a quick, sidewise look, lest his father should see and notice the imperfection of his gift.

Poor father! He would feel so bad after he had taken all that pains and spent all that money—and for something not absolutely necessary, too! And then to get cheated like that. For, of course, he had been cheated—such horrid print that nobody could read.

But it was only a day or two later that Keith found some more horrid print. This time it was in his father's weekly journal that came every Saturday morning. He found it again that night in a magazine, and yet again the next day in the Sunday newspaper.

Then, before he had evolved a satisfactory explanation in his own mind of this phenomenon, he heard Susan Betts talking with Mrs. McGuire over the back-yard fence.

Susan Betts began the conversation. But that was nothing strange: Susan Betts always began the conversation.

"Have you heard about poor old Harrington?" she demanded in what Keith called her "excitingest" voice. Then, as was always the case when she spoke in that voice, she plunged on without waiting for a reply, as if fearful lest her bit of news fall from the other pair of lips first. "Well, he's blind—stone blind. He couldn't see a dollar bill—not if you shook it right before his eyes."

"Sho! you don't say!" Mrs. McGuire dropped the wet sheet back into the basket and came to the fence on her side concernedly. "Now, ain't that too bad?"

"Yes, ain't it? An' he so kind, an' now so blind! It jest makes me sick." Susan whipped open the twisted folds of a wet towel. Susan seldom stopped her work to talk. "But I saw it comin' long ago. An' he did, too, poor man!"

Mrs. McGuire lifted a bony hand to her face and tucked a flying wisp of hair behind her right ear.

"Then if he saw it comin', why couldn't he do somethin' to stop it?" she demanded.

"I don't know. But he couldn't. Dr. Chandler said he couldn't. An' they had a man up from Boston—one of them eye socialists what doesn't doctor anythin' but eyes—an' he said he couldn't."

Keith, on his knees before the beet-bed adjoining the

Eleanor H. Porter

clothes-yard, sat back on his heels and eyed the two women with frowning interest.

He knew old Mr. Harrington. So did all the boys. Never was there a kite or a gun or a jack-knife so far gone that Uncle Joe Harrington could not "fix it" somehow. And he was always so jolly about it, and so glad to do it. But it took eyes to do such things, and if now he was going to be blind—

"An' you say it's been comin' on gradual?" questioned Mrs. McGuire. "Why, I hadn't heard-"

"No, there hain't no one heard," interrupted Susan. "He didn't say nothin' ter nobody, hardly, only me, I guess, an' I suspicioned it, or he wouldn't 'a' said it to me, probably. Ye see, I found out he wa'n't readin' 'em—the papers Mr. Burton has me take up ter him every week. An' he owned up, when I took him ter task for it, that he couldn't read 'em. They was gettin' all blurred."

"Blurred?" It was a startled little cry from the boy down by the beet-bed; but neither Susan nor Mrs. McGuire heard—perhaps because at almost the same moment Mrs. McGuire had excitedly asked the same question.

"Blurred?" she cried.

"Yes; all run tergether like—the printin', ye know—so he couldn't tell one letter from t'other. 'T wa'n't only a little at first. Why, he thought 't was jest somethin' the matter with the printin' itself; an'—"

"And WASN'T it the printing at ALL?"

The boy was on his feet now. His face was a little white and strained-looking, as he asked the question.

"Why, no, dearie. Didn't you hear Susan tell Mis' McGuire jest now? 'T was his EYES, an' he didn't know it. He was gettin' blind, an' that was jest the beginnin'."

Susan's capable hands picked up another wet towel and snapped it open by way of emphasis.

"The b-beginning?" stammered the boy. "But—but ALL beginnings don't—don't end like that, do they?"

Susan Betts laughed indulgently and jammed the clothespin a little deeper on to the towel.

"Bless the child! Won't ye hear that, now?" she laughed with a shrug. "An' how should I know? I guess if Susan Betts could tell the end of all the beginnin's as soon as they're begun, she wouldn't be hangin' out your daddy's washin', my boy. She'd be sittin' on a red velvet sofa with a gold cupola over her head a-chargin' five dollars apiece for tellin' yer fortune. Yes, sir, she would!"

"But—but about Uncle Joe," persisted the boy. "Can't he really see—at all, Susan?"

"There, there, child, don't think anything more about it. Indeed, forsooth, I'm tellin' the truth, but I s'pose I hadn't oughter told it before you. Still, you'd 'a' found it out quick enough—an' you with your tops an' balls always runnin' up there. An' that's what the poor soul seemed to feel the worst about," she went on, addressing Mrs. McGuire, who was still leaning on the division fence.

"'If only I could see enough ter help the boys!' he moaned over an' over again. It made me feel awful bad. I was that upset I jest couldn't sleep that night, an' I had ter get up an' write. But it made a real pretty poem. My fuse always works

Eleanor H. Porter

better in the night, anyhow. 'The wail of the toys'—that's what I called it—had the toys tell the story, ye know, all the kites an' jack-knives an' balls an' bats that he's fixed for the boys all these years, an' how bad they felt because he couldn't do it any more. Like this, ye know:

'Oh, woe is me, said the baseball bat,
Oh, woe is me, said the kite.'

'T was real pretty, if I do say it, an' touchy, too."

"For mercy's sake, Susan Betts, if you ain't the greatest!" ejaculated Mrs. McGuire, with disapproving admiration. "If you was dyin' I believe you'd stop to write a poem for yer gravestone!"

Susan Betts chuckled wickedly, but her voice was gravity itself.

"Oh, I wouldn't have ter do that, Mis' McGuire. I've got that done already."

"Susan Betts, you haven't!" gasped the scandalized woman on the other side of the fence.

"Haven't I? Listen," challenged Susan Betts, striking an attitude. Her face was abnormally grave, though her eyes were merry.

"Here lieth a woman whose name was Betts,
An' I s'pose she'll deserve whatever she gets;
But if she hadn't been Betts she might 'a' been Better,
She might even been Best if her name would 'a' let her."

"Susan!" gasped Mrs. McGuire once more; but Susan only chuckled again wickedly, and fell to work on her basket of clothes in good earnest.

A moment later she was holding up with stern disapproval two socks with gaping heels.

"Keith Burton, here's them scandalous socks again! Now, do you go tell your father that I won't touch 'em. I won't mend 'em another once. He must get you a new pair—two new pairs, right away. Do you hear?"

But Keith did not hear. Keith was not there to hear. Still with that strained, white look on his face he had hurried out of the yard and through the gate.

Mrs. McGuire, however, did hear.

"My stars, Susan Betts, it's lucky your bark is worse than your bite!" she exclaimed. "Mend 'em, indeed! They won't be dry before you've got your darnin' egg in 'em."

Susan laughed ruefully. Then she sighed:—at arms' length she was holding up another pair of yawning socks.

"I know it. And look at them, too," she snapped, in growing wrath. "But what's a body goin' to do? The boy'd go half-naked before his father would sense it, with his nose in that paint-box. Much as ever as he's got sense enough ter put on his own clothes—and he WOULDN'T know WHEN ter put on CLEAN ones, if I didn't spread 'em out for him!"

"I know it. Too bad, too bad," murmured Mrs. McGuire, with a virtuous shake of her head. "An' he with his fine bringin'-up, an' now to be so shiftless an' good-for-nothin', an'—"

But Susan Betts was interrupting, her eyes flashing.

Eleanor H. Porter

"If you please, I'll thank you to say no more like that about my master," she said with dignity. "He's neither shiftless, nor good-for-nothin'. His character is unbleachable! He's an artist an' a scholar an' a gentleman, an' a very superlative man. It's because he knows so much that—that he jest hain't got room for common things like clothes an' holes in socks."

"Stuff an' nonsense!" retorted Mrs. McGuire nettled in her turn. "I guess I've known Dan'l Burton as long as you have; an' as for his bein' your master—he can't call his soul his own when you're around, an' you know it."

But Susan, with a disdainful sniff, picked up her now empty clothes-basket and marched into the house.

Down the road Keith had reached the turn and was climbing the hill that led to old Mr. Harrington's shabby cottage.

The boy's eyes were fixed straight ahead. A squirrel whisked his tail alluringly from the bushes at the left, and a robin twittered from a tree branch on the right. But the boy neither saw nor heard—and when before had Keith Burton failed to respond to a furred or feathered challenge like that?

To-day there was an air of dogged determination about even the way he set one foot before the other. He had the air of one who sees his goal ahead and cannot reach it soon enough. Yet when Keith arrived at the sagging, open gate before the Harrington cottage, he stopped short as if the gate were closed; and his next steps were slow and hesitant. Walking on the grass at the edge of the path he made no sound as he approached the stoop, on which sat an old man.

At the steps, as at the gate, Keith stopped and waited, his gaze on the motionless figure in the rocking-chair. The old man sat with hands folded on his cane-top, his eyes apparently looking straight ahead.

Slowly the boy lifted his right arm and waved it soundlessly. He lifted his left—but there was no waving flourish. Instead it fell impotently almost before it was lifted. On the stoop the old man still sat motionless, his eyes still gazing straight ahead.

Again the boy hesitated; then, with an elaborately careless air, he shuffled his feet on the gravel walk and called cheerfully:

"Hullo, Uncle Joe."

"Hullo! Oh, hullo! It's Keith Burton, ain't it?"

The old head turned with the vague indecision of the newly blind, and a trembling hand thrust itself aimlessly forward. "It IS Keith—ain't it?"

"Oh, yes, sir, I'm Keith."

The boy, with a quick look about him, awkwardly shook the fluttering fingers—Keith was not in the habit of shaking hands with people, least of all with Uncle Joe Harrington. He sat down then on the step at the old man's feet.

"What did ye bring ter-day, my boy?" asked the man eagerly; then with a quick change of manner, he sighed, "but I'm afraid I can't fix it, anyhow."

"Oh, no, sir, you don't have to. I didn't bring anything to be mended to-day." Unconsciously Keith had raised his voice. He was speaking loudly, and very politely.

The old man fell back in his chair. He looked relieved,

Eleanor H. Porter

yet disappointed.

"Oh, well, that's all right, then. I'm glad. That is, of course, if I could have fixed it for you—His sentence remained unfinished. A profound gloom settled over his countenance.

"But I didn't bring anything for you to fix," reiterated the boy, in a yet louder tone.

"There, there, my boy, you don't have to shout." The old man shifted uneasily hi his seat. "I ain't deaf. I'm only—I suppose you know, Keith, what's come to me in my old age."

"Yes, sir, I—I do." The boy hitched a little nearer to the two ill-shod feet on the floor near him. "And—and I wanted to ask you. Yours hurt a lot, didn't they?—I mean, your eyes; they—they ached, didn't they, before they—they got—blind?" He spoke eagerly, almost hopefully.

The old man shook his head.

"No, not much. I s'pose I ought to be thankful I was spared that."

The boy wet his dry lips and swallowed.

"But, Uncle Joe, 'most always, I guess, when—when folks are going to be blind, they—they DO ache, don't they?"

Again the old man stirred restlessly.

"I don't know. I only know about—myself."

"But—well, anyhow, it never comes till you're old—real old, does it?" Keith's voice vibrated with confidence this time.

"Old? I ain't so very old. I'm only seventy-five," bridled Harrington resentfully. "Besides anyhow, the doctor said age didn't have nothin' ter do with this kind of blindness. It comes ter young folks, real young folks, sometimes."

"Oh-h!" The boy wet his lips and swallowed again a bit convulsively. With eyes fearful and questioning he searched the old man's face. Twice he opened his mouth as if to speak; but each time he closed it again with the words left unsaid. Then, with a breathless rush, very much like desperation, he burst out:

"But it's always an awful long time comin', isn't it? Blindness is. It's years and years before it really gets here, isn't it?"

"Hm-m; well, I can't say. I can only speak for myself, Keith."

"Yes, sir, I know, sir; and that's what I wanted to ask—about you," plunged on Keith feverishly. "When did you notice it first, and what was it?"

The old man drew a long sigh.

"Why, I don't know as I can tell, exactly. 'T was quite a spell comin' on—I know that; and't wasn't much of anything at first. 'T was just that I couldn't see ter read clear an' distinct. It was all sort of blurred."

"Kind of run together?" Just above his breath Keith asked the question.

"Yes, that's it exactly. An' I thought somethin' ailed my glasses, an' so I got some new ones. An' I thought at first maybe it helped. But it didn't. Then it got so that't wa'n't only the printin' ter books an' papers that was blurred, but ev'rything a little ways off was in a fog, like, an' I couldn't

Eleanor H. Porter

see anything real clear an' distinct."

"Oh, but things—other things—don't look a mite foggy to me," cried the boy.

"'Course they don't! Why should they? They didn't to me—once," retorted the man impatiently. "But now—" Again he left a sentence unfinished.

"But how soon did—did you get—all blind, after that?" stammered the boy, breaking the long, uncomfortable silence that had followed the old man's unfinished sentence.

"Oh, five or six months—maybe more. I don't know exactly. I know it came, that's all. I guess if 't was you it wouldn't make no difference HOW it came, if it came, boy." "N-no, of course not," chattered Keith, springing suddenly to his feet. "But I guess it isn't coming to me—of course't isn't coming to me! Well, good-bye, Uncle Joe, I got to go now. Good-bye!"

He spoke fearlessly, blithely, and his chin was at a confident tilt. He even whistled as he walked down the hill. But in his heart—in his heart Keith knew that beside him that very minute stalked that shadowy, intangible creature that had dogged his footsteps ever since his fourteenth birthday-gift from his father; and he knew it now by name—The Great Terror.

CHAPTER II

DAD

Keith's chin was still high and his gaze still straight ahead when he reached the foot of Harrington Hill. Perhaps that explained why he did not see the two young misses on the fence by the side of the road until a derisively gleeful shout called his attention to their presence.

"Well, Keith Burton, I should like to know if you're blind!" challenged a merry voice.

The boy turned with a start so violent that the girls giggled again gleefully. "Dear, dear, did we scare him? We're so sorry!"

The boy flushed painfully. Keith did not like girls—that is, he SAID he did not like them. They made him conscious of his hands and feet, and stiffened his tongue so that it would not obey his will. The prettier the girls were, the more acute was his discomfiture. Particularly, therefore, did he dislike these two girls—they were the prettiest of the lot. They were Mazie Sanborn and her friend Dorothy Parkman.

Mazie was the daughter of the town's richest manufacturer, and Dorothy was her cousin from Chicago, who made such long visits to her Eastern relatives that it seemed sometimes almost as if she were as much of a Hinsdale girl as was Mazie herself.

To-day Mazie's blue eyes and Dorothy's brown ones were full of mischief.

"Well, why don't you say something? Why don't you apologize?" demanded Mazie.

"'Pol—pologize? What for?" In his embarrassed misery Keith resorted to bravado in voice and manner.

"Why, for passing us by in that impertinent fashion," returned Mazie loftily. "Do you think that is the way ladies should be treated?" (Mazie was thirteen and Dorothy fourteen.) "The idea!"

For a minute Keith stared helplessly, shifting from one foot to the other. Then, with an inarticulate grunt, he turned away.

But Mazie was not to be so easily thwarted. With a mere flit of her hand she tossed aside a score of years, and became instantly nothing more than a wheedling little girl coaxing a playmate.

"Aw, Keithie, don't get mad! I was only fooling. Say, tell me, HAVE you been up to Uncle Joe Harrington's?"

Because Mazie had caught his arm and now held it tightly, the boy perforce came to a stop.

"Well, what if I have?" he resorted to bravado again.

"And is he blind, honestly?" Mazie's voice became hushed and awestruck.

"Uh-huh." The boy nodded his head with elaborate unconcern, but he shifted his feet uneasily.

"And he can't see a thing—not a thing?" breathed Mazie.

"'Course he can't, if he's blind!" Keith showed irritation now, and pulled not too gently at the arm still held in Mazie's firm little fingers.

"Blind! Ugghh!" interposed Miss Dorothy, shuddering visibly. "Oh, how can you bear to look at him, Keith Burton? I couldn't!"

A sudden wave of red surged over the boy's face. The next instant it had receded, leaving only a white, strained terror.

"Well, he ain't to blame for it, if he is blind, is he?" chattered the boy, a bit incoherently. "If you're blind you're blind, and you can't help yourself." And with a jerk he freed himself from Mazie's grasp and hurried down the road toward home.

But when he reached the bend of the road he turned and looked back. The two girls had returned to their perch on the fence, and were deeply absorbed in something one of them held in her hand.

"And she said she couldn't bear—to look at 'em—if they were blind," he whispered. Then, wheeling about, he ran down the road as fast as he could. Nor did he stop till he had entered his own gate.

"Well, Keith Burton, I should like to know where you've been," cried the irate voice of Susan Betts from the doorway.

"Oh, just walking. Why?"

Eleanor H. Porter

"Because I've been huntin' and huntin' for you.

> But, oh, dear me,
> You're worse'n a flea,
> So what's the use of talkin'?
> You always say,
> As you did to-day,
> I've just been out a-walkin'!"

"But what did you want me for?"

"I didn't want you. Your pa wanted you. But, then, for that matter, he's always wantin' you. Any time, if you look at him real good an' hard enough to get his attention, he'll stare a minute, an' then say: 'Where's Keith?' An' when he gets to the other shore, I suppose he'll do it all the more."

"Oh, no, he won't—not if it's talking poetry. Father never talks poetry. What makes you talk it so much, Susan? Nobody else does."

Susan laughed good-humoredly.

"Lan' sakes, child, I don't know, only I jest can't help it. Why, everything inside of me jest swings along to a regular tune—kind of keeps time, like. It's always been so. Why, Keithie, boy, it's been my joy—There, you see—jest like that! I didn't know that was comin'. It jest—jest came. That's all. I can make a rhyme 'most any time. Oh, of course, most generally, when I write real poems, I have to sit down with a pencil an' paper, an' write 'em out. It's only the spontaneous combustion kind that comes all in a minute, without predisposed thinkin'. Now, run along to your pa, child. He wants you. He's been frettin' the last hour for you, jest because he didn't know exactly where you was. Goodness me! I only hope I'll never have to live with him if anything happens to you."

The boy had crossed the room; but with his hand on the door knob he turned sharply.

"W-what do you mean by that?"

Susan Betts gave a despairing gesture.

"Lan' sakes, child, how you do hold a body up! I meant what I said—that I didn't want the job of livin' with your pa if anything happened to you. You know as well as I do that he thinks you're the very axle for the earth to whirl 'round on. But, there, I don't know as I wonder—jest you left, so!"

The boy abandoned his position at the door, and came close to Susan Betts's side.

"That's what I've always wanted to know. Other boys have brothers and sisters and—a mother. But I can't ever remember anybody only dad. Wasn't there ever any one else?"

Susan Betts drew a long sigh.

"There were two brothers, but they died before you was born. Then there was—your mother."

"But I never—knew her?"

"No, child. When they opened the door of Heaven to let you out she slipped in, poor lamb. An' then you was all your father had left. So of course he dotes on you. Goodness me, there ain't no end to the fine things he's goin' ter have you be when you grow up."

"Yes, I know." The boy caught his breath convulsively and

turned away. "I guess I'll go—to dad."

At the end of the hall upstairs was the studio. Dad would probably be there. Keith knew that. Dad was always there, when he wasn't sleeping or eating, or out tramping through the woods. He would be sitting before the easel now "puttering" over a picture, as Susan called it. Susan said he was a very "insufficient, uncapacious" man—but that was when she was angry or tried with him. She never let any one else say such things about him.

Still, dad WAS very different from other dads. Keith had to acknowledge that—to himself. Other boys' dads had offices and stores and shops and factories where they worked, or else they were doctors or ministers; and there was always money to get things with—things that boys needed; shoes and stockings and new clothes, and candy and baseball bats and kites and jack-knives.

Dad didn't have anything but a studio, and there never seemed to be much money. What there was, was an "annual," Susan said, whatever that was. Anyway, whatever it was, it was too small, and not nearly large enough to cover expenses. Susan had an awful time to get enough to buy their food with sometimes. She was always telling dad that she'd GOT to have a little to buy eggs or butter or meat with.

And there were her wages—dad was always behind on those. And when the bills came in at the first of the month, it was always awful then: dad worried and frowning and unhappy and apologetic and explaining; Susan cross and half-crying. Strange men, not overpleasant-looking, ringing the doorbell peremptorily. And never a place at all where a boy might feel comfortable to stay. Dad was always talking then, especially, how he was sure he was going to sell THIS picture. But he never sold it. At least, Keith never knew him to. And after a while he would begin a new picture, and be SURE he was going to sell THAT.

But not only was dad different from other boys' dads, but the house was different. First it was very old, and full of very old furniture and dishes. Then blinds and windows and locks and doors were always getting out of order; and they were apt to remain so, for there was never any money to fix things with. There was also a mortgage on the house. That is, Susan said there was; and by the way she said it, it would seem to be something not at all attractive or desirable. Just what a mortgage was, Keith did not exactly understand; but, for that matter, quite probably Susan herself did not. Susan always liked to use big words, and some of them she did not always know the meaning of, dad said.

To-day, in the hallway, Keith stood a hesitant minute before his father's door. Then slowly he pushed it open.

"Did you want me, dad?" he asked.

The man at the easel sprang to his feet. He was a tall, slender man, with finely cut features and a pointed, blond beard. Susan had once described him as "an awfully nice man to take care of, but not worth a cent when it comes to takin' care of you." Yet there was every evidence of loving protection in the arm he threw around his boy just now.

"Want you? I always want you!" he cried affectionately. "Look! Do you remember that moss we brought home yesterday? Well, I've got its twin now." Triumphantly he pointed to the lower left-hand corner of the picture on the easel, where was a carefully blended mass of greens and browns.

"Oh, yes, why, so't is." (Keith had long since learned to see

Eleanor H. Porter

in his father's pictures what his father saw.) "Say, dad, I wish't you'd tell me about—my little brothers. Won't you, please?"

"And, Keith, look—do you recognize that little path? It's the one we saw yesterday. I'm going to call this picture 'The Woodland Path'—and I think it's going to be about the very best thing I ever did."

Keith was not surprised that his question had been turned aside: questions that his father did not like to answer were always turned aside. Usually Keith submitted with what grace he could muster; but to-day he was in a persistent mood that would not be denied.

"Dad, WHY won't you tell me about my brothers? Please, what were their names, and how old were they, and why did they die?"

"God knows why they died—I don't!" The man's arm about the boy's shoulder tightened convulsively.

"But how old were they?"

"Ned was seven and Jerry was four, and they were the light of my eyes, and—But why do you make me tell you? Isn't it enough, Keith, that they went, one after the other, not two days apart? And then the sun went out and left the world gray and cold and cheerless, for the next day—your mother went."

"And how about me, dad?"

The man did not seem to have heard. Still with his arm about the boy's shoulder, he had dropped back into the seat before the easel. His eyes now were somberly fixed out the window.

"Wasn't I—anywhere, dad?"

With a start the man turned. His arm tightened again. His eyes grew moist and very tender.

"Anywhere? You're everywhere now, my boy. I'm afraid, at the first, the very first, I didn't like to see you very well, perhaps because you were ALL there was left. Then, little by little, I found you were looking at me with your mother's eyes, and touching me with the fingers of Ned and Jerry. And now—why, boy, you're everything. You're Ned and Jerry and your mother all in one, my boy, my boy!"

Keith stirred restlessly. A horrible tightness came to his throat, yet there was a big lump that must be swallowed.

"Er—that—that Woodland Path picture is going to be great, dad, great!" he said then, in a very loud, though slightly husky, voice. "Come on, let's—"

From the hall Susan's voice interrupted, chanting in a high-pitched singsong:

> "Dinner's ready, dinner's ready,
> Hurry up, or you'll be late,
> Then you'll sure be cross and heady
> If there's nothin' left to ate."

Keith gave a relieved whoop and bounded toward the door. Never had Susan's "dinner-bell" been a more welcome sound. Surely, at dinner, his throat would have to loosen up, and that lump could then be swallowed.

More slowly Keith's father rose from his chair.

"How impossible Susan is," he sighed. "I believe she grows

worse every day. Still I suppose I ought to be thankful she's good-natured—which that absurd doggerel of hers proves that she is. However, I should like to put a stop to it. I declare, I believe I will put a stop to it, too! I'm going to insist on her announcing her meals in a proper manner. Oh, Susan," he began resolutely, as he flung open the dining-room door.

"Well, sir?" Susan stood at attention, her arms akimbo.

"Susan, I—I insist—that is, I wish—"

"You was sayin'—" she reminded him coldly, as he came to a helpless pause.

"Yes. That is, I was saying—" His eyes wavered and fell to the table. "Oh, hash—red-flannel hash! That's fine, Susan!"

But Susan was not to be cajoled. Her eyes still regarded him coldly.

"Yes, sir, hash. We most generally does have beet hash after b'iled dinner, sir. You was sayin'?"

"Nothing, Susan, nothing. I—I've changed my mind," murmured the man hastily, pulling out his chair. "Well, Keith, will you have some of Susan's nice hash?"

"Yes, sir," said Keith.

Susan said nothing. But was there a quiet smile on her lips as she left the room? If so, neither the man nor the boy seemed to notice it.

As for the very obvious change of attitude on the part of the man—Keith had witnessed a like phenomenon altogether too often to give it a second thought. And as for the doggerel that had brought about the situation—that, also, was too familiar to cause comment.

It had been years since Susan first called them to dinner with her "poem"; but Keith could remember just how pleased she had been, and how gayly she had repeated it over and over, so as not to forget it.

"Oh, of course I know that 'ate' ain't good etiquette in that place," she had admitted at the time. "It should be 'eat.' But 'eat' don't rhyme, an' 'ate' does. So I'm goin' to use it. An' I can, anyhow. It's poem license; an' that'll let you do anything."

Since then she had used the verse for every meal—except when she was out of temper—and by substituting breakfast or supper for dinner, she had a call that was conveniently universal.

The fact that she used it ONLY when she was good-natured constituted an unfailing barometer of the atmospheric condition of the kitchen, and was really, in a way, no small convenience—especially for little boys in quest of cookies or bread-and-jam. As for the master of the house—this was not the first time he had threatened an energetic warfare against that "absurd doggerel" (which he had cordially abhorred from the very first); neither would it probably be the last time that Susan's calm "Well, sir?" should send him into ignominious defeat before the battle was even begun. And, really, after all was said and done, there was still that one unfailing refuge for his discomforted recollection: he could be thankful, when he heard it, that she was good-natured; and with Susan that was no small thing to be thankful for, as everybody knew—who knew Susan.

Eleanor H. Porter

To-day, therefore, the defeat was not so bitter as to take all the sweetness out of the "red-flannel" hash, and the frown on Daniel Burton's face was quite gone when Susan brought in the dessert. Nor did it return that night, even when Susan's shrill voice caroled through the hall:

"Supper's ready, supper's ready,
Hurry up, or you'll be late,
Then you'll sure be cross and heady
If there's nothin' left to ate."

CHAPTER III

FOR JERRY AND NED

It was Susan Betts who discovered that Keith was not reading so much that summer.

"An' him with his nose always in a book before," as she said one day to Mrs. McGuire. "An' he don't act natural, somehow, neither, ter my way of thinkin'. Have YOU noticed anything?"

"Why, no, I don't know as I have," answered Mrs. McGuire from the other side of the fence, "except that he's always traipsin' off to the woods with his father. But then, he's always done that, more or less."

"Indeed he has! But always before he's lugged along a book, sometimes two; an' now—why he hain't even read the book his father give him on his birthday. I know, 'cause I asked him one day what 't was about, an' he said he didn't know; he hadn't read it."

"Deary me, Susan! Well, what if he hadn't? I shouldn't fret about that. My gracious, Susan, if you had four children same as I have, instead of one, I guess you wouldn't do no worryin' jest because a boy didn't read a book. Though, as

Eleanor H. Porter

for my John, he—"

Susan lifted her chin.

"I wasn't talkin' about your children, Mis' McGuire," she interrupted. "An' I reckon nobody'd do no worryin' if they didn't read. But Master Keith is a different supposition entirely. He's very intelligible, Master Keith is, and so is his father before him. Books is food to them—real food. Hain't you ever heard of folks devourin' books? Well, they do it. Of course I don't mean literaryly, but metaphysically."

"Oh, land o' love, Susan Betts!" cried Mrs. McGuire, throwing up both hands and turning away scornfully. "Of course, when you get to talkin' like that, NOBODY can say anything to you! However in the world that poor Mr. Burton puts up with you, I don't see. *I* wouldn't—not a day—not a single day!" And by way of emphasis she entered her house and shut the door with a slam.

Susan Betts, left alone, shrugged her shoulders disdainfully.

"Well, 'nobody asked you, sir, she said,'" she quoted, under her breath, and slammed her door, also, by way of emphasis.

Yet both Susan and Mrs. McGuire knew very well that the next day would find them again in the usual friendly intercourse over the back-yard fence.

Susan Betts was a neighbor's daughter. She had lived all her life in the town, and she knew everybody. Just because she happened to work in Daniel Burton's kitchen was no reason, to her mind, why she should not be allowed to express her opinion freely on all occasions, and on all subjects, and to all persons. Such being her conviction she conducted herself accordingly. And Susan always lived up to her convictions.

In the kitchen to-day she found Keith.

"Oh, I say, Susan, I was looking for you. Dad wants you."

"What for?"

"I don't know; but I GUESS it's because he wants to have something besides beans and codfish and fish-hash to eat. Anyhow, he SAID he was going to speak to you about it."

Susan stiffened into inexorable sternness.

"So he's goin' ter speak ter me, is he? Well, 't will be mighty little good that'll do, as he ought to know very well. Beefsteaks an' roast fowls cost money. Has he got the money for me?"

Without waiting for an answer to her question, she strode through the door leading to the dining-room and shut it crisply behind her.

The boy did not follow her. Alone, in the kitchen he drummed idly on the window-pane, watching the first few drops of a shower that had been darkening the sky for an hour past.

After a minute he turned slowly and gazed with listless eyes about the kitchen. On the table lay a folded newspaper. After a moment's hesitation he crossed the room toward it. He had the air of one impelled by some inner force against his will.

He picked the paper up, but did not at once look at it. In fact, he looked anywhere but at it. Then, with a sudden jerk, he faced it. Shivering a little he held it nearer, then farther away, then nearer again. Then, with an inarticulate little cry he dropped the paper and hurried from the room.

No one knew better than Keith himself that he was not reading much this summer. Not that he put it into words, but he had a feeling that so long as he was not SEEING how blurred the printed words were, he would not be sure that they were blurred. Yet he knew that always, whenever he saw a book or paper, his fingers fairly tingled to pick it up—and make sure. Most of the time, however, Keith tried not to notice the books and papers. Systematically he tried to forget that there were books and papers—and he tried to forget the Great Terror.

Sometimes he persuaded himself that he was doing this. He contrived to keep himself very busy that summer. Almost every day, when it did not rain, he was off for a long walk with his father in the woods. His father liked to walk in the woods. Keith never had to urge him to do that. And what good times they had!—except that Keith did wish that his father would not talk quite so much about what great things he, Keith, was going to do when he should have become a man—and a great artist.

One day he ventured to remonstrate.

"But, dad, maybe I—I shan't be a great artist at all. Maybe I shan't be even a little one. Maybe I shall be just a—a man."

Keith never forgot his father's answer nor his father's anguished face as he made that answer.

"Keith, I don't ever want you to let me hear you say that again. I want you to KNOW that you're going to succeed. And you will succeed. God will not be so cruel as to deny me that. *I* have failed. You needn't shake your head, boy, and say 'Oh, dad!' like that. I know perfectly well what I'm talking about. *I* HAVE FAILED—though it is not often that I'll admit it, even to myself. But when I heard you say to-day—

"Keith, listen to me. You've got to succeed. You've got to succeed not only for yourself, but for Jerry and Ned, and for—me. All my hopes for Jerry and Ned and for—myself are in you, boy. That's why, in all our walks together, and at home in the studio, I'm trying to teach you something that you will want to know by and by."

Keith never remonstrated with his father after that. He felt worse than ever now when his father talked of what great things he was going to do; but he knew that remonstrances would do no good, but rather harm; and he did not want to hear his father talk again as he had talked that day, about Jerry and Ned and himself. As if it were not bad enough, under the best of conditions, to have to be great and famous for one's two dead brothers and one's father; while if one were blind—

But Keith refused to think of that. He tried very hard, also, to absorb everything that his father endeavored to teach him. He listened and watched and said "yes, sir," and he did his best to make the chalks and charcoal that were put into his hands follow the copy set for him.

To be sure, in this last undertaking, his efforts were not always successful. The lines wavered and blurred and were far from clear. Still, they were not half so bad as the print in books; and if it should not get any worse—Besides, had he not always loved to draw cats and dogs and faces ever since he could hold a pencil?

And so, with some measure of hope as to the results, he was setting himself to be that great and famous artist that his father said he must be.

But it was not all work for Keith these summer days. There were games and picnics and berry expeditions with the boys

Eleanor H. Porter

and girls, all of which he hailed with delight—one did not have to read, or even study wavering lines and figures, on picnics or berrying expeditions! And that WAS a relief. To be sure, there was nearly always Mazie, and if there was Mazie, there was bound to be Dorothy. And Dorothy had said—Some way he could never see Dorothy without remembering what she did say on that day he had come home from Uncle Joe Harrington's.

Not that he exactly blamed her, either. For was not he himself acting as if he felt the same way and did not like to look at blind persons? Else why did he so persistently keep away from Uncle Joe now? Not once, since that first day, had he been up to see the poor old blind man. And before— why, before he used to go several times a week.

CHAPTER IV

SCHOOL

And so the summer passed, and September came. And September brought a new problem—school. And school meant books.

Two days before school began Keith sought Susan Betts in the kitchen.

"Say, Susan, that was awfully good johnny-cake we had this morning."

Susan picked up another plate to dry and turned toward her visitor. Her face was sternly grave, though there was something very like a twinkle in her eye.

"There ain't no cookies, if that's what you're wantin'," she said.

"Aw, Susan, I never said a word about cookies."

"Then what is it you want? It's plain to be seen there's something, I ween."

"My, how easy you do make rhymes, Susan. What's that 'I

ween' mean?"

"Now, Keith Burton, this beatin' the bush like this don't do one mite of good. You might jest as well out with it first as last. Now, what is it you want?"

Keith drew a long sigh.

"Well, Susan, there IS something—a little something—only I meant what I said about the johnny-cake and the rhymes; truly, I did."

"Well?" Susan was smiling faintly.

"Susan, you know you can make dad do anything."

Susan began to stiffen, and Keith hastened to disarm her.

"No, no, truly! This is the part I want. You CAN make dad do anything; and I want you to do it for me."

"Do what?"

"Make him let me off from school any more."

"Let you off from school!" In her stupefied amazement Susan actually forgot to pick up another plate from the dishpan.

"Yes. Tell him I'm sick, or 't isn't good for me. And truly, 't isn't good for me. And truly, I am quite a little sick, Susan. I don't feel well a bit. There's a kind of sinking feeling in my stomach, and—"

But Susan had found her wits and her tongue by this time, and she gave free rein to her wrath.

"Let you off from school, indeed! Why, Keith Burton, I'm ashamed of you—an' you that I've always boasted of! What do you want to do—grow up a perfect ignominious?"

Keith drew back resentfully, and uptilted his chin.

"No, Susan Betts, I'm not wanting to be a—a ignominious, and I don't intend to be one, either. I'm going to be an artist—a great big famous artist, and I don't NEED school for that. How are multiplication tables and history and grammar going to help me paint big pictures? That's what I want to know. But I'm afraid that dad—Say, WON'T you tell dad that I don't NEED books any more, and—"But he stopped short, so extraordinary was the expression that had come to Susan Betts's face. If it were possible to think of Susan Betts as crying, he should think she was going to cry now.

"Need books? Why, child, there ain't nobody but what needs books. An' I guess I know! What do you suppose I wouldn't give now if I could 'a' had books an' book-learnin' when I was young? I could 'a' writ real poetry then that would sell. I could 'a' spoke out an' said things that are in my soul, an' that I CAN'T say now, 'cause I don't know the words that—that will impress what I mean. Now, look a-here, Keith Burton, you're young. You've got a chance. Do you see to it that you make good. An' it's books that will help you do it."

"But books won't help me paint, Susan."

"They will, too. Books will help you do anything."

"Then you won't ask dad?"

"Indeed, I won't."

"But I don't see how books—" With a long sigh Keith

turned away.

In the studio the next morning he faced his father.

"Dad, you can't learn to paint pictures by just READING how to do it, can you?"

"You certainly cannot, my boy."

"There! I told Susan Betts so, but she wouldn't LISTEN to me. And so—I don't have to go to school any more, do I?"

"Don't have to go to school any more! Why, Keith, what an absurd idea! Of course you've got to go to school!"

"But just to be an artist and paint pictures, I don't see—"

But his father cut him short and would not listen.

Five minutes later a very disappointed, disheartened young lad left the studio and walked slowly down the hall.

There was no way out of it. If one were successfully to be Jerry and Ned and dad and one's self, all in one, there was nothing but school and more school, and, yes, college, that would give one the proper training. Dad had said it.

Keith went to school the next morning. With an oh-well-I-don't-care air he slung his books over his shoulder and swung out the gate, whistling blithely.

It might not be so bad, after all, he was telling himself. Perhaps the print would be plainer now. Anyway, he could learn a lot in class listening to the others; and maybe some of the boys would study with him, and do the reading part.

But it was not to be so easy as Keith hoped for. To begin with, the print had not grown any clearer. It was more blurred than ever. To be sure, it was much worse with one eye than with the other; but he could not keep one eye shut all the time. Besides—his eyes ached now if he tried to use them much, and grew red and inflamed, and he was afraid his father would notice them. He began to see strange flashes of rainbow light now, too. And sometimes little haloes around the lamp flame. As if one could study books with all that!

True, he learned something in class—but naturally he was never called upon to recite what had already been given, so he invariably failed miserably when it came to his turn. Even the "boy to study with" proved to be a delusion and a snare, for no boy was found who cared to do "all the reading," without being told the reason why it was expected of him— and that was exactly what Keith was straining every nerve to keep to himself.

And so week in and week out Keith stumbled along through those misery-filled days, each one seemingly a little more unbearable than the last. Of course, it could not continue indefinitely, and Keith, in his heart, knew it. Almost every lesson was more or less of a failure, and recitation hour was a torture and a torment. The teacher alternately reproved and reproached him, with frequent appeals to his pride, holding up for comparison his splendid standing of the past. His classmates gibed and jeered mercilessly. And Keith stood it all. Only a tightening of his lips and a new misery in his eyes showed that he had heard and understood. He made neither apology nor explanation. Above all, by neither word nor sign did he betray that, because the print in his books was blurred, he could not study.

Then came the day when his report card was sent to his

father, and he himself was summoned to the studio to answer for it.

"Well, my son, what is the meaning of that?"

Keith had never seen his father look so stern. He was holding up the card, face outward. Keith knew that the damning figures were there, and he suspected what they were, though he could see only a blurred mass of indistinct marks. With one last effort he attempted still to cling to his subterfuge.

"What—what is it?" he stammered.

"'What is it?'—and in the face of a record like that!" cried his father sternly. "That's exactly what I want to know. What is it? Is this the way, Keith, that you're showing me that you don't want to go to school? I haven't forgotten, you see, that you tried to beg off going this fall. Now, what is the matter?"

Keith shifted his position miserably. His face grew white and strained-looking.

"I—I couldn't seem to get my lessons, dad."

"Couldn't! You mean you wouldn't, Keith. Surely, you're not trying to make me think you couldn't have made a better record than this, if you'd tried."

There was no answer.

"Keith!" There was only pleading in the voice now— pleading with an unsteadiness more eloquent than words. "Have you forgotten so soon what I told you?—how now you hold all the hopes of Jerry and Ned and of—dad in your own two hands? Keith, do you think, do you really think you're treating Jerry and Ned and dad—square?"

For a moment there was no answer; then a very faint, constrained voice asked:

"What were those figures, dad?"

"Read for yourself." With the words the card was thrust into his hand.

Keith bent his head. His eyes apparently were studying the card.

"Suppose you read them aloud, Keith."

There was a moment's pause; then with a little convulsive breath the words came.

"I—can't—dad."

The man smiled grimly.

"Well, I don't know as I wonder. They are pretty bad. However, I guess we'll have to have them. Read them aloud, Keith."

"But, honest, dad, I can't. I mean—they're all blurred and run together." The boy's face was white like paper now.

Daniel Burton gave his son a quick glance.

"Blurred? Run together?" He reached for the card and held it a moment before his own eyes. Then sharply he looked at his son again. "You mean—Can't you read any of those figures —the largest ones?"

Keith shook his head.

"Why, Keith, how long—" A sudden change came to his face. "You mean—is that the reason you haven't been able to get your lessons, boy?"

Keith nodded dumbly, miserably.

"But, my dear boy, why in the world didn't you say so? Look here, Keith, how long has this been going on?"

There was no answer.

"Since the very first of school?"

"Before that."

"How long before that?"

"Last spring on my—birthday. I noticed it first—then."

"Good Heavens! As long as that, and never a word to me? Why, Keith, what in the world possessed you? Why didn't you tell me? We'd have had that fixed up long ago."

"Fixed up?" Keith's eyes were eager, incredulous.

"To be sure. We'd have had some glasses, of course."

Keith shook his head. All the light fled from his face.

"Uncle Joe Harrington tried that, but it didn't help—any."

"Uncle Joe! But Uncle Joe is—" Daniel Burton stopped short. A new look came to his eyes. Into his son's face he threw a glance at once fearful, searching, rebellious. Then he straightened up angrily.

"Nonsense, Keith! Don't get silly notions into your head," he snapped sharply. "It's nothing but a little near-sightedness, and we'll have some glasses to remedy that in no time. We'll go down to the optician's to-morrow. Meanwhile I'll drop a note to your teacher, and you needn't go to school again till we get your glasses."

Near-sightedness! Keith caught at the straw and held to it fiercely. Near-sightedness! Of course, it was that, and not blindness, like Uncle Joe's at all. Didn't dad know? Of course, he did! Still, if it was near-sightedness he ought to be able to see near to; and yet it was just as blurred—But, then, of course it WAS near-sightedness. Dad said it was.

They went to the optician's the next morning. It seemed there was an oculist, too, and he had to be seen. When the lengthy and arduous examinations were concluded, Keith drew a long breath. Surely now, after all that—

Just what they said Keith did not know. He knew only that he did not get any glasses, and that his father was very angry, and very much put out about something, and that he kept declaring that these old idiots didn't know their business, anyway, and the only thing to do was to go to Boston where there was somebody who DID know his business.

They went to Boston a few days later. It was not a long journey, but Keith hailed it with delight, and was very much excited over the prospect of it. Still, he did not enjoy it very well, for with his father he had to go from one doctor to another, and none of them seemed really to understand his business—that is, not well enough to satisfy his father, else why did he go to so many? And there did not seem to be anywhere any glasses that would do any good.

Keith began to worry then, for fear that his father had been wrong, and that it was not near-sightedness after all. He could not forget Uncle Joe—and Uncle Joe had not been able to find any glasses that did any good. Besides, he heard his father and the doctors talking a great deal about "an accident," and a "consequent injury to the optic nerve"; and he had to answer a lot of questions about the time when he was eleven years old and ran into the big maple tree with his sled, cutting a bad gash in his forehead. But as if that, so long ago, could have anything to do with things looking blurred now!

But it did have something to do with it—several of the doctors said that; and they said it was possible that a slight operation now might arrest the disease. They would try it. Only one eye was badly affected at present.

So it was arranged that Keith should stay a month with one of the doctors, letting his father go back to Hinsdale.

It was not a pleasant experience, and it seemed to Keith anything but a "slight operation"; but at the end of the month the bandages were off, and his father had come to take him back home.

The print was not quite so blurred now, though it was still far from clear, and Keith noticed that his father and the doctors had a great deal to say to each other in very low tones, and that his father's face was very grave.

Then they started for home. On the journey his father talked cheerfully, even gayly; but Keith was not at all deceived. For perhaps half an hour he watched his father closely. Then he spoke.

"Dad, you might just as well tell me."

"Tell you what?"

"About those doctors—what they said."

"Why, they said all sorts of things, Keith. You heard them yourself." The man spoke lightly, still cheerily.

"Oh, yes, they said all sorts of things, but they didn't say anything PARTICULAR before me. They always talked to you soft and low on one side. I want to know what they said then."

"Why, really, Keith, they—"

"Dad," interposed the boy a bit tensely, when his father's hesitation left the sentence unfinished, "you might just as well tell me. I know already it isn't good, or you'd have told me right away. And if it's bad—I might just as well know it now, 'cause I'll have to know it sometime. Dad, what did they say? Don't worry. I can stand it—honest, I can. I've GOT to stand it. Besides, I've been expecting it—ever so long. 'Keith, you're going to be blind.' I wish't you'd say it right out like that—if you've got to say it."

But the man shuddered and gave a low cry.

"No, no, Keith, never! I'll not say it. You're not going to be blind!"

"But didn't they say I was?"

"They said—they said it MIGHT be. They couldn't tell yet." The man wet his lips and cleared his throat huskily. "They said—it would be some time yet before they could tell, for sure. And even then, if it came, there might be another operation that—But for now, Keith, we've got to wait—that's all. I've got some drops, and there are certain things you'll have to do each day. You can't go to school, and you can't read, of course; but there are lots of things you can do. And there are lots of things we can do together—you'll see. And it's coming out all right. It's bound to come out all right."

"Yes, sir." Keith said the two words, then shut his lips tight. Keith could not trust himself to talk much just then. Babies and girls cried, of course; but men, and boys who were almost men—they did not cry.

For a long minute he said nothing; then, with his chin held high and his breath sternly under control, he said:

"Of course, dad, if I do get blind, you won't expect me to be Jerry, and Ned, and—and you, all in a bunch, then, will you?"

This time it was dad who could not speak—except with a strong right arm that clasped with a pressure that hurt.

CHAPTER V

WAITING

Not for some days after his return from Boston did Keith venture out upon the street. He knew then at once that the whole town had heard all about his trip to Boston and what the doctors had said. He tried not to see the curious glances cast in his direction. He tried not to care that the youngest McGuire children stood at their gate and whispered, with fingers plainly pointing toward himself.

He did not go near the schoolhouse, and he stayed at the post-office until he felt sure all the scholars must have reached home. Then, just at the corner of his own street, he met Mazie Sanborn and Dorothy Parkman face to face. He would have passed quickly, with the briefest sort of recognition, but Mazie stopped him short.

"Keith, oh, Keith, it isn't true, is it?" she cried breathlessly. "You aren't going to be blind?"

"Mazie, how could you!" cried Dorothy sharply. And because she shuddered and half turned away, Keith saw only the shudder and the turning away, and did not realize that it was rebuke and remonstrance, and not aversion, that Dorothy was expressing so forcibly.

Keith stiffened.

"Say, Keith, I'm awfully sorry, and so's Dorothy. Why, she hasn't talked about a thing, hardly, but that, since she heard of it."

"Mazie, I have, too," protested Dorothy sharply.

"Well, anyway, it was she who insisted on coming around this way to-day," teased Mazie wickedly; "and when I—"

"I'm going home, whether you are or not," cut in Miss Dorothy, with dignity. And with a low chuckle Mazie tossed a good-bye to Keith and followed her lead.

Keith, his chin aggressively high, strode in the opposite direction.

"I suppose she wanted to see how really bad I did look," he was muttering fiercely, under his breath. "Well, she needn't worry. If I do get blind, I'll take good care she don't have to look at me, nor Mazie, nor any of the rest of them."

Keith went out on the street very little after that, and especially he kept away from it after school hours. They were not easy—those winter days. The snow lay deep in the woods, and it was too cold for long walks. He could not read, nor paint, nor draw, nor use his eyes about anything that tried them. But he was by no means idle. He had found now "the boy to do the reading"—his father. For hours every day they studied together, Keith memorizing, where it was necessary, what his father read, always discussing and working out the problems together. That he could not paint or draw was a great cross to his father, he knew.

Keith noticed, too,—and noticed it with a growing heartache,—

that nothing was ever said now about his being Jerry and Ned and dad himself all in a bunch. And he understood, of course, that if he was going to be blind, he could not be Jerry and—

But Keith was honestly trying not to think of that; and he welcomed most heartily anything or anybody that helped him toward that end.

Now there was Susan. Not once had Susan ever spoken to him of his eyes, whether he could or could not see. But Susan knew about it. He was sure of that. First he suspected it when he found her, the next day after his return from Boston, crying in the pantry.

SUSAN CRYING! Keith stood in the doorway and stared unbelievingly. He had not supposed that Susan could cry.

"Why, Susan!" he gasped. "What IS the matter?"

He never forgot the look on Susan's face as she sprang toward him, or the quick cry she gave.

"Oh, Keith, my boy, my boy!" Then instantly she straightened back, caught up a knife, and began to peel an onion from a pan on the shelf before her. "Cryin'? Nonsense!" she snapped quaveringly. "Can't a body peel a pan of onions without being accused of cryin' about somethin'? Shucks! What should I be cryin' for, anyway, to be sure?

> Some things need a knife,
> An' some things need a pill,
> An' some things jest a laugh'll make a cure.
> But jest you bet your life,
> You may cry jest fit to kill,
> An' never cure nothin'—that is sure.

Eleanor H. Porter

That's what I always say when I see folks cryin'. An' it's so, too. Here, Keith, want a cooky? An' take a jam tart, too. I made 'em this mornin', 'specially for you."

With which astounding procedure—for her—Susan pushed a plate of cookies and tarts toward him, then picked up her pan of onions and hurried into the kitchen.

Once again Keith stared. Cookies and jam tarts, and made for him? If anything, this was even more incomprehensible than were the tears in Susan's eyes. Then suddenly the suspicion came to him—SUSAN KNEW. And this was her way—

The suspicion did not become a certainty, however, until two days later. Then he overheard Susan and Mrs. McGuire talking in the kitchen. He had slipped into the pantry to look for another of those cookies made for him, when he heard Mrs. McGuire burst into the kitchen and accost Susan agitatedly. And her first words were such that he could not bring himself to step out into view.

"Susan," she had cried, "it ain't true, is it? IS it true that Keith Burton is going—BLIND? My John says—"

"Sh-h! You don't have to shout it out like that, do ye?" demanded Susan crossly, yet in a voice that was far from steady. "Besides, that's a very extravagated statement."

"You mean exaggerated, I suppose," retorted Mrs. McGuire impatiently. "Well, I'm sure I'm glad if it is, of course. But can't you tell me anything about it? Or, don't you know?"

Keith knew—though he could not see her—just how Susan was drawing herself up to her full height.

"I guess I know—all there is to know, Mis' McGuire," she said then coldly. "But there ain't anybody KNOWS anything. We're jest waitin' to see." Her voice had grown unsteady again.

"You mean he MAY be blind, later?"

"Yes."

"Oh, the poor boy! Ain't that terrible? How CAN they stand it?"

"I notice there are things in this world that have to be stood. An' when they have to be stood, they might as well be—stood, an' done with it."

"Yes, I suppose so," sighed Mrs. McGuire. Then, after a pause: "But what is it—that's makin' him blind?"

"I don't know. They ain't sayin'. I thought maybe't was a catamount, but they say't ain't that."

"But when is it liable to come?"

"Come? How do I know? How does anybody know?" snapped Susan tartly. "Look a-here, Mis' McGuire, you must excuse me from discoursin' particulars. We don't talk 'em here. None of us don't."

"Well, you needn't be so short about it, Susan Betts. I'm only tryin' to show a little sympathy. You don't seem to realize at all what a dreadful thing this is. My John says—"

"Don't I—DON'T I?" Susan's voice shook with emotion. "Don't you s'pose that I know what it would be with the sun put out, an' the moon an' the stars, an' never a thing to look at but black darkness all the rest of your life? Never to be able to see the blue sky, or your father's face, or—But talkin' about it don't help any. Look a-here, if somethin' awful was goin' to happen to you, would YOU want folks to be talkin' to you all the time about it? No, I guess you wouldn't. An' so we don't talk here. We're just—waitin'. It may come in a year, it may come sooner, or later. It may not come at all. An' while we ARE waitin' there ain't nothin' we can do except to do ev'rything the doctor tells us, an' hope—'t won't ever come."

Even Mrs. McGuire could have had no further doubt about Susan's "caring." No one who heard Susan's voice then could have doubted it. Mrs. McGuire, for a moment, made no answer; then, with an inarticulate something that might have passed for almost any sort of comment, she rose to her feet and left the house.

In the pantry, Keith, the cookies long since forgotten, shamelessly listened at the door and held his breath to see which way Susan's footsteps led. Then, when he knew that the kitchen was empty, he slipped out, still cookyless, and hurried upstairs to his own room.

Keith understood, after that, why Susan did not talk to him about his eyes; and because he knew she would not talk, he felt at ease and at peace with her.

It was not so with others. With others (except with his father) he never knew when a dread question or a hated comment was to be made. And so he came to avoid those others more and more.

At the first signs of spring, and long before the snow was off the ground, Keith took to the woods. When his father did not care to go, he went alone. It was as if he wanted to fill his inner consciousness with the sights and sounds of his beloved out-of-doors, so that when his outer eyes were darkened, his inner eyes might still hold the pictures. Keith did not say this, even to himself; but when every day Susan questioned him minutely as to what he had seen, and begged him to describe every budding tree and every sunset, he wondered; was it possible that Susan, too, was trying to fill that inner consciousness with visions?

Keith was thrown a good deal with Susan these days. Sometimes it seemed as if there were almost no one but Susan. Certainly all those others who talked and questioned—he did not want to be with them. And his father—sometimes it seemed to Keith that his father did not like to be with him as well as he used to. And, of course, if he was going to be blind—Dad never had liked disagreeable subjects. Had HE become—a disagreeable subject?

And so there seemed, indeed, at times, no one but Susan. Susan, however, was a host in herself. Susan was never cross now, and almost always she had a cooky or a jam tart for him. She told lots of funny stories, and there were always her rhymes and jingles. She had a new one every day, sometimes two or three a day.

There was no subject too big or too little for Susan to put into rhyme. Susan said that something inside of her was a gushing siphon of poems, anyway, and she just had to get them out of her system. And she told Keith that spring always made the siphon gush worse than ever, for some reason. She didn't know why.

Keith suspected that she said this by way of an excuse for repeating so many of her verses to him just now. But Keith was not deceived. He had not forgotten what Susan had said to Mrs. McGuire in the kitchen that day; and he knew very well that all this especial attention to him was only Susan's way of trying to help him "wait."

CHAPTER VI

LIGHTS OUT

And so Keith waited, through the summer and into another winter. And April came. Keith was not listening to Susan's rhymes and jingles now, nor was he tramping through the woods in search of the first sign of spring. Both eyes had become badly affected now. Keith knew that and—

THE FOG HAD COME. Keith had seen the fog for several days before he knew what it was. He had supposed it to be really—fog. Then one day he said to Susan:

"Where's the sun? We haven't had any BRIGHT sun for days and days—just this horrid old foggy fog."

"Fog? Why, there ain't any fog!" exclaimed Susan. "The sun is as bright—" She stopped short. Keith could not see her face very clearly—Keith was not seeing anything clearly these days. "Nonsense, Keith, of course, the sun is shinin'!" snapped Susan. "Now don't get silly notions in your head!" Then she turned and hurried from the room.

And Keith knew. And he knew that Susan knew.

Keith did not mention the fog to his father—dad did not like disagreeable subjects. But somebody must have mentioned it—Susan, perhaps. At all events, before the week was out Keith went with his father again to Boston.

It was a sorry journey. Keith did not need to go to Boston. Keith knew now. There was no one who could tell him anything. Dad might laugh and joke and call attention to everything amusing that he wanted to—it would make no difference. Besides, as if he could not hear the shake in dad's voice under all the fun, and as if he could not feel the tremble in dad's hand on his shoulder!

Boston was the same dreary round of testing, talk, and questions, hushed voices and furtive glances, hurried trips from place to place; only this time it was all sharper, shorter, more decisive, and there was no operation. It was not the time for that now, the doctors said. Moreover, this time dad did not laugh, or joke, or even talk on the homeward journey. But that, too, made no difference. Keith already knew.

He knew so well that he did not question him at all. But if he had not known, he would have known from Susan the next day. For he found Susan crying three times the next forenoon, and each time she snapped out so short and sharp about something so entirely foreign from what he asked her that he would have known that Susan knew.

Keith did wonder how many months it would be. Some way he had an idea it would be very few now. As long as it was coming he wished it would come, and come quick. This waiting business—On the whole he was glad that Susan was cross, and that his father spent his days shut away in his own room with orders that he was not to be disturbed. For, as for talking about this thing—

It was toward the last of July that Keith discovered how

Eleanor H. Porter

indistinct were growing the outlines of the big pictures on the wall at the end of the hall. Day by day he had to walk nearer and nearer before he could see them at all. He wondered just how many steps would bring him to the wall itself. He was tempted once to count them—but he could not bring himself to do that; so he knew then that in his heart he did not want to know just how many days it would be before—

But there came a day when he was but two steps away. He told himself it would be in two days then. But it did not come in two days. It did not come in a week. Then, very suddenly, it came.

He woke up one morning to find it quite dark. For a minute he thought it WAS dark; then the clock struck seven—and it was August.

Something within Keith seemed to snap then. The long-pent strain of months gave way. With one agonized cry of "Dad, it's come—it's come!" he sprang from the bed, then stood motionless in the middle of the room, his arms outstretched. But when his father and Susan reached the room he had fallen to the floor in a dead faint.

It was some weeks before Keith stood upright on his feet again. His illness was a long and serious one. Late in September, Mrs. McGuire, hanging out her clothes, accosted Susan over the back-yard fence.

"I heard down to the store last night that Keith Burton was goin' to get well."

"Of course he's goin' to get well," retorted Susan with emphasis. "I knew he was, all the time."

"All the same, I think it's a pity he is." Mrs. McGuire's lips came together a bit firmly. "He's stone blind, I hear, an' my John says—"

"Well, what if he is?" demanded Susan, almost fiercely. "You wouldn't kill the child, would you? Besides SEEIN' is only one of his facilities. He's got all the rest left. I reckon he'll show you he can do somethin' with them."

Mrs. McGuire shook her head mournfully.

"Poor boy, poor boy! How's he feel himself? Has he got his senses, his real senses yet?"

"He's just beginnin' to." The harshness in Susan's voice betrayed her difficulty in controlling it. "Up to now he hain't sensed anything, much. Of course, part of the time he hain't known ANYTHING—jest lay there in a stupid. Then, other times he's jest moaned of-of the dark—always the dark.

"At first he—when he talked—seemed to be walkin' through the woods; an' he'd tell all about what he saw; the 'purple sunsets,' an' 'dancin' leaves,' an' the merry little brooks hurryin' down the hillside,' till you could jest SEE the place he was talkin' about. But now—now he's comin' to full conscientiousness, the doctor says; an' he don't talk of anything only—only the dark. An' pretty quick he'll—know."

"An' yet you want that poor child to live, Susan Betts!"

"Of course I want him to live!"

"But what can he DO?"

"Do? There ain't nothin' he can't do. Why, Mis' McGuire, listen! I've been readin' up. First, I felt as you do—a little.

I—I didn't WANT him to live. Then I heard of somebody who was blind, an' what he did. He wrote a great book. I've forgotten its name, but it was somethin' about Paradise. PARADISE—an' he was in prison, too. Think of writin' about Paradise when you're shut up in jail—an' blind, at that! Well, I made up my mind if that man could see Paradise through them prison bars with his poor blind eyes, then Keith could. An' I was goin' to have him do it, too. An' so I went down to the library an' asked Miss Hemenway for a book about him. An' I read it. An' then she told me about more an' more folks that was blind, an' what they had done. An' I read about them, too."

"Well, gracious me, Susan Betts, if you ain't the limit!" commented Mrs. McGuire, half admiringly, half disapprovingly.

"Well, I did. An'—why, Mis' McGuire, you hain't any inception of an idea of what those men an' women an'—yes, children—did. Why, one of 'em wasn't only blind, but deaf an' dumb, too. She was a girl. An' now she writes books an' gives lecturin's, an', oh, ev'rything."

"Maybe. I ain't sayin' they don't. But I guess somebody else has to do a part of it. Look at Keith right here now. How are you goin' to take care of him when he gets up an' begins to walk around? Why, he can't see to walk or—or feed himself, or anything. Has the nurse gone?"

Susan shook her head. Her lips came together grimly.

"No. Goes next week, though. Land's sakes, but I hope that woman is expulsive enough! Them entrained nurses always cost a lot, I guess. But we've just had to have her while he was so sick. But she's goin' next week."

"But what ARE you goin' to do? You can't tag him around all day an' do your other work, too. Of course, there's his father—"

"His father! Good Heavens, woman, I wonder if you think I'd trust that boy to his father?" demanded Susan indignantly. "Why, once let him get his nose into that paint-box, an' he don't know anything—not anything. Why, I wouldn't trust him with a baby rabbit—if I cared for the rabbit. Besides, he don't like to be with Keith, nor see him, nor think of him. He feels so bad."

"Humph! Well, if he does feel bad I don't think that's a very nice way to show it. Not think of him, indeed! Well, I guess he'll find SOME one has got to think of him now. But there! that's what you might expect of Daniel Burton, I s'pose, moonin' all day over those silly pictures of his. As my John says—"

"They're not silly pictures," cut in Susan, flaring into instant wrath. "He HAS to paint pictures in order to get money to live, don't he? Well, then, let him paint. He's an artist—an extinguished artist—not just a common storekeeper." (Mr. McGuire, it might be mentioned in passing, kept a grocery store.) "An' if you're artistical, you're different from other folks. You have to be."

"Nonsense, Susan! That's all bosh, an' you know it. What if he does paint pictures? That hadn't ought to hinder him from takin' proper care of his own son, had it?"

"Yes, if he's blind." Susan spoke with firmness and decision. "You don't seem to understand at all, Mis' McGuire. Mr. Burton is an artist. Artists like flowers an' sunsets an' clouds an' brooks. They don't like disagreeable things. They don't want to see 'em or think about 'em. I know. It's that way with

Mr. Burton. Before, when Keith was all right, he couldn't bear him out of his sight, an' he was goin' to have him do such big, fine, splendid things when he grew up. Now, since he's blind, he can't bear him IN his sight. He feels that bad. He just won't be with him if he can help it. But he ain't forgettin' him. He's thinkin' of him all the time. *I* KNOW. An' it's tellin' on him. He's lookin' thin an' bad an' sick. You see, he's so disappointed, when he'd counted on such big things for that boy!"

"Humph! Well, I'll risk HIM. It's Keith I'm worry in' about. Who is going to take care of him?"

Susan Betts frowned.

"Well, *I* could, I think. But there's a sister of Mr. Burton's— she's comin'."

"Not Nettie Colebrook?"

"Yes, Mis' Colebrook. That's her name. She's a widow, an' hain't got anything needin' her. She wrote an' offered, an' Mr. Burton said yes, if she'd be so kind. An' she's comin'."

"When?"

"Next week. The day the nurse goes. Why? What makes you look so queer? Do you know—Mis' Colebrook?"

"Know Nettie Burton Colebrook? Well, I should say I did! I went to boardin'-school with her."

"Humph!" Susan threw a sharp glance into Mrs. McGuire's face. Susan looked as if she wanted to ask another question. But she did not ask it. "Humph!" she grunted again; and turned back to the sheet she was hanging on the line.

There was a brief pause, then Mrs. McGuire commented dryly:

"I notice you ain't doin' no rhymin' to-day, Susan."

"Ain't I? Well, perhaps I ain't. Some way, they don't come out now so natural an' easy-like."

"What's the matter? Ain't the machine workin'?"

Susan shook her head. Then she drew a long sigh. Picking up her empty basket she looked at it somberly.

"Not the way it did before. Some way, there don't seem anything inside of me now only dirges an' funeral marches. Everywhere, all day, everything I do an' everywhere I go I jest hear: 'Keith's blind, Keith's blind!' till it seems as if I jest couldn't bear it."

With something very like a sob Susan turned and hurried into the house.

CHAPTER VII

SUSAN TO THE RESCUE

It was when the nurse was resting and Susan was with Keith that the boy came to a full, realizing sense of himself, on his lips the time-worn question asked by countless other minds back from that mysterious land of delirium:

"Where am I?"

Susan sprang to her feet, then dropped on her knees at the bedside.

"In your own bed—honey."

"Is that—Susan?" No wonder he asked the question. Whenever before had Susan talked like that?

"Sure it's Susan."

"But I can't—see you—or anything. Oh-h!" With a shudder and a quivering cry the boy flung out his hands, then covered his eyes with them. "I know, now, I know! It's come—it's come! I am—BLIND!"

"There, there, honey, don't, please don't. You'll break Susan's heart. An' you're SO much better now."

"Better?"

"Yes. You've been sick—very sick."

"How long?"

"Oh, several weeks. It's October now."

"And I've been blind all that time?"

"Yes."

"But I haven't known I was blind!"

"No."

"I want to go back—I want to go back, where I didn't know—again."

"Nonsense, Keith!" (Susan was beginning to talk more like herself.) "Go back to be sick? Of course you don't want to go back an' be sick! Listen!

> Don't you worry, an' don't you fret.
> Somethin' better is comin' yet.
> Somethin' fine! What'll you bet?
> It's jest the thing you're wantin' ter get!

Come, come! We're goin' to have you up an' out in no time, now, boy!"

"I don't want to be up and out. I'm blind, Susan."

"An' there's your dad. He'll be mighty glad to know you're

better. I'll call him."

"No, no, Susan—don't! Don't call him. He won't want to see me. Nobody will want to see me now. I'm blind, Susan—blind!"

"Shucks! Everybody will want to see you, so's to see how splendid you are, even if you are blind. Now don't talk any more—please don't; there's a good boy. You're gettin' yourself all worked up, an' then, oh, my, how that nurse will scold!"

"I shan't be splendid," moaned the boy. "I shan't be anything, now. I shan't be Jerry or Ned or dad. I shall be just ME. And I'll be pointed at everywhere; and they'll whisper and look and stare, and say, 'He's blind—he's blind—he's blind.' I tell you, Susan, I can't stand it. I can't—I can't! I want to go back. I want to go back to where I didn't—KNOW!"

The nurse came in then, and of course Susan was banished in disgrace. Of course, too, Keith was almost in hysterics, and his fever had gone away up again. He still talked in a high, shrill voice, and still thrashed his arms wildly about, till the little white powder the nurse gave him got in its blessed work. And then he slept.

Keith was entirely conscious the next day when Susan came in to sit with him while the nurse took her rest. But it was a very different Keith. It was a weary, spent, nerveless Keith that lay back on the pillow with scarcely so much as the flutter of an eyelid to show life.

"Is there anything I can get you, Keith?" she asked, when a long-drawn sigh convinced her that he was awake.

Only a faint shake of the head answered her.

"The doctor says you're lots better, Keith."

There was no sort of reply to this; and for another long minute Susan sat tense and motionless, watching the boy's face. Then, with almost a guilty look over her shoulder, she stammered:

"Keith, I don't want you to talk to me, but I do wish you'd just SPEAK to me."

But Keith only shook his head again faintly and turned his face away to the wall.

By and by the nurse came in, and Susan left the room. She went straight to the kitchen, and she did not so much as look toward Keith's father whom she met in the hall. In the kitchen Susan caught up a cloth and vigorously began to polish a brass faucet. The faucet was already a marvel of brightness; but perhaps Susan could not see that. One cannot always see clearly—through tears.

Keith was like this every day after that, when Susan came in to sit with him—silent, listless, seemingly devoid of life. Yet the doctor declared that physically the boy was practically well. And the nurse was going at the end of the week.

On the last day of the nurse's stay, Susan accosted her in the hall somewhat abruptly.

"Is it true that by an' by there could be an operator on that boy's eyes?"

"Oper—er—oh, operation! Yes, there might be, if he could only get strong enough to stand it. But it might not be successful, even then."

"But there's a chance?"

"Yes, there's a chance."

"I s'pose it—it would be mighty expulsive, though."

"Expulsive?" The young woman frowned slightly; then suddenly she smiled. "Oh! Oh, yes, I—I'm afraid it would—er—cost a good deal of money," she nodded over her shoulder as she went on into Keith's room.

That evening Susan sought her employer in the studio. Daniel Burton spent all his waking hours in the studio now. The woods and fields were nothing but a barren desert of loneliness to Daniel Burton—without Keith.

The very poise of Susan's head spelt aggressive determination as she entered the studio; and Daniel Burton shifted uneasily in his chair as he faced her. Nor did he fail to note that she carried some folded papers in her hand.

"Yes, yes, Susan, I know. Those bills are due, and past due," he cried nervously, before Susan could speak. "And I hoped to have the money, both for them and for your wages, long before this. But—"

Susan stopped him short with an imperative gesture.

"T ain't bills, Mr. Burton, an't ain't wages. It's—it's somethin' else. Somethin' very importune." There was a subdued excitement in Susan's face and manner that was puzzling, yet most promising.

Unconsciously Daniel Burton sat a little straighter and lifted his chin—though his eyes were smiling.

"Something else?"

"Yes. It's—poetry."

"Oh, SUSAN!" It was as if a bubble had been pricked, leaving nothing but empty air.

"But you don't know—you don't understand, yet," pleaded Susan, unerringly reading the disappointment in her employer's face. "It's to sell—to get some money, you know, for the operator on the poor lamb's eyes. I—I wanted to help, some way. An' this is REAL poetry—truly it is!—not the immaculate kind that I jest dash off! I've worked an' worked over this, an' I'm jest sure it'll sell, It's GOT to sell, Mr. Burton. We've jest got to have that money. An' now, I—I want to read 'em to you. Can't I, please?"

And this from Susan—this palpitating, pleading "please"! Daniel Burton, with a helpless gesture that expressed embarrassment, dismay, bewilderment, and resignation, threw up both hands and settled back in his chair.

"Why, of—of course, Susan, read them," he muttered as clearly as he could, considering the tightness that had come into his throat.

And Susan read this:

SPRING

Oh, gentle Spring, I love thy rills,
I love thy wooden, rocky rills,
I love thy budsome beauty.
But, oh, I hate o'er anything,
Thy mud an' slush, oh, gentle Spring,
When rubbers are a duty.

"That's the shortest—the other is longer," explained Susan, still the extraordinary, palpitating Susan, with the shining, pleading eyes.

"Yes, go on." Daniel Burton had to clear his throat before he could say even those two short words.

"I called this 'Them Things That Plague,'" said Susan. "An' it's really true, too. Don't you know? Things DO plague worse nights, when you can't sleep. An' you get to thinkin' an' thinkin'. Well, that's what made me write this." And she began to read:

THEM THINGS THAT PLAGUE

They come at night, them things that plague,
An' gather round my bed.
They cluster thick about the foot,
An' lean on top the head.

They like the dark, them things that plague,
For then they can be great,
They loom like doom from out the gloom,
An' shriek: "I am your Fate!"

But, after all, them things that plague
Are cowards—Say not you?—
To strike a man when he is down,
An' in the darkness, too.

For if you'll watch them things that plague,
Till comin' of the dawn,
You'll find, when once you're on your feet,
Them things that plague—are gone!

"There, ain't that true—every word of it?" she demanded.

"An' there ain't hardly any poem license in it, too. I think they're a ways lots better when there ain't; but sometimes, of course, you jest have to use it. There! an' now I've read 'em both to you—an' how much do you s'pose I can get for 'em— the two of 'em, either singly or doubly?" Susan was still breathless, still shining-eyed—a strange, exotic Susan, that Daniel Burton had never seen before. "I've heard that writers—some writers—get lots of money, Mr. Burton, an' I can write more—lots more. Why, when I get to goin' they jest come autocratically—poems do—without any thinkin' at all; an'—But how much DO you think I ought to get?"

"Get? Good Heavens woman!" Daniel Burton was on his feet now trying to shake off the conflicting emotions that were all but paralyzing him. "Why, you can't get anything for those da—" Just in time he pulled himself up. At that moment, too, he saw Susan's face. He sat down limply.

"Susan." He cleared his throat and began again. He tried to speak clearly, judiciously, kindly. "Susan, I'm afraid—that is, I'm not sure—Oh, hang it all, woman"—he was on his feet now—"send them, if you want to—but don't blame me for the consequences." And with a gesture, as of flinging the whole thing far from him, he turned his back and walked away.

"You mean—you don't think I can get hardly anything for 'em?" An extraordinarily meek, fearful Susan asked the question.

Only a shrug of the back-turned shoulders answered her.

"But, Mr. Burton, we—we've got to have the money for that operator; an', anyhow, I—I mean to try." With a quick indrawing of her breath she turned abruptly and left the studio.

That evening, in her own room, Susan pored over the two inexpensive magazines that came to the house. She was searching for poems and for addresses.

As she worked she began to look more cheerful. Both the magazines published poems, and if they published one poem they would another, of course, especially if the poem were a better one—and Susan could not help feeling that they were better (those poems of hers) than almost any she saw there in print before her. There was some SENSE to her poems, while those others—why, some of them didn't mean anything, not anything!—and they didn't even rhyme!

With real hope and courage, therefore, Susan laboriously copied off the addresses of the two magazines, directed two envelopes, and set herself to writing the first of her two letters. That done, she copied the letter, word for word— except for the title of the poem submitted.

It was a long letter. Susan told first of Keith and his misfortune, and the imperative need of money for the operation. Then she told something of herself, and of her habit of turning everything into rhyme; for she felt it due to them, she said, that they know something of the person with whom they were dealing. She touched again on the poverty of the household, and let it plainly be seen that she had high hopes of the money these poems were going to bring. She did not set a price. She would leave that to their own indiscretion, she said in closing.

It was midnight before Susan had copied this letter and prepared the two manuscripts for mailing. Then, tired, but happy, she went to bed.

It was the next day that the nurse went, and that Mrs. Colebrook came.

The doctor said that Keith might be dressed now, any day—that he should be dressed, in fact, and begin to take some exercise. He had already sat up in a chair every day for a week—and he was in no further need of medicine, except a tonic to build him up. In fact, all efforts now should be turned toward building him up, the doctor said. That was what he needed.

All this the nurse mentioned to Mr. Burton and to Susan, as she was leaving. She went away at two o'clock, and Mrs. Colebrook was not to come until half-past five. At one minute past two Susan crept to the door of Keith's room and pushed it open softly. The boy, his face to the wall, lay motionless. But he was not asleep. Susan knew that, for she had heard his voice not five minutes before, bidding the nurse good-bye. For one brief moment Susan hesitated. Then, briskly, she stepped into the room with a cheery:

"Well, Keith, here we are, just ourselves together. The nurse is gone an' I am on—how do you like the weather?"

"Yes, I know, she said she was going." The boy spoke listlessly, wearily, without turning his head.

"What do you say to gettin' up?"

Keith stirred restlessly.

"I was up this morning."

"Ho!" Susan tossed her head disdainfully. "I don't mean THAT way. I mean up—really up with your clothes on."

The boy shook his head again.

"I couldn't. I—I'm too tired."

"Nonsense! A great boy like you bein' too tired to get up! Why Keith, it'll do you good. You'll feel lots better when you're up an' dressed like folks again."

The boy gave a sudden cry.

"That's just it, Susan. Don't you see? I'll never be—like folks again."

"Nonsense! Jest as if a little thing like bein' blind was goin' to keep you from bein' like folks again!" Susan was speaking very loudly, very cheerfully—though with first one hand, then the other, she was brushing away the hot tears that were rolling down her cheeks. "Why, Keith, you're goin' to be better than folks—jest common folks. You're goin' to do the most wonderful things that—"

"But I can't—I'm blind, I tell you!" cut in the boy. "I can't do—anything, now."

"But you can, an' you're goin' to," insisted Susan again. "You jest wait till I tell you; an' it's because you ARE blind that it's goin' to be so wonderful. But you can't do it jest lyin' abed there in that lazy fashion. Come, I'm goin' to get your clothes an' put 'em right on this chair here by the bed; then I'm goin' to give you twenty minutes to get into 'em. I shan't give you but fifteen tomorrow." Susan was moving swiftly around the room now, opening closet doors and bureau drawers.

"No, no, Susan, I can't get up," moaned the boy turning his face back to the wall. "I can't—I can't!"

"Yes, you can. Now, listen. They're all here, everything you need, on these two chairs by the bed."

"But how can I dress me when I can't see a thing?"

"You can feel, can't you?"

"Y-yes. But feeling isn't seeing. You don't KNOW."

Susan gave a sudden laugh—she would have told you it was a laugh—but it sounded more like a sob.

"But I do know, an' that's the funny part of it, Keith," she cried. "Listen! What do you s'pose your poor old Susan's been doin'? You'd never guess in a million years, so I'm goin' to tell you. For the last three mornin's she's tied up her eyes with a handkerchief an' then DRESSED herself, jest to make sure it COULD be done, you know."

"Susan, did you, really?" For the first time a faint trace of interest came into the boy's face.

"Sure I did! An' Keith, it was great fun, really, jest to see how smart I could be, doin' it. An' I timed myself, too. It took me twenty-five minutes the first time. Dear, dear, but I was clumsy! But I can do it lots quicker now, though I don't believe I'll ever do it as quick as you will."

"Do you think I could do it, really?"

"I know you could."

"I could try," faltered Keith dubiously.

"You ain't goin' to TRY, you're goin' to DO it," declared Susan. "Now, listen. I'm goin' out, but in jest twenty minutes I'm comin' back, an' I shall expect to find you all dressed. I—I shall be ashamed of you if you ain't." And without another glance at the boy, and before he could possibly protest, Susan hurried from the room.

Her head was still high, and her voice still determinedly clear—but in the hall outside the bedroom, Susan burst into such a storm of sobs that she had to hurry to the kitchen and shut herself in the pantry lest they be heard.

Later, when she had scornfully lashed herself into calmness, she came out into the kitchen and looked at the clock.

"An' I've been in there five minutes, I'll bet ye, over that fool cry in'," she stormed hotly to herself. "Great one, I am, to take care of that boy, if I can't control myself better than this!"

At the end of what she deemed to be twenty minutes, and after a fruitless "puttering" about the kitchen, Susan marched determinedly upstairs to Keith's room. At the door she did hesitate a breathless minute, then, resolutely, she pushed it open.

The boy, fully dressed, stood by the bed. His face was alight, almost eager.

"I did it—I did it, Susan! And if it hasn't been more than twenty minutes, I did it sooner than you!"

Susan tried to speak; but the tears were again chasing each other down her cheeks, and her face was working with emotion.

"Susan!" The boy put out his hand gropingly, turning his head with the pitiful uncertainty of the blind. "Susan, you are there, aren't you?"

Susan caught her breath chokingly, and strode into the room with a brisk clatter.

"Here? Sure I'm here—but so dumb with amazement an' admiration that I couldn't open my head—to see you standin' there all dressed like that! What did I tell you? I knew you could do it. Now, come, let's go see dad." She was at his side now, her arm linked into his.

But the boy drew back.

"No, no, Susan, not there. He—he wouldn't like it. Truly, he—he doesn't want to see me. You know he—he doesn't like to see disagreeable things."

"'Disagreeable things,' indeed!" exploded Susan, her features working again. "Well, I guess if he calls it disagreeable to see his son dressed up an' walkin' around—"

But Keith interrupted her once more, with an even stronger protest, and Susan was forced to content herself with leading her charge out on to the broad veranda that ran across the entire front of the house. There they walked back and forth, back and forth.

She was glad, afterward, that this was all she did, for at the far end of the veranda Daniel Burton stepped out from a door, and stood for a moment watching them. But it was for only a moment. And when she begged mutely for him to come forward and speak, he shook his head fiercely, covered his eyes with his hand, and plunged back into the house.

"What was that, Susan? What was that?" demanded the boy.

"Nothin', child, nothin', only a door shuttin' somewhere, or a window."

At that moment a girl's voice caroled shrilly from the street.

"Hullo, Keith, how do you do? We're awfully glad to see you out again."

The boy started violently, but did not turn his head—except to Susan.

"Susan, I—I'm tired. I want to go in now," he begged a little wildly, under his breath.

"Keith, it's Mazie—Mazie and Dorothy," caroled the high-pitched voice again.

But Keith, with a tug so imperative that Susan had no choice but to obey, turned his head quite away as he groped for the door to go in.

In the hall he drew a choking breath.

"Susan, I don't want to go out there to walk any more—NOT ANY MORE! I don't want to go anywhere where anybody'll see me."

"Shucks!" Susan's voice was harshly unsteady again. "See you, indeed! Why, we're goin' to be so proud of you we'll want the whole world to see you.

> You jest wait
> An' see the fate
> That I've cut out for you.
> We'll be so proud
> We'll laugh aloud,
> An' you'll be laughin', too!

I made that up last night when I laid awake thinkin' of all the fine things we was goin' to have you do."

But Keith only shook his head again and complained of feeling, oh, so tired. And Susan, looking at his pale, constrained face, did not quote any more poetry to him, or talk about the glorious future in store for him. She led him to the easiest chair in his room and made him as comfortable as she could. Then she went downstairs and shut herself in the pantry—until she could stop her "fool cryin' over nothin'."

CHAPTER VIII

AUNT NETTIE MEETS HER MATCH

Mrs. Nettie Colebrook came at half-past five. She was a small, nervous-looking woman with pale-blue eyes and pale-yellow hair. She greeted her brother with a burst of tears.

"Oh, Daniel, Daniel, how can you stand it—how can you stand it!" she cried, throwing herself upon the man's somewhat unresponsive shoulder.

"There, there, Nettie, control yourself, do!" besought the man uncomfortably, trying to withdraw himself from the clinging arms.

"But how CAN you stand it!—your only son—blind!" wailed Mrs. Colebrook, with a fresh burst of sobs.

"I notice some things have to be stood," observed Susan grimly. Susan, with Mrs. Colebrook's traveling-bag in her hand, was waiting with obvious impatience to escort her visitor upstairs to her room.

Susan's terse comment accomplished what Daniel Burton's admonition had been quite powerless to bring about. Mrs. Colebrook stopped sobbing at once, and drew herself somewhat haughtily erect.

"And, pray, who is this?" she demanded, looking from one to the other.

"Well, 'this' happens to be the hired girl, an' she's got some biscuits in the oven," explained Susan crisply. "If you'll be so good, ma'am, I'll show you upstairs to your room."

"Daniel!" appealed Mrs. Colebrook, plainly aghast.

But her brother, with a helpless gesture, had turned away, and Susan, bag in hand, was already halfway up the stairs. With heightened color and a muttered "Impertinence!" Mrs. Colebrook turned and followed Susan to the floor above.

A little way down the hall Susan threw open a door.

"I swept, but I didn't have no time to dust," she announced as she put down the bag. "There's a duster in that little bag there. Don't lock the door. Somethin' ails it. If you do you'll have to go out the window down a ladder. There's towels in the top drawer, an' you'll have to fill the pitcher every day, 'cause there's a crack an' it leaks, an' you can't put in the water only to where the crack is. Is there anything more you want?"

"Thank you. If you'll kindly take me to Master Keith's room, that will be all that I require," answered Mrs. Colebrook frigidly, as she unpinned her hat and laid that on top of her coat on the bed.

"All right, ma'am. He's a whole lot better. He's been up an' dressed to-day, but he's gone back to bed now. His room is right down here, jest across the hall," finished Susan, throwing wide the door.

Eleanor H. Porter

There was a choking cry, a swift rush of feet, then Mrs. Colebrook, on her knees, was sobbing at the bedside.

"Oh, Keithie, Keithie, my poor blind boy! What will you do? How will you ever live? Never to see again, never to see again! Oh, my poor boy, my poor blind boy!"

Susan, at the door, flung both hands above her head, then plunged down the stairs.

"Fool! FOOL! FOOL!" she snarled at the biscuits in the oven. "Don't you know ANYTHING?" Yet the biscuits in the oven were puffing up and browning beautifully, as the best of biscuits should.

When Susan's strident call for supper rang through the hall, Mrs. Colebrook was with her brother in the studio. She had been bemoaning and bewailing the cruel fate that had overtaken "that dear boy," and had just asked for the seventh time how he could stand it, when from the hall below came:

"Supper's ready, supper's ready,
Hurry up or you'll be late.
Then you'll sure be cross an' heady,
If there's nothin' left to ate."

"Daniel, what in the world is the meaning of that?" she interrupted sharply.

"That? Oh, that is Susan's—er—supper bell," shrugged the man, with a little uneasy gesture.

"You mean that you've heard it before?—that that is her usual method of summoning you to your meals?"

"Y-yes, when she's good-natured," returned the man, with a

still more uneasy shifting of his position. "Come, shall we go down?"

"DANIEL! And you stand it?"

"Oh, come, come! You don't understand—conditions here. Besides, I've tried to stop it."

"TRIED to stop it!"

"Yes. Oh, well, try yourself, if you think it's so easy. I give you my full and free permission. Try it."

"TRY it! I shan't TRY anything of the sort. I shall STOP it."

"Humph!" shrugged the man. "Oh, very well, then. Suppose we go down."

"But what does that poor little blind boy eat? How can he eat—anything?"

"Why, I—I don't know." The man gave an irritably helpless gesture. "The nurse—she used to—You'll have to ask Susan. She'll know."

"Susan! That impossible woman! Daniel, how DO you stand her?"

Daniel Burton shrugged his shoulders again. Then suddenly he gave a short, grim laugh.

"I notice there are some things that have to be stood," he observed, so exactly in imitation of Susan that it was a pity only Mrs. Nettie Colebrook's unappreciative ears got the benefit of it.

In the dining-room a disapproving Susan stood by the table.

"I thought you wasn't never comin'. The hash is gettin' cold."

Mrs. Colebrook gasped audibly.

"Yes, yes, I know," murmured Mr. Burton conciliatingly. "But we're here now, Susan."

"What will Master Keith have for his supper?" questioned Mrs. Colebrook, lifting her chin a little.

"He's already had his supper, ma'am. I took it up myself."

"What was it?" Mrs. Colebrook asked the question haughtily, imperiously.

Susan's eyes grew cold like steel.

"It was what he asked for, ma'am, an' he's ate it. Do you want your tea strong or weak, ma'am?"

Mrs. Colebrook bit her lip.

"I'll not take any tea at all," she said coldly. "And, Susan!"

"Yes, ma'am." Susan turned, her hand on the doorknob.

"Hereafter I will take up Master Keith's meals myself. He is in my charge now."

There was no reply—in words. But the dining-room door after Susan shut with a short, crisp snap.

After supper Mrs. Colebrook went out into the kitchen.

"You may prepare oatmeal and dry toast and a glass of milk for Master Keith to-morrow morning, Susan. I will take them up myself."

"He won't eat 'em. He don't like 'em—not none of them things."

"I think he will if I tell him to. At all events, they are what he should eat, and you may prepare them as I said."

"Very well, ma'am."

Susan's lips came together in a thin, white line, and Mrs. Colebrook left the kitchen.

Keith did not eat his toast and oatmeal the next morning, though his aunt sat on the edge of the bed, called him her poor, afflicted, darling boy, and attempted to feed him herself with a spoon.

Keith turned his face to the wall and said he didn't want any breakfast. Whereupon his aunt sighed, and stroked his head; and Keith hated to have his head stroked, as Susan could have told her.

"Of course, you don't want any breakfast, you poor, sightless lamb," she moaned. "And I don't blame you. Oh, Keithie, Keithie, when I see you lying there like that, with your poor useless eyes—! But you must eat, dear, you must eat. Now, come, just a weeny, teeny mouthful to please auntie!"

But Keith turned his face even more determinedly to the wall, and moved his limbs under the bed clothes in a motion very much like a kick. He would have nothing whatever to do with the "weeny, teeny mouthfuls," not even to please auntie. And after a vain attempt to remove his tortured head, entirely away from those gently stroking ringers, he said he guessed he would get up and be dressed.

"Oh, Keithie, are you well enough, dear? Are you sure you are strong enough? I'm sure you must be ill this morning. You haven't eaten a bit of breakfast. And if anything should happen to you when you were in MY care—"

"Of course I'm well enough," insisted the boy irritably.

"Then I'll get your clothes, dear, and help you dress, if you will be careful not to overdo."

"I don't want any help."

"Why, Keithie, you'll HAVE to have some one help you. How do you suppose your poor blind eyes are going to let you dress yourself all alone, when you can't see a thing? Why, dear child, you'll have to have help now about everything you do. Now I'll get your clothes. Where are they, dear? In this closet?"

"I don't know. I don't want 'em. I—I've decided I don't want to get up, after all."

"You ARE too tired, then?"

"Yes, I'm too tired." And Keith, with another spasmodic jerk under the bedclothes, turned his face to the wall again.

"All right, dear, you shan't. That's the better way, I think myself," sighed his aunt. "I wouldn't have you overtax yourself for the world. Now isn't there anything, ANYTHING I can do for you?"

And Keith said no, not a thing, not a single thing. And his

face was still to the wall.

"Then if you're all right, absolutely all right, I'll go out to walk and get a little fresh air. Now don't move. Don't stir. TRY to go to sleep if you can. And if you want anything, just ring. I'll put this little bell right by your hand on the bed; and you must ring if you want anything, ANYTHING. Then Susan will come and get it for you. There, the bell's right here. See? Oh, no, no, you CAN'T see!" she broke off suddenly, with a wailing sob. "Why will I keep talking to you as if you could?"

"Well, I wish you WOULD talk to me as if I could see," stormed Keith passionately, sitting upright in bed and flinging out his arms. "I tell you I don't want to be different! It's because I AM different that I am so—"

But his aunt, aghast, interrupted him, and pushed him back.

"Oh, Keithie, darling, lie down! You mustn't thrash yourself around like that," she remonstrated. "Why, you'll make yourself ill. There, that's better. Now go to sleep. I'm going out before you can talk any more, and get yourself all worked up again," she finished, hurrying out of the room with the breakfast tray.

A little later in the kitchen she faced Susan a bit haughtily.

"Master Keith is going to sleep," she said, putting down the breakfast tray. "I have left a bell within reach of his hand, and he will call you if he wants anything. I am going out to get a little air."

"All right, ma'am." Susan kept right on with the dish she was drying.

Eleanor H. Porter

"You are sure you can hear the bell?"

"Oh, yes, my hearin' ain't repaired in the least, ma'am." Susan turned her back and picked up another dish. Plainly, for Susan, the matter was closed.

Mrs. Colebrook, after a vexed biting of her lip and a frowning glance toward Susan's substantial back, shrugged her shoulders and left the kitchen. A minute later, still hatless, she crossed the yard and entered the McGuires' side door.

"Take the air, indeed!" muttered Susan, watching from the kitchen window. "A whole lot of fresh air she'll get in Mis' McGuire's kitchen!"

With another glance to make sure that Mrs. Nettie Colebrook was safely behind the McGuires' closed door, Susan crossed the kitchen and lifted the napkin of the breakfast tray.

"Humph!" she grunted angrily, surveying the almost untouched breakfast. "I thought as much! But I was ready for you, my lady. Toast an' oatmeal, indeed!" With another glance over her shoulder at the McGuire side door Susan strode to the stove and took from the oven a plate of crisply browned hash and a hot corn muffin. Two minutes later, with a wonderfully appetizing-looking tray, she tapped at Keith's door and entered the room.

"Here's your breakfast, boy," she announced cheerily.

"I didn't want any breakfast," came crossly from the bed.

"Of course you didn't want THAT breakfast," scoffed Susan airily; "but you just look an' see what I'VE brought you!"

Look and see! Susan's dismayed face showed that she fully

realized what she had said, and that she dreaded beyond words its effect on the blind boy in the bed.

She hesitated, and almost dropped the tray in her consternation. But the boy turned with a sudden eagerness that put to rout her dismay, and sent a glow of dazed wonder to her face instead.

"What HAVE you got? Let me see." He was sitting up now. "Hash—and—johnny-cake!" he crowed, as she set the tray before him, and he dropped his fingers lightly on the contents of the tray. "And don't they smell good! I don't know—I guess I am hungry, after all."

"Of course you're hungry!" Susan's voice was harsh, and she was fiercely brushing back the tears. "Now, eat it quick, or I'll be sick! Jest think what'll happen to Susan if that blessed aunt of yours comes an' finds me feedin' you red-flannel hash an' johnny-cake! Now I'll be up in ten minutes for the tray. See that you eat it up—every scrap," she admonished him, as she left the room.

Susan had found by experience that Keith ate much better when alone. She was not surprised, therefore, though she was very much pleased—at sight of the empty plates awaiting her when she went up for the tray at the end of the ten minutes.

"An' now what do you say to gettin' up?" she suggested cheerily, picking up the tray from the bed and setting it on the table.

"Can I dress myself?"

"Of course you can! What'll you bet you won't do it five minutes quicker this time, too? I'll get your clothes."

Halfway back across the room, clothes in hand, she was brought to a sudden halt by a peremptory: "What in the world is the meaning of this?" It was Mrs. Nettie Colebrook in the doorway.

"I'm gettin' Keith's clothes. He's goin' to get up."

"But MASTER Keith said he did not wish to get up."

"Changed his mind, maybe." The terseness of Susan's reply and the expression on her face showed that the emphasis on the "Master" was not lost upon her.

"Very well, then, that will do. You may go. I will help him dress."

"I don't want any help," declared Keith.

"Why, Keithie, darling, of course you want help! You forget, dear, you can't see now, and—"

"Oh, no, I don't forget," cut in Keith bitterly. "You don't let me forget a minute—not a minute. I don't want to get up now, anyhow. What's the use of gettin' up? I can't DO anything!" And he fell back to his old position, with his face to the wall.

"There, there, dear, you are ill and overwrought," cried Mrs. Colebrook, hastening to the bedside. "It is just as I said, you are not fit to get up." Then, to Susan, sharply: "You may put Master Keith's clothes back in the closet. He will not need them to-day."

"No, ma'am, I don't think he will need them—now." Susan's eyes flashed ominously. But she hung the clothes back in the closet, picked up the tray, and left the room.

Susan's eyes flashed ominously, indeed, all the rest of the morning, while she was about her work; and at noon, when she gave the call to dinner, there was a curious metallic incisiveness in her voice, which made the call more strident than usual.

It was when Mrs. Colebrook went into the kitchen after dinner for Keith's tray that she said coldly to Susan:

"Susan, I don't like that absurd doggerel of yours."

"Doggerel?" Plainly Susan was genuinely ignorant of what she meant.

"Yes, that extraordinary dinner call of yours. As I said before, I don't like it."

There was a moment's dead silence. The first angry flash in Susan's eyes was followed by a demure smile.

"Don't you? Why, I thought it was real cute, now."

"Well, I don't. You'll kindly not use it any more, Susan," replied Mrs. Colebrook, with dignity.

Once again there was the briefest of silences, then quietly came Susan's answer:

"Oh, no, of course not, ma'am. I won't—when I work for you. There, Mis' Colebrook, here's your tray all ready."

And Mrs. Colebrook, without knowing exactly how it happened, found herself out in the hall with the tray in her hands.

Eleanor H. Porter

CHAPTER IX

SUSAN SPEAKS HER MIND

"How's Keith?"

It was Monday morning, and as usual Mrs. McGuire, seeing Susan in the clothes-yard, had come out, ostensibly to hang out her own clothes, in reality to visit with Susan while she was hanging out hers.

"About as usual." Susan snapped out the words and a pillow-case with equal vehemence.

"Is he up an' dressed?"

"I don't know. I hain't seen him this mornin'—but it's safe to say he ain't."

"But I thought he was well enough to be up an' dressed right along now."

"He is WELL ENOUGH—or, rather he WAS." Susan snapped open another pillow-case and hung it on the line with spiteful jabs of two clothespins.

"Why, Susan, is he worse? You didn't say he was any worse.

You said he was about as usual."

"Well, so he is. That's about as usual. Look a-here, Mis' McGuire," flared Susan, turning with fierce suddenness, "wouldn't YOU be worse if you wasn't allowed to do as much as lift your own hand to your own head?"

"Why, Susan, what do you mean? What are you talkin' about?"

"I'm talkin' about Keith Burton an' Mis' Nettie Colebrook. I've GOT to talk about 'em to somebody. I'm that full I shall sunburst if I don't. She won't let him do a thing for himself—not a thing, that woman won't!"

"But how can he do anything for himself, with his poor sightless eyes?" demanded Mrs. McGuire. "I don't think I should complain, Susan Betts, because that poor boy's got somebody at last to take proper care of him."

"But it AIN'T takin' proper care of him, not to let him do things for himself," stormed Susan hotly. "How's he ever goin' to 'mount to anything—that's what I want to know—if he don't get a chance to begin to 'mount? All them fellers—them fellers that was blind an' wrote books an' give lecturin's an' made things—perfectly wonderful things with their hands—how much do you s'pose they would have done if they'd had a woman 'round who said, 'Here, let me do it; oh, you mustn't do that, Keithie, dear!' every time they lifted a hand to brush away a hair that was ticklin' their nose?"

"Oh, Susan!"

"Well, it's so. Look a-here, listen!" Susan dropped all pretense of work now, and came close to the fence. She was obviously very much in earnest. "That boy hain't been dressed but twice since that woman came a week ago. She won't let him dress himself alone an' now he don't want to be dressed. Says he's too tired. An' she says, 'Of course, you're too tired, Keithie, dear!' An' there he lies, day in an' day out, with his poor sightless eyes turned to the wall. He won't eat a thing hardly, except what I snuggle up when she's out airin' herself. He ain't keen on bein' fed with a spoon like a baby. No boy with any spunk would be."

"But can he feed himself?"

"Of course he can—if he gets a chance! But that ain't all. He don't want to be told all the time that he's different from other folks. He can't forget that he's blind, of course, but he wants you to act as if you forgot it. I know. I've seen him. But she don't forget it a minute—not a minute. She's always cryin' an' wringin' her hands, an' sighin', 'Oh, Keithie, Keithie, my poor boy, my poor blind boy!' till it's enough to make a saint say, 'Gosh!'"

"Well, that's only showin' sympathy, Susan," defended Mrs. McGuire. "I'm sure she ought not to be blamed for that."

"He don't want sympathy—or, if he does, he hadn't ought to have it."

"Why, Susan Betts, I'm ashamed of you—grudgin' that poor blind boy the comfort of a little sympathy! My John said yesterday—"

"'T ain't sympathy he needs. Sympathy's a nice, soft little paw that pats him to sleep. What he needs is a good sharp scratch that will make him get up an' do somethin'."

"Susan, how can you talk like that?"

"'Cause somebody's got to." Susan's voice was shaking now. Her hands were clenched so tightly on the fence pickets that the knuckles showed white with the strain. "Mis' McGuire, there's a chance, maybe, that that boy can see. There's somethin' they can do to his eyes, if he gets strong enough to have it done."

"Really? To see again?"

"Maybe. There's a chance. They ain't sure. But they can't even TRY till he gets well an' strong. An' how's he goin' to get well an' strong lyin' on that bed, face to the wall? That's what I want to know!"

"Hm-m, I see," nodded Mrs. McGuire soberly. Then, with a sidewise glance into Susan's face, she added: "But ain't that likely to cost—some money?"

"Yes, 't is." Susan went back to her work abruptly. With stern efficiency she shook out a heavy sheet and hung it up. Stooping, she picked up another one. But she did not shake out this. With the same curious abruptness that had characterized her movements a few moments before, she dropped the sheet back into the basket and came close to the fence again. "Mis' McGuire, won't you please let me take a copy of them two women's magazines that you take? That is, they—they do print poetry, don't they?"

"Why, y-yes, Susan, I guess they do. Thinkin' of sendin' 'em some of yours?" The question was asked in a derision that was entirely lost on Susan.

"Yes, to get some money." It was the breathless, palpitating Susan that Daniel Burton had seen a week ago, and like Daniel Burton on that occasion, Mrs. McGuire went down now in defeat before it.

"To—to get some money?" she stammered.

"Yes—for Keith's eyes, you know," panted Susan. "An' when I sell these, I'm goin' to write more—lots more. Only I've got to find a place, first, of course, to sell 'em. An' I did send 'em off last week. But they was jest cheap magazines; an' they sent a letter all printed sayin' as how they regretted very much they couldn't accept 'em. Like enough they didn't have money enough to pay much for 'em, anyway; but of course they didn't say that right out in so many words. But, as I said, they wasn't anything but cheap magazines, anyway. That's why I want yours, jest to get the addressin's of, I mean. THEY'RE first-class magazines, an' they'll pay me a good price, I'm sure. They'll have to, to get 'em! Why, Mis' McGuire, I've got to have the money. There ain't nobody but me TO get it. An' you don't s'pose we're goin' to let that boy stay blind all his life, do you, jest for the want of a little money?"

"'A little money'! It'll cost a lot of money, an' you know it, Susan Betts," cried Mrs. McGuire, stirred into sudden speech. "An' the idea of you tryin' to EARN it writin' poetry. For that matter, the idea of your earnin' it, anyway, even if you took your wages."

"Oh, I'd take my wages in a minute, if—" Susan stopped short. Her face had grown suddenly red. "That is, I—I think I'd rather take the poetry money, anyway," she finished lamely.

But Mrs. McGuire was not to be so easily deceived.

"Poetry money, indeed!" she scoffed sternly. "Susan Betts, do you know what I believe? I believe you don't GET any wages. I don't believe that man pays you a red cent from one week's end to the other. Now does he? You don't dare to answer!"

Susan drew herself up haughtily. But her face was still very red.

"Certainly I dare to answer, Mis' McGuire, but I don't care to. What Mr. Burton pays me discerns him an' me an' I don't care to discourse it in public. If you'll kindly lend me them magazines I asked you for a minute ago, I'll be very much obliged, an' I'll try to retaliate in the same way for you some time, if I have anything you want."

"Oh, good lan', Susan Betts, if you ain't the beat of 'em!" ejaculated Mrs. McGuire. "I'd like to shake you—though you don't deserve a shakin', I'll admit. You deserve—well, never mind. I'll get the magazines right away. That's the most I CAN do for you, I s'pose," she flung over her shoulder, as she hurried into the house.

CHAPTER X

AND NETTIE COLEBROOK SPEAKS HERS

Mrs. Colebrook had been a member of the Burton household a day less than two weeks when she confronted her brother in the studio with this terse statement:

"Daniel, either Susan or I leave this house tomorrow morning. You can choose between us."

"Nonsense, Nettie, don't be a fool," frowned the man. "You know very well that we need both you and Susan. Susan's a trial, I'll admit, in a good many ways; but I'll wager you'd find it more of a trial to get along without her, and try to do her work and yours, too."

"Nobody thought of getting along without SOMEBODY," returned Mrs. Colebrook, with some dignity. "I merely am asking you to dismiss Susan and hire somebody else—that is, of course, if you wish me to stay. Change maids, that's all."

The man made an impatient gesture.

"All, indeed! Very simple, the way you put it. But—see here, Nettie, this thing you ask is utterly out of the question. You don't understand matters at all."

"You mean that you don't intend to dismiss Susan?"

"Yes, if you will have it put that way—just that."

"Very well. Since that is your decision I shall have to govern myself accordingly, of course. I will see you in the morning to say good-bye." And she turned coldly away.

"What do you mean by that?"

"Why, that I am going home, of course—since you think more of having that impossible, outrageously impertinent servant girl here than you do me." Mrs. Colebrook was nearing the door how.

"Shucks! You know better than that! Come, come, if you're having any trouble with Susan, settle it with the girl herself, won't you? Don't come to me with it. You KNOW how I dislike anything like this."

At the door Mrs. Colebrook turned back suddenly with aggressive determination.

"Yes, I do know. You dislike anything that's disagreeable. You always have, from the time when you used to run upstairs to the attic and let us make all the explanations to pa and ma when something got lost or broken. But, see here, Daniel Burton, you've GOT to pay attention to this. It's your son, and your house, and your maid. And you shall listen to me."

"Well, well, all right, go ahead," sighed the man despairingly, throwing himself back in his chair. "What is the trouble? What is it that Susan does that annoys you so?"

"What does she do? What doesn't she do?" retorted Mrs.

Colebrook, dropping herself wearily into a chair facing her brother. "In the first place, she's the most wretchedly impertinent creature I ever dreamed of. It's always 'Keith' instead of 'Master Keith,' and I expect every day it'll be 'Daniel' and 'Nettie' for you and me. She shows no sort of respect or deference in her manner or language, and—well, what are you looking like that for?" she interrupted herself aggrievedly.

"I was only thinking—or rather I was TRYING to think of Susan—and deference," murmured the man dryly.

"Yes, that's exactly it," Mrs. Colebrook reproved him severely. "You're laughing. You've always laughed, I suspect, at her outrageous behavior, and that's why she's so impossible in every way. Why, Daniel Burton, I've actually heard her refuse—REFUSE to serve you with something to eat that you'd ordered."

"Oh, well, well, what if she has? Very likely there was something we had to eat up instead, to keep it from spoiling. Susan is very economical, Nettie."

"I dare say—at times, when it suits her to be so, especially if she can assert her authority over you. Why, Daniel, she's a perfect tyrant to you, and you know it. She not only tells you what to eat, but what to wear, and when to wear it—your socks, your underclothes. Why, Daniel, she actually bosses you!"

"Yes, yes; well, never mind," shrugged the man, a bit irritably. "We're talking about how she annoys YOU, not me, remember."

"Well, don't you suppose it annoys me to see my own brother so completely under the sway of this serving-maid? And such a maid! Daniel, will you tell me where she gets those long words of hers that she mixes up so absurdly?"

Daniel Burton laughed.

"Susan lived with Professor Hinkley for ten years before she came to me. The Hinkleys never used words of one or two syllables when they could find one of five or six that would do just as well. Susan loves long words."

"So I should judge. And those ridiculous rhymes of hers— did she learn those, also, from Professor Hinkley?" queried Mrs. Colebrook. "And as for that atrocious dinner-call of hers, it's a disgrace to any family—a positive disgrace!"

"Well, well, why don't you stop her doing it, then?" demanded Daniel Burton, still more irritably. "Go to HER, not me. Tell her not to."

"I have."

The tone of her voice was so fraught with meaning that the man looked up sharply.

"Well?"

"She said she wouldn't do it—when she worked for me."

Daniel Burton gave a sudden chuckle.

"I can imagine just how she'd say that," he murmured appreciatively.

"Daniel Burton, are you actually going to abet that girl in her wretched impertinence?" demanded Mrs. Colebrook angrily. "I tell you I will not stand it! Something has got to be done.

Why, she even tries to interfere with the way I take care of your son—presumes to give me counsel and advice on the subject, if you please. Dares to criticize me—ME! Daniel Burton, I tell you I will not stand it. You MUST give that woman her walking papers. Why, Daniel, I shall begin to think she has hypnotized you—that you're actually afraid of her!"

Was it the scorn in her voice? Or was it that Daniel Burton's endurance had snapped at this last straw? Whatever it was, the man leaped to his feet, threw back his shoulders, and thrust his hands into his pockets.

"Nettie, look here. Once for all let us settle this matter. I tell you I cannot dismiss Susan; and I mean what I say when I use the words 'can not.' I literally CAN NOT. To begin with, she's the kindest-hearted creature in the world, and she's been devotion itself all these years since—since Keith and I have been alone. But even if I could set that aside, there's something else I can't overlook. I—I owe Susan considerable money."

"You owe her—MONEY?"

"Yes, her wages. She has not had them for some time. I must owe her something like fifty or sixty dollars. You see, we—we have had some very unusual and very heavy expenses, and I have overdrawn my annuity—borrowed on it. Susan knew this and insisted on my letting her wages go on, for the present. More than that, she has refused a better position with higher wages—I know that. The pictures I had hoped to sell—"He stopped, tried to go on, failed obviously to control his voice; then turned away with a gesture more eloquent than any words could have been.

Mrs. Colebrook stared, frowned, and bit her lip. Nervously

she tapped her foot on the floor as she watched with annoyed eyes her brother tramping up and down, up and down, the long, narrow room. Then suddenly her face cleared.

"Oh, well, that's easily remedied, after all." She sprang to her feet and hurried from the room. Almost immediately she was back—a roll of bills in her hand. "There, I thought I had enough money to do it," she announced briskly as she came in. "Now, Daniel, I'LL pay Susan her back wages."

"Indeed you will not!" The man wheeled sharply, an angry red staining his cheeks.

"Oh, but Daniel, don't you see?—that'll simplify everything. She'll be working for ME, then, and I—"

"But I tell you I won't have—" interrupted the man, then stopped short. Susan herself stood in the doorway.

"I guess likely you was talkin' so loud you didn't hear me call you to dinner," she was saying. "I've called you two times already. If you want anything fit to eat you'd better come quick. It ain't gettin' any fitter, waitin'."

"Susan!" Before Susan could turn away, Mrs. Colebrook detained her peremptorily." Mr. Burton tells me that he owes you for past wages. Now—"

"NETTIE!" warned the man sharply.

But with a blithe "Nonsense, Daniel, let me manage this!" Mrs. Colebrook turned again to Susan. The man, not unlike the little Daniel of long ago who fled to the attic, shrugged his shoulders with a gesture of utter irresponsibility, turned his back and walked to the farther side of the room.

Eleanor H. Porter

"Susan," began Mrs. Colebrook again, still blithely, but with just a shade of haughtiness, "my brother tells me your wages are past due; that he owes you at least fifty dollars. Now I'm going to pay them for him, Susan. In fact, I'm going to pay you sixty dollars, so as to be sure to cover it. Will that be quite satisfactory?"

Susan stared frankly.

"You mean ME—take money from you, ma'am,—to pay my back wages?" she asked.

"Yes."

"But—" Susan paused and threw a quick glance toward the broad back of the man at the end of the room. Then she turned resolutely to Mrs. Colebrook, her chin a little higher than usual. "Oh, no, thank you. I ain't needin' the money, Mis' Colebrook, an' I'd ruther wait for Mr. Burton, anyway," she finished cheerfully, as she turned to go.

"Nonsense, Susan, of COURSE you need the money. Everybody can make use of a little money, I guess. Surely, there's SOMETHING you want."

With her hand almost on the doorknob Susan suddenly whisked about, her face alight.

"Oh, yes, yes, I forgot, Mis' Colebrook," she cried eagerly. "There is somethin' I want; an' I'll take it, please, an' thank you kindly."

"There, that's better," nodded Mrs. Colebrook. "And I've got it right here, so you see you don't have to wait, even a minute," she smiled, holding out the roll of bills.

Still with the eager light on her face, Susan reached for the money.

"Thank you, oh, thank you! An' it will go quite a ways, won't it?—for Keith, I mean. The—" But with sudden sharpness Mrs. Colebrook interrupted her.

"Susan, how many times have I told you to speak of my nephew as 'Master Keith'? Furthermore, I shall have to remind you once more that you are trying to interfere altogether too much in his care. In fact, Susan, I may as well speak plainly. For some time past you have failed to give satisfaction. You are paid in full now, I believe, with some to spare, perhaps. You may work the week out. After that we shall no longer require your services."

The man at the end of the room wheeled sharply and half started to come forward. Then, with his habitual helpless gesture, he turned back to his old position.

Susan, her face eloquent with amazed unbelief, turned from one to the other.

"You mean—you don't mean—Mis' Colebrook, be you tryin' to—dismissal me?"

Mrs. Colebrook flushed and bit her lip.

"I am dismissing you—yes."

Once more Susan, in dazed unbelief, looked from one to the other. Her eyes dwelt longest on the figure of the man at the end of the room.

"Mr. Burton, do you want me to go?" she asked at last.

The man turned irritably, with a shrug, and a swift out-flinging of his hands.

"Of course, I don't want you to go, Susan. But what can I do? I have no money to pay you, as you know very well. I have no right to keep you—of course—I should advise you to go." And he turned away again.

Susan's face cleared.

"Pooh! Oh, that's all right then," she answered pleasantly. "Mis' Colebrook, I'm sorry to be troublin' you, but I shall have to give back that 'ere notice. I ain't goin'."

Once again Mrs. Colebrook flushed and bit her lip.

"That will do, Susan. You forget. You're not working for Mr. Burton now. You're working for me."

"For YOU?"

"Certainly. Didn't I just pay you your wages for some weeks past?"

Susan's tight clutch on the roll of bills loosened so abruptly that the money fell to the floor. But at once Susan stooped and picked it up. The next moment she had crossed the room and thrust the money into Mrs. Colebrook's astonished fingers.

"I don't want your money, Mis' Colebrook—not on them terms, even for Keith. I know I hain't earned any the other way, yet, but I hain't tried all the magazines. There's more—lots more." Her voice faltered, and almost broke. "I'll do it yet some way, you see if I don't. But I won't take this. Why, Mis' Colebrook, do you think I'd leave NOW, with that poor boy blind, an' his father so wrought up he don't have even his extraordinary common sense about his flannels an' socks an' what to eat, an' no money to pay the bills with, either? An' him bein' pestered the life out of him with them intermittent, dunnin' grocers an' milkmen? Well, I guess not! You couldn't hire me to go, Mis' Colebrook."

"Daniel, are you going to stand there and permit me to be talked to like this?" appealed Mrs. Colebrook.

"What can I do?" (Was there a ghost of a twinkle in Daniel Burton's eyes as he turned with a shrug and a lift of his eyebrows?) "If YOU haven't the money to hire her—" But Mrs. Colebrook, with an indignant toss of her head, had left the room.

"Mr. Burton!" Before the man could speak Susan had the floor again. "Can't you do somethin', sir? Can't you?"

"Do something, Susan?" frowned the man.

"Yes, with your sister," urged Susan. "I don't mean because she's so haughty an' impious. I can stand that. It's about Keith I'm talkin' about. Mr. Burton, Keith won't never get well, never, so's he can have that operator on his eyes, unless he takes some exercise an' gets his strength back. The nurse an' the doctor—they both said he wouldn't."

"Yes, yes, I know, Susan," fumed the man impatiently, beginning to pace up and down the room. "And that's just what we're trying to do—get his strength back."

"But he ain't—he won't—he can't," choked Susan feverishly. "Mr. Burton, I KNOW you don't want to talk about it, but you've got to. I'm all Keith's got to look out for him." The father of Keith gave an inarticulate gasp, but Susan plunged on unheeding. "An' he'll never get well if he ain't let to get up an' stand an' walk an' eat an' sit down himself. But Mis' Colebrook won't let him. She won't let him do anything. She keeps sayin', 'Don't do it, oh, don't do it,' all the time,—when she ought to say, 'Do it, do it, do it!' Mr. Burton, cryin' an' wringin' your hands an' moanin', 'Oh, Keithie, darling!' won't make a boy grow red blood an' make you feel so fine you want to knock a man down! Mr. Burton, I want you to tell that woman to let me take care of that boy for jest one week—ONE WEEK, an' her not to come near him with her snivelin' an'—"

But Daniel Burton, with two hands upflung, and a head that ducked as if before an oncoming blow, had rushed from the room. For the second time that day Daniel Burton had fled— to the attic.

CHAPTER XI

NOT PATS BUT SCRATCHES

Mrs. Colebrook went home the next day. She wore the air of an injured martyr at breakfast. She told her brother that, of course, if he preferred to have an ignorant servant girl take care of his poor afflicted son, she had nothing to say; but that certainly he could not expect HER to stay, too, especially after being insulted as she had been.

Daniel Burton had remonstrated feebly, shrugged his shoulders and flung his arms about in his usual gestures of impotent annoyance.

Susan, in the kitchen, went doggedly about her work, singing, meanwhile, what Keith called her "mad" song. When Susan was particularly "worked up" over something, "jest b'ilin' inside" as she expressed it, she always sang this song—her own composition, to the tune of "When Johnny Comes Marching Home":

> "I've taken my worries, an' taken my woes,
> I have, I have,
> An' shut 'em up where nobody knows,
> I have, I have.
> I chucked 'em down, that's what I did,

An' now I'm sittin' upon the lid,
An' we'll all feel gay when Johnny comes marchin' home.
I'm sittin' upon the lid, I am,
Hurrah! Hurrah!

I'm tryin' to be a little lamb,
Hurrah! Hurrah!
But I'm feelin' more like a great big slam
Than a nice little peaceful woolly lamb,
But we'll all feel gay when Johnny comes marchin'
home."

When Daniel Burton, this morning, therefore, heard Susan singing this song, he was in no doubt as to Susan's state of mind—a fact which certainly did not add to his own serenity.

Upstairs, Keith, wearily indifferent as to everything that was taking place about him, lay motionless as usual, his face turned toward the wall.

And at ten o'clock Mrs. Colebrook went. Five minutes later Daniel Burton entered the kitchen—a proceeding so extraordinary that Susan broke off her song in the middle of a "Hurrah" and grew actually pale.

"What is it?—KEITH? Is anything the matter with Keith?" she faltered.

Ignoring her question the man strode into the room.

"Well, Susan, this time you've done it," he ejaculated tersely.

"Done it—to Keith—ME? Why, Mr. Burton, what do you mean? Is Keith—worse?" chattered Susan, with dry lips. "It was only a little hash I took up. He simply won't eat that oatmeal stuff, an'—"

"No, no, I don't mean the hash," interrupted the man irritably. "Keith is all right—that is, he is just as he has been. It's my sister, Mrs. Colebrook. She's gone."

"Gone—for good?"

"Yes, she's gone home."

"Glory be!" The color came back to Susan's face in a flood, and frank delight chased the terror from her eyes. "Now we can do somethin' worthwhile."

"I reckon you'll find you have to do something, Susan. You know very well I can't afford to hire a nurse—now."

"I don't want one."

"But there's all the other work, too."

"Work! Why, Mr. Burton, I won't mind a little work if I can have that blessed boy all to myself with no one to feed him oatmeal mush with a spoon, an' snivel over him. You jest wait. The first elemental thing is to learn him self-defiance, so he can do things for himself. Then he'll begin to get his health an' strength for the operator."

"You're forgetting the money, Susan. It costs money for that."

Susan's face fell.

"Yes, sir, I know." She hesitated, then went on, her color deepening. "An' I hain't sold—none o' them poems yet. But there's other magazines, a whole lot of 'em, that I hain't tried. Somebody's sure to take 'em some time."

"I'm glad your courage is still good, Susan; but I'm afraid the dear public is going to appreciate your poems about the way it does—my pictures," shrugged the man bitterly, as he turned and left the room.

Not waiting to finish setting her kitchen in order, Susan ran up the back stairs to Keith's room.

"Well, your aunt is gone, an' I'm on,
An' here we are together.
We'll chuck our worries into pawn,
An' how do you like the weather?"

she greeted him gayly. "How about gettin' up? Come on! Such a lazy boy! Here it is away in the middle of the forenoon, an' you abed like this!"

But it was not to be so easy this time. Keith was not to be cajoled into getting up and dressing himself even to beat Susan's record. Steadfastly he resisted all efforts to stir him into interest or action; and a dismayed, disappointed Susan had to go downstairs in acknowledged defeat.

"But, land's sake, what could you expect?" she muttered to herself, after a sorrowful meditation before the kitchen fire. "You can't put a backbone into a jellyfish by jest showin' him the bone—an' that's what his aunt has made him—a flappy, transparallel jellyfish. Drat her! But I ain't goin' to give up. Not much I ain't!" And Susan attacked the little kitchen stove with a vigor that would have brought terror to the clinkers of a furnace fire pot.

Susan did not attempt again that day to get Keith up and dressed; and she gave him his favorite "pop-overs" for supper with a running fire of merry talk and jingles that contained never a reference to the unpleasant habit of putting on clothes, But the next morning, after she had given Keith his breakfast (not of toast and oatmeal) she suggested blithely that he get up and be dressed. When he refused she tried coaxing, mildly, then more strenuously. When this failed she tried to sting his pride by telling him she did not believe he could get up now, anyhow, and dress himself.

"All right, Susan, let it go that I can't. I don't want to, anyhow," sighed the boy with impatient weariness. "Say, can't you let a fellow alone?"

Susan drew a long breath and held it suspended for a moment. She had the air of one about to make a dreaded plunge.

"No, I can't let you alone, Keith," she replied, voice and manner now coldly firm.

"Why not? What's the use when I don't want to get up?"

"How about thinkin' for once what somebody else wants, young man?" Susan caught her breath again, and glanced furtively at the half-averted face on the pillow. Then doggedly she went on. "Maybe you think I hain't got anything to do but trespass up an' down them stairs all day waitin' on you, when you are perfectly capacious of waitin' on yourself SOME."

"Why, SUSAN!" There was incredulous, hurt amazement in the boy's voice; but Susan was visibly steeling herself against it.

"What do you think?—that I'm loafin' all day, an' your aunt gone now, an' me with it all on my hands?" she demanded, her stony gaze carefully turned away from the white face on the pillow. "An' to have to keep runnin' up here all the mornin' when I've got to do the dishes, an' bake bread, an' make soap, an'—"

"If you'll get my clothes, Susan, I'll get up," said Keith very quietly from the bed.

And Susan, not daring to unclose her lips, wrested the garments from the hooks, dropped them on to the chair by the bed, and fled from the room. But she had not reached the hall below when the sobs shook her frame.

"An' me talkin' like that when I'd be willin' to walk all day on my hands an' knees, if't would help him one little minute," she choked.

Barely had Susan whipped herself into presentable shape again when Keith's voice at the kitchen door caused her to face about with a startled cry.

"I'm downstairs, Susan." The boy's voice challenged hers for coldness now. "I'll take my meals down here, after this."

"Why, Keith, however in the world did you—" Then Susan pulled herself up. "Good boy, Keith! That WILL make it lots easier," she said cheerfully, impersonally, turning away and making a great clatter of pans in the sink.

But later, at least once every half-hour through that long forenoon, Susan crept softly through the side hall to the half-open living-room door, where she could watch Keith. She watched him get up and move slowly along the side of the room, picking his way. She watched him pause and move hesitating fingers down the backs of the chairs that he encountered. But when she saw him stop and finger the books on the little table by the window, she crept back to her kitchen—and rattled still more loudly the pots and pans in the sink.

Just before the noon meal Keith appeared once more at the kitchen door.

"Susan, would it bother you very much if I ate out here—with you?" he asked.

"With me? Nonsense! You'll eat in the dinin'-room with your dad, of course. Why, what would he say to your eatin' out here with me?"

"That's just it. It's dad. He'd like it, I'm sure," insisted the boy feverishly. "You know sometimes I—I don't get any food on my fork, when I eat, an' I have to—to feel for things, an' it—it must be disagreeable to see me. An' you know he never liked disagreeable—"

"Now, Keith Burton, you stop right where you are," interrupted Susan harshly. "You're goin' to eat with your father where you belong. An' do you now run back to the settin'-room. I've got my dinner to get."

Keith had not disappeared down the hall, however, before Susan was halfway up the back stairs. A moment later she was in the studio.

"Daniel Burton, you're goin' to have company to dinner," she panted.

"Company?"

"Yes. Your son." "KEITH?" The man drew back perceptibly.

"There, now, Daniel Burton, don't you go to scowlin' an' lookin' for a place to run, just because you hate to see him feel 'round for what he eats."

"But, Susan, it breaks my heart," moaned the man, turning quite away.

"What if it does? Ain't his broke, too? Can't you think of him a little? Let me tell you this, Daniel Burton—that boy has more consolation for your feelin's than you have for his, every time. Didn't he jest come to me an' beg to eat with me, 'cause his dad didn't like to see disagreeable things, an'—"

The man wheeled sharply.

"Did Keith—do that?"

"He did, jest now, sir."

"All right, Susan. I—I don't think you'll have to say—any more."

And Susan, after a sharp glance into the man's half-averted face, said no more. A moment later she had left the room.

At dinner that day, with red eyes but a vivacious manner, she waited on a man who incessantly talked of nothing in particular, and a boy who sat white-faced and silent, eating almost nothing.

CHAPTER XII

CALLERS FOR "KEITHIE"

And so inch by inch Susan fought her way, and inch by inch she gained ground. Sometimes it was by coaxing, sometimes by scolding; perhaps most often by taunts and dares, and shrewd appeals to Keith's pride. But by whatever it was, each day saw some stride forward, some new victory that Keith had won over his blindness, until by the end of the week the boy could move about the house and wait upon himself with a facility almost unbelievable when one remembered his listless helplessness of a week before.

Then one day there entered into the case a brand-new element, a dainty element in white muslin and fluttering blue ribbons—Mazie Sanborn and Dorothy Parkman.

"We heard Keithie was lots better and up and dressed now," chirped Mazie, when Susan answered her ring; "and so we've brought him some flowers. Please can't we see him?"

Susan hesitated. Susan had not forgotten Keith's feverish retreat from Mazie's greeting called up to the veranda the month before. But then, for that matter, had he not retreated from everything until she determinedly took him in hand? And he must some time begin to mingle with the world

Eleanor H. Porter

outside the four walls of his house!

Why not now? What better chance could she hope to have for him to begin than this? Where could she find two more charmingly alluring ambassadors of that outside world than right here on the door-step now?

Susan's lips snapped together with a little defiant nod of her head, then parted in a cordial smile.

"Sure, you may see him," she cried, "an' it's glad that I am to have you come! It'll do him good. Come in, come in!" And with only a heightened color to show her trepidation as to the reception that might be accorded her charges, she threw open the sitting-room door. "Well, Keith, here's company come on purpose to see you. An' they've brought you some flowers," she announced gayly.

"No, no, Susan, I—I don't want to see them," stammered the boy. He had leaped to his feet, a painful red flooding his face.

"Well, I like that!" bridled Mazie, with playful indignation; "and when Dorothy and I have taken all this trouble to come and—"

"Is Dorothy here, too?" interrupted the boy sharply.

"Yes, Keith I am—here." Dorothy was almost crying, and her voice sounded harsh and unnatural.

"And we brought you these," interposed Mazie brightly, crossing the room to his side and holding out the flowers. Then, with a little embarrassed laugh, as he did not take them, she thrust them into his fingers. "Oh, I forgot. You can't see them, can you?"

"Mazie!" remonstrated the half-smothered voice of Dorothy.

But it was Susan who came promptly to the rescue.

"Yes, an' ain't they pretty?" she cried, taking them from Keith's unresisting fingers. "Here, let me put 'em in water, an' you two sit down. I always did love coronation pinks," she declared briskly, as she left the room.

She was not gone long. Very quickly she came back, with the flowers in a vase. Keith had dropped back into his chair; but he was plainly so unwilling a host that Susan evidently thought best to assist him. She set the vase on a little stand near Keith's chair, then dropped herself on to the huge haircloth sofa near by.

"My, but I don't mind settin' myself awhile," she smiled. "Guess I'm tired."

"I should think you would be." Mazie, grown suddenly a bit stiff and stilted, was obviously trying to be very polite and "grown up." "There must be an awful lot to do here. Mother says she don't see how you stand it."

"Pooh! Not so very much!" scoffed Susan, instantly on her guard. "Keith here's gettin' so smart he won't let me do anything hardly for him now."

Oh, but there must be a lot of things," began Mazie," that he can't do, and—"

"Er—what a lovely big, sunny room," interrupted Dorothy hastily, so hastily that Susan threw a sharp glance into her face to see if she were really interrupting Mazie for a purpose. "I love big rooms."

"Yes, so do I," chimed in Mazie. "And I always wanted to see the inside of this house, too."

"What for?" Keith's curiosity got the better of his vexed reticence, and forced the question from his lips.

"Oh, just 'cause I've heard folks say 'twas so wonderful—old, you know, and full of rare old things, and there wasn't another for miles around like it. But I don't see—That is," she corrected herself, stumbling a little, "you probably don't keep them in this room, anyway."

"Why, they do, too," interfered Dorothy, with suddenly pink cheeks. "This room is just full of the loveliest kind of old things, just like the things father is always getting—only nicer. Now that, right there in the corner, all full of drawers—We've got one almost just exactly like that out home, and father just dotes on it. That IS a—a highboy, isn't it?" she appealed to Susan. "And it is very old, isn't it?"

"A highboy? Old? Lan' sakes, child," laughed Susan. "Maybe 'tis. I ain't sayin' 'tisn't, though I'm free to confess I never heard it called that. But it's old enough, if that's all it needs; it's old enough to be a highMAN by this time, I reckon," chuckled Susan. "Mr. Burton was tellin' me one day how it belonged to his great-grand-mother."

"Kind of funny-looking, though, isn't it?" commented Mazie.

"Father'd love it, so'd Aunt Hattie," avowed Dorothy, evidently not slow to detect the lack of appreciation in Mazie's voice. "And I do, too," she finished, with a tinge of defiance.

Mazie laughed.

"Well, all right, you may, for all I care," she retorted. Then to Keith she turned with sudden disconcerting abruptness: "Say, Keith, what do you do all day?"

It was Susan who answered this. Indeed, it was Susan who answered a good many of the questions during the next fifteen minutes. Some she answered because she did not want Keith to answer them. More she answered because Keith would not answer them. To tell the truth, Keith was anything but a polite, gracious host. He let it be plainly understood that he was neither pleased at the call nor interested in the conversation. And the only semblance of eagerness in his demeanor that afternoon was when his young visitors rose to go.

In spite of Keith's worse than indifference, however, Susan was convinced that this call, and others like it, were exactly what was needed for Keith's best welfare and development. With all her skill and artifice, therefore, she exerted herself to make up for Keith's negligence. She told stories, rattled off absurd jingles, and laughed and talked with each young miss in turn, determined to make the call so great a success that the girls would wish to come again.

When she had bowed them out and closed the door behind them, she came back to Keith, intending to remonstrate with him for his very ungracious behavior. But before she could open her lips Keith himself had the floor.

"Susan Betts," he began passionately, as soon as she entered the room, "don't you ever let those girls in again. I won't have them. I WON'T HAVE THEM, I tell you!

"Oh, for shame, Keith!—and when they were so kind and thoughtful, too!"

"It wasn't kindness and thoughtfulness," resented the boy. "It was spying out. They came to see how I took it. I know 'em. And that Dorothy Parkman—I don't know WHY she came. She said long ago that she couldn't bear—to look at 'em."

"Look at them?"

"Yes—blind folks. Her father is a big oculist—doctors eyes, you know. She told me once. And she said she couldn't bear to look at them; that—"

"An eye doctor?—a big one?" Susan was suddenly excited, alert.

"Yes, yes. And—"

"Where's he live?"

"I don't know. Where she does, I s'pose. I don't know where that is. She's here most of the time, and—"

"Is he a real big one?—a really, truly big one?"

"Yes, yes, I guess so." Keith had fallen wearily back in his chair, his strength spent. "Dad said he was one of the biggest in the country. And of course lots of—of blind people go there, and she sees them. Only she says she can't bear to see them, that she won't look at them. And—and she shan't come here—she shan't, Susan, to look at me, and—"

But Susan was not listening now. With chin up-tilted and a new fire in her eyes, she had turned toward the kitchen door.

Two days later, on her way to the store, Susan spied Dorothy Parkman across the street. Without hesitation or ceremony she went straight across and spoke to her.

"Is it true that your father is a big occultist, one of the biggest there is?" she demanded.

"A—what?" Dorothy frowned slightly.

"Occultist—doctors folks' eyes, you know. Is he? I heard he was."

"Oh! Y-yes—yes, he is." Miss Dorothy was giggling a bit now.

"Then, listen!" In her eagerness Susan had caught the girl's sleeve and held it. "Can't you get him to come on an' see you, right away, quick? Don't he want to take you home, or—or something?"

Dorothy laughed merrily.

"Why, Susan, are you in such a hurry as all that to get rid of me? Did I act so bad the other day that—"A sudden change crossed her face. Her eyes grew soft and luminous. "Was it for—Keith that you wanted father, Susan?"

"Yes." Susan's eyes blurred, and her voice choked.

"Well, then I'm glad to tell you he is coming by and by. He's coming to take me home for Christmas. But—he isn't going to stay long."

"That's all right—that's all right," retorted Susan, a little breathlessly. "If he'd jest look at the boy's eyes an' tell if—if he could fix 'em later. You see, we—we couldn't have it done now, 'cause there ain't any money to pay. But we'll have it later. We'll sure have it later, an' then—"

"Of course he'll look at them," interrupted Dorothy eagerly.

"He'll love to, I know. He's always so interested in eyes, and new cases. And—and don't worry about the other part—the money, you know," nodded Dorothy, hurrying away then before Susan could protest.

As it happened Keith was more "difficult" than usual that afternoon, and Susan, thinking to rouse him from his lassitude, suddenly determined to tell him all about the wonderful piece of good fortune in store for him.

"How'd you like to have that little Miss Dorothy's daddy see your eyes, honey," she began eagerly, "an' tell—"

"I wouldn't let him see them." Keith spoke coldly, decisively.

"Oh, but he's one of the biggest occultists there is, an'—"

"I suppose you mean 'oculist,' Susan," interrupted Keith, still more coldly; "but that doesn't make any difference. I don't want him."

"But, Keith, if he—"

"I tell you I won't have him," snapped Keith irritably.

"But you've got to have somebody, an' if he's the biggest!" All the eager light had died out of Susan's face.

"I don't care if he is the biggest, he's Dorothy Parkman's father, and that's enough. I WON'T HAVE HIM!"

"No, no; well, all right!" And Susan, terrified and dismayed, hurried from the room.

But though Susan was dismayed and terrified, she was far from being subdued. In the kitchen she lifted her chin defiantly.

"All right, Master Keith," she muttered to herself. "You can say what you want to, but you'll have him jest the same—only you won't know he's HIM. I'll jest tell him to call hisself another name for you. An' some time I'll find out what there is behind that Dorothy Parkman business. But 'tain't till Christmas, an' that's 'most two months off yet. Time enough for trouble when trouble knocks at the door; an' till it does knock, jest keep peggin' away."

CHAPTER XIII

FREE VERSE—A LA SUSAN

And persistently, systematically Susan did, indeed, keep "peggin' away." No sooner had she roused Keith to the point of accomplishing one task than she set for him another. No sooner could he pilot himself about one room than she inveigled him into another. And when he could go everywhere about the house she coaxed him out into the yard. It was harder here, for Keith had a morbid fear of being stared at. And only semi-occasionally would he consent at all to going out.

It was then that with stern determination Susan sought Daniel Burton.

"Look a-here, Daniel Burton," she accosted him abruptly, "I've done all I can now, an' it's up to you."

The man looked up, plainly startled.

"Why, Susan, you don't mean—you aren't—GOING, are you?"

"Goin' nothin'—shucks!" tossed Susan to one side disdainfully. "I mean that Keith ain't goin' to get that good red blood he's needin' sittin' 'round the house here. He's got to go off in the woods an' walk an' tramp an' run an' scuff leaves. An' you've got to go with him. I can't, can I?"

The man shifted his position irritably.

"Do you think that boy will let me lead him through the streets, Susan? Well, I know he won't."

"I didn't say 'lead him.' I said go WITH him. There's an awful lot of difference between leadin' an' accommodatin'. We don't none of us like to be led, but we don't mind goin' WITH folks 'most anywheres. Put your arm into his an' walk together. He'll walk that way. I've tried it. An' to see him you wouldn't know he was blind at all. Oh, yes, I know you're hangin' back an' don't want to. I know you hate to see him or be with him, 'cause it makes you KNOW what a terrible thing it is that's come to you an' him. But you've got to, Daniel Burton. You an' me is all he's got to stand between him an' utter misery. I can feed his stomach an' make him do the metaphysical things, but it's you that's got to feed his soul an' make him do the menial things."

"Oh, Susan, Susan!" half groaned the man. There was a smile on his lips, but there were tears in his eyes.

"Well, it's so," argued Susan earnestly. "Oh, I read to him, of course. I read him everything I can get hold of, especially about men an' women that have become great an' famous an' extinguished, even if they was blind or deaf an' dumb, or lame—especially blind. But I can't learn him books, Mr. Burton. You've got to do that. You've got to be eyes for him, an' he's got to go to school to you. Mr. Burton,"—Susan's voice grew husky and unsteady,—"you've got a chance now to paint bigger an' grander pictures than you ever did before, only you won't be paintin' 'em on canvas backs. You'll be paintin' 'em on that boy's soul, an' you'll be usin' words instead of them little brushes."

"You've put that—very well, Susan." It was the man who spoke unsteadily, huskily, now.

"I don't know about that, but I do know that them pictures you're goin' to paint for him is goin' to be the makin' of him. Why, Mr. Burton, we can't have him lazin' behind, 'cause when he does get back his eyes we don't want him to be too far behind his class."

"But what—if he doesn't ever get his eyes", Susan?"

"Then he'll need it all the more. But he's goin' to get 'em, Mr. Burton. Don't you remember? The nurse said if he got well an' strong he could have somethin' done. I've got the doctor, an' all I need now is the money. An'—an' that makes me think." She hesitated, growing suddenly pink and embarrassed. Then resolutely she put her hand into the pocket of her apron and pulled out two folded papers.

"I was goin' to tell you about these, anyhow, so I might as well do it now," she explained. "You know, them—them other poems didn't sell much—there was only one went, an' the man wouldn't take that till he'd made me promise he could print my letter, too, that I'd wrote with it—jest as if that was worth anything!—but he only paid a measly dollar anyhow. "Susan's voice faltered a little, though her chin was at a brave tilt. "An' I guess now I know the reason. Them kind of poems ain't stylish no longer. Rhymes has gone out. Everything's 'free verse' now. I've been readin' up about it. So I've wrote some of 'em. They're real easy to do—jest lines chopped off free an' easy, anywheres that it happens, only have some long, an' some short, for notoriety, you know, like this." And she read:

"A great big cloud
That was black
Came up
Out of the West. An' I knew
Then For sure
That a storm was brewin'.
An' it brewed."

"Now that was dead easy—anybody could see that. But it's kind of pretty, I think, too, jest the same. Them denatured poems are always pretty, I think—about trees an' grass an' flowers an' the sky, you know. Don't you?"

"Why, er—y-yes, of course," murmured the man faintly.

"I tried a love poem next. I don't write them very often. They're so common. You see 'em everywhere, you know. But I thought I would try it—'twould be different, anyhow, in this new kind of verses. So I wrote this:

Oh, love of mine,
I love
Thee.
Thy hair is yellow like the
Golden squash.
Thy neck so soft
An' slender like a goose,
Is encompassed in filtered lace
So rich an'
Rare.
Thy eyes in thy pallid face like
Blueberries in a
Saucer of milk.
Oh, love of mine,
I love
Thee."

"Have you sent—any of these away yet, Susan?" Daniel Burton was on his feet now, his back carefully turned.

"No, not yet; but I'm goin' to pretty quick, an' I guess them will sell." Susan nodded happily, and smiled. But almost instantly her face grew gravely earnest again. "But all the money in the world ain't goin' to do no good Mr. Burton, unless we do our part, an' our part is to get him well an' strong for that operator. Now I'm goin' to send Keith in to you. I ain't goin' to TELL him he's goin' to walk with you, 'cause if I did he wouldn't come. But I'm expectin' you to take him, jest the same," she finished severely, as she left the room.

Keith and his father went to walk. It was the first of many such walks. Almost every one of these crisp November days found the two off on a tramp somewhere. And because Daniel Burton was careful always to accompany, never to lead, the boy's step gained day by day in confidence and his face in something very like interest. And always, for cold and stormy days, there were the books at home.

Daniel Burton was not painting pictures—pigment pictures—these days. His easel was empty. "The Woodland Path," long since finished, had been sent away "to be sold." Most of Daniel Burton's paintings were "sent away to be sold," so that was nothing new. What was new, however, was the fact that no fresh canvas was placed on the easel to take the place of the picture sent away. Daniel Burton had begun no new picture. The easel, indeed, was turned face to the wall. And yet Daniel Burton was painting pictures, wonderful pictures. His brushes were words, his colors were the blue and gold and brown and crimson of the wide autumn landscape, his inspiration was the hungry light on a boy's face, and his canvas was the soul of the boy behind it. Most assuredly Daniel Burton was giving himself now, heart and mind and body, to his son. Even the lynx-eyed, alert Susan had no fault to find. Daniel Burton, most emphatically, was "doing his part."

CHAPTER XIV

A SURPRISE ALL AROUND

The week before Christmas Dorothy Parkman brought a tall, dignified-looking man to the Burtons' shabby, but still beautiful, colonial doorway.

Dorothy had not seen Keith, except on the street, since her visit with Mazie in October. Two or three times the girls had gone to the house with flowers or fruit, but Keith had stubbornly refused to see them, in spite of Susan's urgings. To-day Dorothy, with this evidently in mind, refused Susan's somewhat dubious invitation to come in.

"Oh, no, thank you, I'll not come in," she smiled. "I only brought father, that's all. And—oh, I do hope he can do something," she faltered unsteadily. And Susan saw that her eyes were glistening with tears as she turned away.

In the hall Susan caught the doctor's arm nervously.

"Dr. Parkman, there's somethin'—"

"My name is Stewart," interrupted the doctor.

"What's that? What's that?" cried Susan, unconsciously

tightening her clasp on his arm. "Ain't you Dorothy Parkman's father?"

"I'm her stepfather. She was nine when I married Mrs. Parkman, her mother."

"Then your name ain't Parkman, at all! Oh, glory be!" ejaculated Susan ecstatically. "Well, if that ain't the luckiest thing ever!"

"Lucky?" frowned the doctor, looking thoroughly mystified, and not altogether pleased.

Susan gave an embarrassed laugh.

"There, now, if that ain't jest like me, to fly off on a tandem like that, without a word of exploitation. It's jest that I'm so glad I won't have to ask you to come under a resumed name."

"Under a what, madam?" The doctor was looking positively angry now. Moreover, with no uncertain determination, he was trying to draw himself away from Susan's detaining fingers.

"Oh, please, doctor, please, don't be mad!" Susan had both hands hold of his arm now. "'Twas for Keith, an' I knew you'd be willin' to do anything for him, when you understood, jest as I am. You see, I didn't want him to know you was Dorothy's father," she plunged on breathlessly, "an' so I was goin' to ask you to let me call you somethin' else—not Parkman. An' then, when I found that you didn't have to have a resumed name, that you was already somebody else—that is, that you was really you, only Keith wouldn't know you was you, I was so glad."

"Oh, I see." The doctor was still frowning, though his lips were twitching a little. "But—er—do you mind telling me why I can't be I? What's the matter with Dorothy's father?"

"Nothin' sir. It's jest a notion. Keith won't see Dorothy, nor Mazie, nor none of 'em. He thinks they come jest to spy out how he looks an' acts; an' he got it into his head that if you was Dorothy's father, he wouldn't see you. He hates to be pitied an' stared at."

"Oh, I see." A sympathetic understanding came into the doctor's eyes. The anger was all gone now. "Very well. As it happens I'm really Dr. Stewart. So you may call me that with all honesty, and we'll be very careful not to let the boy know I ever heard of Dorothy Parkman. How about the boy's father? Does he—know?"

"Yes, sir. I told him who you was, an' that you was comin'; an' I told him we wasn't goin' to let Keith know. An' he said 'twas absurd, an' we couldn't help lettin' him know. But I told him I knew better an' 'twas all right."

"Oh, you did!" The doctor was regarding Susan with a new interest in his eyes.

"Yes, an' 'tis, you see."

"Where is Mr. Burton?"

"In his studio—shut up. He'll see you afterwards. I told him he'd GOT to do that."

"Eh? What?" The doctor's eyes flew wide open.

"See you afterwards. I told him he'd ought to be in the room with you, when you was examplin' Keith's eyes. But I knew he wouldn't do that. He never will do such-like things—makes him feel too bad. An' he wanted ME to find out what you said. But I told him HE'D got to do that. But, oh, doctor, I do hope—oh, please, please say somethin' good if you can. An' now I'll take you in. It's right this way through the sittin'-room."

"By Jove, what a beauty!" Halfway across the living-room the doctor had come to a pause before the mahogany highboy.

"THAT?"

"Yes, 'that'!" The whimsical smile in the doctor's eyes showed that he was not unappreciative of the scorn in Susan's voice. "By George, it IS a beauty! I've got one myself, but it doesn't compare with that, for a minute. H-m! And that's not the only treasure you have here, I see," he finished, his admiring gaze roving about the room. "We've got some newer, better stuff in the parlor. These are awful old things in here," apologized Susan.

"Yes, I see they are—old things." The whimsical smile had come back to the doctor's eyes as he followed Susan through the doorway.

"Keith's upstairs in his room, an' I'm takin' you up the back way so's Mr. Burton won't hear. He asked me to. He didn't want to know jest exactly when you was here."

"Mr. Burton must be a brave man," commented the doctor dryly.

"He ain't—not when it comes to seein' disagreeable things, or folks hurt," answered the literal Susan cheerfully. "But he'll see you all right, when it's over." Her lips came together with a sudden grimness.

The next moment, throwing open Keith's door, her whole expression changed. She had eyes and thoughts but for the blind boy over by the window.

The doctor, too, obviously, by the keen, professional alertness that transfigured his face at that moment, had eyes and thoughts but for that same blind boy over by the window.

"Well, Keith, here's Dr. Stewart to see you boy."

"Dr.—Stewart?" Keith was on his feet, startled, uncertain.

"Yes, Dr. Stewart.'" Susan repeated the name with clear emphasis. "He was in town an' jest came up to look at you. He's a big, kind doctor, dear, an' you'll like him, I know." At the door Susan turned to the doctor. "An' when—when you're done, sir, if you'll jest come down them stairs to the kitchen, please—TO THE KITCHEN," she repeated, hurrying out before Keith could remonstrate.

Down in the kitchen Susan took a pan of potatoes to peel— and when, long hours later, after the doctor had come downstairs, had talked with Mr. Burton, and had gone, Susan went to get those potatoes to boil for dinner, she found that all but two of them had been peeled and peeled and peeled, until there was nothing left but—peelings.

Susan was peeling the next to the last potato when the doctor came down to the kitchen.

"Well?" She was on her feet instantly.

The doctor's face was grave, yet his eyes were curiously

alight. They seemed to be looking through and beyond Susan.

"I don't know. I THINK I have good news, but I'm not—sure."

"But there's a chance?"

"Yes; but-" There was a moment's silence; then, with an indrawing of his breath, the doctor's soul seemed to come back from a long journey. "I think I know what is the matter." The doctor was looking at Susan, now, not through her. "If it's what I think it is, it's a very rare disease, one we do not often find."

"But could you—can you—is it possible to—to cure it?"

"We can operate—yes; but it's six to half a dozen whether it's successful or not. They've just about broken even so far—the cases I've known about. But they've been interesting, most interesting." The doctor was far away again.

"But there's a chance; and if there is a chance I'd want to take it," cried Susan. "Wouldn't you?"

There was no answer.

Susan hesitated, threw a hurried glance into the doctor's preoccupied face, then hurried on again feverishly.

"Doctor, there's somethin' I've got to—to speak to you about before you see Mr. Burton. It—it—it'll cost an awful lot, I s'pose."

There was no answer.

Eleanor H. Porter

Susan cleared her throat.

"It—it'll cost an awful lot, won't it, doctor?" she asked in a louder voice.

"Eh? What? Cost? Oh, yes, yes; it is an expensive operation." The doctor spoke unconcernedly. He merely glanced at Susan, then resumed his fixed gaze into space.

"Well, doctor." Susan cleared her throat again. This time she caught hold of the doctor's sleeve as if to pull him bodily back to a realizing sense of her presence. "About the money—we haven't got it. An' that's what I wanted to speak to you about. Mr. Burton hain't got any. He's already spent more'n he's got—part of next year's annual, I mean. Some day he'll have more—a whole lot more—when Mis' Holworthy, his third cousin, dies. 'Twas her husband that gave him the annual, you understand, an' when she dies it'll come to him in a plump sum. But 'tain't his now, an' 'course it won't be till she goes; an' 'course 'tain't for us to dodge her footsteps hopin' she'll jest naturally stop walkin' some day— though I'm free to confess she has lost most all her facilities, bein' deaf an' lame an' some blind; an' I can't exactly see the harm in wishin' she had got 'em all back—in Heaven, I mean. But 'course I don't say so to him. An' as I said before, we hain't got money now—not any.

"An'—an' his last pictures didn't sell any better than the others," she went on a little breathlessly. "Then there was me—that is, I WAS goin' to get some money; but—but, well MY pictures didn't sell, either." She paused to wet her lips. "But I've thought it all out, an' there's a way.

You—you'd have to have Keith with you, somewheres, wouldn't you?"

"To operate? Oh, yes, yes."

"A long time?"

"Eh? What? Oh, yes, we would have to have him a long time, probably. In fact, time is one of the very biggest factors in such cases—for the after-treatment, you know. And we must have him where we can watch him, of course."

"Oh! Then that's all right, then. I can manage it fine," sighed Susan, showing by the way her whole self relaxed how great had been the strain. "Then I'll come right away to work for you."

"To what?" The doctor suddenly came back to earth.

"To work for you—in your kitchen, I mean," nodded Susan. "I'll send Mr. Burton to his sister's, then I'll come to you, an' I'll come impaired to stay till I've paid it up—every cent."

"Good Heavens, woman!" ejaculated the man. "What are you talking about?"

"Oh, please, please don't say that I can't," besought Susan, her fearful eyes on his perturbed face. "I'll work real well— truly I will. An' I'm a real good cook, honest I am, when I have a super-abundance to do it with—butter, an' eggs, an' nice roasts. An' I won't bother you a mite with my poetry. I don't make it much now, anyhow. An'—oh, doctor, you've GOT to let me do it; it's the only way there is to p-pay." Her voice choked into silence. Susan turned her back abruptly. Not even for Keith could Susan let any one see her cry.

"Pay! And do you think you'd live long—" Just in time the doctor pulled himself up short. Thrusting his hands into his pockets he took a nervous turn about the kitchen; then sharply he wheeled about. "My dear woman, let us talk no more about the money question. See here, I shall be glad to take that boy into my charge and take care of him for the sheer love of it—indeed, I shall!"

"Do you mean without ANY pay?" Susan had drawn herself up haughtily.

"Yes. So far as money goes—it is of no consequence, anyway. I'm glad—"

"Thank you, but we ain't charitable folks, Dr. Stewart," cut in Susan coldly. "Maybe it is infinitesimal to you whether we pay or not, but't ain't to us. We don't want—"

"But I tell you it's pay enough just to do it," interrupted the doctor impatiently. "It's a very rare case, and I'm glad—"

A door banged open.

"Susan, hasn't that doctor—" a new voice cut in, then stopped short.

The doctor turned to see a pallid-faced, blond-bearded man with rumpled hair standing in the doorway.

"Mr. Burton?" hazarded the doctor crisply.

"Yes. And you-"

"Dr. Stewart. And I'd like a little talk with you, please—if you can talk sense. "This last was added under his breath; but Daniel Burton was not listening, in any case. He was leading the way to the studio.

In the studio the doctor did not wait for questions, but

plunged at once into his story.

"Without going into technical terms, Mr. Burton, I will say that your son has a very rare trouble. There is only one known relief, and that is a certain very delicate operation. Even with that, the chances are about fifty-fifty that he regains his sight."

"But there's a chance?"

"Yes, there's a chance. And, anyway, it won't do any harm to try. It is the only thing possible, and, if it fails—well, he'll only be blind, as he is now. It must be done right away, however. Even now it may be too late. And I may as well tell you, if it DOESN'T fail—there is a strong probability of another long period of treatment and a second operation, before there's a chance of ultimate success!"

"Could—could that time be spent here?" Daniel Burton's lips had grown a little white.

"No. I should want the boy where I could see him frequently—with me, in fact. And that brings me to what I was going to propose. With your permission I will take the boy back with me next week to Chicago, and operate at once. And let me say that from sheer interest in the case I shall be glad to do this entirely without cost to you."

"Thank you; but of course you must understand that I could not allow that for a moment." A painful color had flamed into Daniel Burton's face.

"Nonsense! Don't be foolish, man. I tell you I'm glad to do it. It'll be worth it to me—the rarity of the case—"

"How much—would it cost?" interposed Daniel Burton

peremptorily, with an unsteadiness of voice that the doctor did not fail to read aright.

"Why, man, alive, it would cost—" With his eyes on Daniel Burton's sternly controlled face, the doctor came to an abrupt pause. Then, turning, he began to tramp up and down the room angrily. "Oh, hang it all, man, why can't you be sensible? I tell you I don't want any—" Once again his tongue stopped. His feet, also, had come to an abrupt pause. He was standing before an old colonial mirror. Then suddenly he wheeled about. "By Jove, there IS something I want. If you'll sell me two or three of these treasures of yours here, you will be more than cancelling your debt, and—"

"Thank you," interrupted the other coldly, but with a still deeper red staining his face. "As I happen to know of the unsalability of these pictures, however, I cannot accept your generosity there, either."

"Pictures!" The doctor, turning puzzled eyes back to the mirror, saw now that a large oil painting hung beside it on the wall. "I wasn't talking about your pictures, man," he scoffed then. "I was looking at that mirror there, and I'd like the highboy downstairs, if I could persuade you to part with them, and—WOULD you be willing to part with them?"

"What do you think!" (So marvelous was the change, and so great was the shining glory in Daniel Burton's face, that the doctor caught himself actually blinking.) "Do you think there's anything, ANYTHING that I wouldn't part with, if I thought I could give that boy a chance? Make your own selection, doctor. I only hope you'll want—really WANT— enough of them to amount to something."

The doctor threw a keen glance into his face.

"Amount to something! Don't you know the value of these things here?"

Daniel Burton laughed and shrugged his shoulders. "Oh, I suppose they are—valuable. But I shall have to confess I DON'T know very much about it. They're very old, I can vouch for that."

"Old! Humph!" The doctor was close to the mirror now, examining it with the appreciative eyes of the real lover of the antique. "I should say they were. Jove, that's a beauty! And I've got just the place that's hungering for it."

"Good! Suppose we look about the house, then, a little," suggested Daniel Burton. "Perhaps we'll find some more things—er—good for a hungry stomach, eh?" And with a light on his face such as had not been there for long months past, Daniel Burton led the way from the studio.

CHAPTER XV

AGAIN SUSAN TAKES A HAND

That evening Daniel Burton told Susan. "Keith is to go home with Dr. Stewart next week. The doctor will operate as soon as possible. Keith will live at the sanatorium connected with the doctor's home and be under his constant supervision."

Susan tried to speak, but instead of speaking she burst into tears.

"Why, Susan!" exclaimed the man.

"I know, I know," she choked, angrily dashing the drops from her eyes. "An' me cryin' like this when I'm gettin' jest what I want, too!"

"But there's no certainty, Susan, that it'll be successful; remember that," warned the man, his face clouding a little. "We can only—hope."

"An' there's the—the pay." Susan looked up, her voice vibrating with fearful doubts.

"Oh, that's all right." The man lifted his head with the air of one who at last has reached firm ground after a dangerous crossing on thin ice. "The doctor's going to buy the highboy and that mirror in the studio, and—oh, several other things."

"You mean that old chest of drawers in the settin'-room?" scorned Susan openly.

"Yes." Daniel Burton's lips twitched a little.

"But will he PAY anything for 'em? Mr. Burton, you can't get nothin', hardly, for second-hand furniture. My mother had a stove an' a real nice bedstead, an' a red-plush parlor set, an' she sold 'em. But she didn't get anything—not hardly anything, for 'em; an' they was 'most new, some of 'em, too."

"That's the trouble, Susan—they were too new, probably," laughed the man. "It's because these are old, very old, that he wants them, I suspect.

"An' he'll really pay MONEY for 'em?" Plainly Susan still had her doubts.

"He certainly will. I'd be almost ashamed to tell you HOW much he'll pay, Susan," smiled the man. "It seemed to me sheer robbery on my part. But he assures me they are very valuable, and that he's more than delighted to have them even at that price."

"Lan' sakes! An' when I'd been worryin' an' worryin' so about the money," sighed Susan; "an' now to have it fall plump into your lap like that. It jest shows you not to hunt for bridges till you get your feet wet, don't it? An' he's goin' jest next week?"

"Yes. The doctor and his daughter start Tuesday."

"You don't mean that girl Dorothy's goin' too?" Susan had

almost bounced out of her chair.

"Why, yes, Dr. Stewart SAID she was. What's the matter?"

"Matter? Matter enough! Why, if she goes—Say, why IS she taggin' along, anyhow?" demanded Susan wrathfully.

"Well, I shouldn't exactly call it 'taggin' along' to go home with her father for the Christmas vacation," shrugged the man. "As I understand it, Dorothy's mother died several years ago. That's why the girl is here in the East so much with her relatives, going to school. The doctor's home has become practically a sanatorium—not the most desirable place in the world to bring up a young daughter in, I should say. Let's see, how old is Miss Dorothy?"

"Sixteen, Keith says. I asked him one day. She's about his age."

"Hm-m; well, however that may be, Susan, I don't see how we can help ourselves very well. I fancy Miss Dorothy'll still—tag along," he finished whimsically.

"Maybe, an' then maybe not," mumbled Susan darkly, as she turned away.

For two days after this Susan's kitchen, and even Keith himself, showed almost neglect; persistently and systematically Susan was running "down street" every hour or two—ostensibly on errands, yet she bought little. She spent most of her time tramping through the streets and stores, scrutinizing especially the face of every young girl she met.

On the afternoon of the second day she met Dorothy Parkman coming out of the post-office.

"Well, I've got you at last," she sighed, "though I'm free to confess I was beginnin' to think I never would see you."

"Oh, yes, about Keith," cried the girl joyously. "Isn't it splendid! I'm so glad! And he's going home with us right away, you know."

"Yes, I know. An' that's what—that is, I wanted—" stammered Susan, growing red in her misery. "Oh, Miss Dorothy, you WOULD do anything for that poor blind boy, wouldn't you?"

"Why, y-yes, of course," faltered Dorothy, stammering in her turn.

"I knew you would. Then please don't go home with your father this time."

"Don't go home—with—my father!" exclaimed the girl, in puzzled wonder.

"No. Because if you do—That is—Oh, I know it's awful for me to say this, but I've got to do it for Keith. You see, if you go,—Keith won't."

"If I go, he—I don't think—I quite understand." The girl drew back a little haughtily. Her face showed a painful flush.

"No, no, of course you don't! An' please, PLEASE don't look like that," begged Susan. "It's jest this. I found out. I wormed it out of him the other day—why he won't let you come to see him. He says that once, long ago, you said how you couldn't bear to look at blind people, an'—"

"Oh, I never, never could have said such a cruel thing to—to a blind boy," interposed the girl.

"He wasn't blind then. He said he wasn't. But, it was when he was 'fraid he was goin' to be blind; an' he see you an' Mazie Sanborn at the foot of Harrington Hill, one day. It was just after the old man had got blind, an' Keith had been up to see him. It seems that Keith was worryin' then for fear HE was goin' to be blind."

"He WAS?"

"Yes—things blurred, an' all that. Well, at the foot of the hill he see you an' Mazie, an' you shuddered at his goin' up to see Mr. Harrington, an' said how could he bear to look at folks that was blind. That YOU couldn't. An' he never forgot it. Bein' worried for fear he himself was goin' blind, you see, he was especially acceptable to anything like that."

"Oh, but I—I—At home I always did hate to see all the poor blind people that came to see father," she stammered. "But it—it was only because I felt so bad—for them. And that's one reason why father doesn't keep me at home any more. He says—But, about Keith—I—I didn't mean to—" Dorothy came to a helpless pause.

"Yes, I know. You didn't mean to hurt him," nodded Susan. "But it did hurt him. An' now he always thinks of it, if he knows you're 'round. You see, worse'n anything else, he hates to be stared at or to have folks think he's different. There ain't anything I can ever say to him that makes him half so happy as to act as if he wa'n't blind."

"Yes, I—see," breathed Dorothy, her eyes brimming.

"An' so now you won't go, will you? Because if you go, he won't."

Miss Dorothy frowned in deep thought for a moment.

"I shall have to go," she said at last, slowly. "Father is just counting on my being there Christmas, and he is so lonely—I couldn't disappoint him. But, Keith—I won't have to see much of him, anyway. I'll explain it to father. He won't mind. He's used to his patients taking notions. It'll be all right. Don't worry," she nodded, her face clearing.

"But you'll have to be with Keith—some."

"Oh, yes, a little. But he won't know who I am. I'm just Dr. Stewart's daughter. Don't you see?"

"But—he'll know your voice."

"I shan't talk much. Besides, he never did hear me talk much. It was always Mazie that talked most. And he hasn't heard me any for a year or more, except that little bit that day at the house."

"But your name, Dorothy," still argued Susan dubiously.

"Father never calls me that. I'm always 'Puss' to him. And there won't be anybody else with us on the journey. Don't you worry. You just send Keith right along, and trust me for the rest. You'll see," she nodded again brightly, as she turned away.

Susan went home then to her neglected work. There seemed really nothing else that she could do. But that she was far from following Miss Dorothy's blithe advice "not to worry" was very evident from her frowning brow and preoccupied air all the rest of the time until Tuesday morning when Keith went—until, indeed, Mr. Burton came home from seeing Keith off on his journey. Then her pent-up perturbation culminated in an onslaught of precipitate questions.

Eleanor H. Porter

"Was he all right? Was that girl there? Did he know who she was? Do you think he'll find out?"

"One at a time, Susan, one at a time," laughed the man. "Yes, he was all right. He went off smiling, with the doctor's arm about his shoulders. Yes, the young lady was there, but she kept well away from Keith, so far as I could see. Friends had come evidently to see her off, but I noticed she contrived to keep herself and them as far away from Keith as possible. Of course, on the journey there'll be just the three of them. The test will come then. But I wouldn't worry, Susan. Remember your own advice about those bridges of yours. He's started, and he's with the doctor. I don't think he'll turn back now."

"No, I s'pose not," sighed Susan. "But I wish I could really KNOW how things are!" she finished, as she took up her work again.

Thirty-six hours later came the telegram from the doctor telling of their safe arrival, and a week later came a letter from Keith himself to Susan. It was written in lead-pencil on paper that had been carefully perforated so as to form lines not too near together.

At the top of the page in parentheses were these words:

DEAR SUSAN: If you think dad would like it you may read him a part or the whole of this letter. I was afraid I wouldn't write very well and that he wouldn't like to see it. So I write to you instead. I know you won't mind.

Below came the letter.

DEAR SUSAN: How do you and dad do? I am well and hope you are the same.

This is an awfully pretty place with trees and big lawns all around it, and walks and seats everywhere in the summer, they say. We aren't sitting outdoors to-day, though. It's only four below!

We had a jolly trip out. The doctor's great. He spent half his time talking to me about the things we were seeing out the window. We went through a wonderful country, and saw lots of interesting things.

The doctor's daughter was along, too. But she didn't have much to say on the trip. I've seen quite a lot of her since we've been here, though, and she's ALL RIGHT. At first I didn't like her very well. It was her voice, I guess. It reminded me of somebody I didn't like to be reminded of. But after I got used to it I found she was really very nice and jolly. She knows lots of games, and we play together a lot now. She's so different from that girl she sounded like that I don't mind her voice now. And I don't think she minds (here a rather unsuccessful erasure showed that "playing with me" had been substituted for "being with blind folks").

She gave me this paper, and told me the folks at home would like a letter, she knew. That's why I'm writing it. And I guess that's enough for this time.

Love to all. KEITH BURTON

P.S. I'm going to have the operation to-morrow, but they won't know for quite a while whether it's successful or not, the doctor says.

KEITH

Susan read this letter, then took it at once to the studio and read it again aloud.

"Now ain't that great?" she crowed, as soon as she had finished. "Y-yes, but he didn't say much about himself or his treatment," demurred the man.

Susan made an impatient gesture.

"Why, yes, he did, too! Lan' sakes, Mr. Burton, he didn't talk about nothin' else but himself an' his treatment, all the way through. Oh, I know he didn't say anything about his occultist treatment, if that's what you mean. But I didn't do no worryin' about that part. It was the other part."

"The other part!"

"Yes. They're treatin' him as if he wa'n't different an' queer. An' didn't you notice the way he wrote? Happy as a king tellin' about what he SAW on the way out, an' the wonderful country they went through. They're all right—them two are. I shan't do no more worryin' about Keith. An' her fixin' that paper so cute for him to write on—I declare I'm that zealous of her I don't know what to do. Why couldn't *I* 'a' thought of that?" she sighed, as she rose to leave the room.

Two days later came a letter from the doctor. The operation had been performed and, so far as they could judge, all was well, though, as Keith had written, the real results would not show until the bandages were removed some time later.

When the schools opened again in January, Dorothy Parkman came back to Hinsdale. Susan had been counting the days ever since Christmas, for she knew Dorothy was coming, and she could scarcely wait to see her. This time, however, she did not have to tramp through the streets and stores looking for her, for Miss Dorothy came at once to the house and rang the bell.

"I knew you'd want to hear all about Mr. Keith," she smiled brightly into Susan's eyes. "And I'm glad to report that he's doing all right."

"Be them bandages off yet? Do you mean—he can see?" demanded Susan excitedly, leading the way to the sitting-room.

"Oh, no—no—not that!" cried the girl quickly. "I mean—he's doing all right so far. It's a week yet before the bandages can be removed, and even then, he probably won't see much—if at all. There'll have to be another one—later—father says—maybe two more."

"Oh!" Susan fell back, plainly disappointed. Then, suddenly, a new interest flamed into her eyes.

"An' he ain't sensed yet who you are?" she questioned.

Miss Dorothy blushed, and Susan noticed suddenly how very pretty she was.

"No. Though I must confess that at first, when he heard my voice, he looked up much startled, and even rose from his seat. But I told him lots of folks thought I talked like Dorothy Parkman; and I just laughed and turned it off, and made nothing of it. And so pretty quick he made nothing of it, too. After that we got along beautifully."

"I should say you did!" retorted Susan, almost enviously. "An' you fixin' up that paper so fine for him to write on!"

Miss Dorothy blushed again—and again Susan noticed how very charming was the combination of brown eyes and yellow-gold hair.

Eleanor H. Porter

"Yes, he did like that paper," smiled the young girl. "He never mentioned the lines, and neither did I. When I first suggested the letter home he was all ready to refuse, I could see; but I wouldn't give him the chance. Before he could even speak I had thrust the paper into his hands, and I could see the wonder, interest, and joy in his face as his fingers discovered the pricked lines and followed their course from edge to edge. But he didn't let ME know he'd found them— not much! 'Well, I don't know but they would like a letter,' was all he said, casually. I knew then that I had won."

"Well, I should say you had. But HOW did you know how?" cried Susan.

"Oh, you told me first that I must talk to him as if he were not blind. Then father told me the same thing. He said lots of his patients were like that. So I always tried to do it that way. And it's wonderful how, when you give it a little thought, you can manage to tell them so much that they can turn about and tell somebody else, just as if they really had seen it."

"I know, I know," nodded Susan. "An'—Miss Dorothy"—her voice grew unsteady—"he really IS goin' to see by an' by, ain't he?"

The girl's face clouded.

"They aren't at all sure of that."

"But they can't tell YET?" Susan had grown a little white.

"Oh, no, not sure."

"An' they're goin' to give him all the chances there is?"

"Certainly. I only spoke because I don't want you to be too

disappointed if—if we lose. You must remember that fully half of the cases do lose."

Susan drew a long sigh. Then, determinedly she lifted her chin.

"Well, I like to think we ain't goin' to belong to that half," she said.

CHAPTER XVI

THE WORRY OF IT

There was a letter from the doctor when the bandages were removed. Daniel Burton began to read the letter, but his eyes blurred and his hand shook, so that Susan had to take it up where he had dropped it.

Yet the letter was very short.

The operation had been as successful, perhaps, as they could expect, under the circumstances. Keith could discern light now—faintly, to be sure, but unmistakably. He was well and happy. Meanwhile he was under treatment for the second operation to come later. But that could not be performed for some time yet, so they must not lose their patience. That was all.

"Well, I s'pose we ought to be glad he can see light even a little," sighed Susan; "but I'm free to confess I was hopin' he could do a little more than that."

"Yes, so was I," said Daniel Burton. And Susan, looking at his face, turned away without another word. There were times when Susan knew enough not to talk.

Then came the days when there were only Keith's letters and an occasional short note from the doctor to break the long months of waiting.

In the Burton homestead at Hinsdale, living was reduced to the simplest formula possible. On the whole, there was perhaps a little more money. Dunning tradesmen were not so numerous. But all luxuries, and some things that were almost necessities, were rigorously left out. And the money was saved always—for Keith. A lodger, a young law student, in Keith's old room helped toward defraying the family expenses.

Susan had given up trying to sell her "poems." She had become convinced at last that a cruel and unappreciative editorial wall was forever to bar her from what she still believed was an eagerly awaiting public. She still occasionally wrote jingles and talked in rhyme; but undeniably she had lost her courage and her enthusiasm. As she expressed it to Mrs. McGuire, she did not feel "a mite like a gushing siphon inside her now."

As the summer came and passed, Susan and Mrs. McGuire talked over the back-yard fence even more frequently. Perhaps because Susan was lonely without Keith. Perhaps because there was so much to talk about.

First there was Keith.

Keith was still under treatment preparatory to the second operation. He had not responded quite as they had hoped, the doctor said, which meant that the operation must be postponed for perhaps several months longer.

All this Susan talked over with Mrs. McGuire; and there was always, too, the hushed discussion as to what would happen if, after all, it failed, and Keith came home hopelessly blind.

"But even that ain't the worst thing that could happen," maintained Susan stoutly. "I can tell you Keith Burton ain't goin' to let a little thing like that floor him!"

Mrs. McGuire, however, did not echo Susan's optimistic prophecies. But Mrs. McGuire's own sky just now was overcast, which perhaps had something to do with it. Mrs. McGuire had troubles of her own.

It was the summer of 1914, and the never-to-be-forgotten August had come and passed, firing the match that was destined to set the whole world ablaze. Mrs. McGuire's eldest son John—of whom she boasted in season and out and whom she loved with an all-absorbing passion—had caught the war-fever, gone to Canada, and enlisted. Mrs. McGuire herself was a Canadian by birth, and all her family still lived there. She was boasting now more than ever about John; but, proud as she was of her soldier boy, his going had plunged her into an abyss of doubt and gloom.

"He'll never come back, he'll never come back," she moaned to Susan. "I can just feel it in my bones that he won't."

"Shucks, a great, strong, healthy boy like John McGuire! Of course, he'll come back," retorted Susan. "Besides, likely the war'll be all over with 'fore he gets there, anyhow. An' as for feelin' it in your bones, Mis' McGuire, that's a very facetious doctrine, an' ain't no more to be depended upon than my flour sieve for an umbrella. They're gay receivers every time—bones are. Why, lan' sakes, Mis' McGuire, if all things happened that my bones told me was goin' to happen, there wouldn't none of us be livin' by now, nor the sun shinin', nor the moon moonin'. I found out, after awhile, how they DIDN'T happen half the time, an' I wrote a poem on it, like this:

Trust 'em not, them fickle bones,
Always talkin' moans an' groans.
Jest as if inside of you,
Lived a thing could tell you true,
Whether it was goin' to rain,
Whether you would have a pain,
Whether him or you would beat,
Whether you'd have 'nuf to eat!
Bones was give to hold us straight,
Not to tell us 'bout our Fate."

"Yes, yes, I s'pose so," sighed Mrs. McGuire. "But when I think of John, my John, lyin' there so cold an' still—"

"Well, he ain't lyin' there yet," cut in Susan impatiently. "Time enough to hunt bears when you see their tracks. Mis' McGuire, CAN'T you see that worryin' don't do no good? You'll have it ALL for nothin', if he don't get hurt; an' if he does, you'll have all this extra for nothin', anyway,—that you didn't need till the time came. Ever hear my poem on worryin'?"

Without waiting for a reply—Susan never asked such questions with a view to having them answered—she chanted this:

"Worry never climbed a hill,
Worry never paid a bill,
Worry never led a horse to water.
Worry never cooked a meal,
Worry never darned a heel,
Worry never did a thing you'd think it oughter!"

"Yes, yes, I know, I know," sighed Mrs. McGuire again. "But John is so—well, you don't know my John. Nobody knows John as I do. He'd have made a big man if he'd lived—John would."

"'If he'd lived'!" repeated Susan severely. "Well, I never, Mis' McGuire, if you ain't talkin' already as if he was dead! You don't have to begin to write his obliquity notice yet, do you?"

"But he is dead," moaned Mrs. McGuire, catching at the one word in Susan's remark and paying no attention to the rest. "He's dead to everything he was goin' to do. He was ambitious,—my John was. He was always studyin' and readin' books nights an' Sundays an' holidays, when he didn't have to be in the store. He was takin' a course, you know."

"Yes, I know—one of them respondin' schools," nodded Susan. "John's a clever lad, he is, I'm free to confess."

Under the sunshine of Susan's appreciation Mrs. McGuire drew a step nearer.

"He was studyin' so he could 'mount to somethin'—John was," declared Mrs. McGuire. "He was goin' to be"—she paused and threw a hurried look over her shoulder—"he was keepin' it secret, but he won't mind my tellin' NOW. He was goin' to be a—writer some day, he hoped."

Susan's instantly alert attention was most flattering.

"Sho! You don't say! Poems?"

"I don't know." Mrs. McGuire drew back and spoke a little coldly. Now that the secret was out, Mrs. McGuire was troubled evidently with qualms of conscience. "He never said much. He didn't want it talked about."

Susan drew a long breath.

"Yes, I know. 'Tain't so pleasant if folks know—when you can't sell 'em. Now in my case—"

But Mrs. McGuire, with a hurried word about the beans in her oven, had hastened into the house.

Mrs. McGuire was not the only one with whom Susan was having long talks. September had come bringing again the opening of the schools, which in turn had brought Miss Dorothy Parkman back to Hinsdale.

Miss Dorothy was seventeen now, and prettier than ever—in Susan's opinion. She had been again to her father's home; and Susan never could hear enough of her visit or of Keith. Nor was Miss Dorothy evidently in the least loath to talk of her visit—or of Keith. Patiently, even interestedly, each time she saw Susan, she would repeat for her the details of Keith's daily life, telling everything that she knew about him.

"But I've told you all there is, before," she said laughingly one day at last, when Susan had stopped her as she was going by the house. "I've told it several times before."

"Yes, I know you have," nodded Susan, drawing a long breath; "but I always get somethin' new in it, just as I do in the Bible, you know. You always tell me somethin' you hadn't mentioned before. Now, to-day—you never told me before about them dominoes you an' him played together."

"Didn't I?" An added color came into Miss Dorothy's cheeks. "Well, we played them quite a lot. Poor fellow! Time hung pretty heavily on his hands, and we HAD to do something for him. There were other games, too, that we played together."

"But how can he play dominoes, an' those others, when—

Eleanor H. Porter

when he can't see?"

"Oh, the points of the dominoes are raised, of course, and the board has little round places surrounded by raised borders for him to keep his dominoes in. The cards are marked with little raised signs in the corners, and there are dice studded with tiny nailheads. The checker-board has little grooves to keep the men from sliding. Of course, we already had all these games, you know. They use them for all father's patients. But, of course, Keith had to be taught first."

"And you taught him?"

"Well, I taught him some of them." The added color was still in Miss Dorothy's cheeks.

"An' you told me last week you read to him."

"Yes, oh, yes. I read to him quite a lot."

The anxiously puckered frown on Susan's face suddenly dissolved into a broad smile.

"Lan' sakes, if that ain't the limit!" she chuckled.

"Well, what do you mean by that?" bridled Miss Dorothy, looking not exactly pleased.

"Nothin'. It's only that I was jest a-thinkin' how you was foolin' him."

"Fooling him?" Miss Dorothy was looking decidedly not pleased now.

"Yes, an' you all the time Dorothy Parkman, an' he not knowin' it."

"Oh!" The color on Miss Dorothy's face was one pink blush now. Then she laughed lightly. "After all, do you know?—I hardly ever thought of that, after the very first. He called me Miss Stewart, of course—but lots of folks out there do that. They don't think, or don't know, about my name being different, you see. The patients, coming and going all the time, know me as the doctor's daughter, and naturally call me 'Miss Stewart.' So it doesn't seem so queer when Mr. Keith does it."

"Good!" exclaimed Susan with glowing satisfaction. "An' now here's to hopin' he won't never find out who you really be!"

"Is he so very bitter, then, against—Dorothy Parkman?" The girl asked the question a little wistfully.

"He jest is," nodded Susan with unflattering emphasis. "If you'd heard him when he jest persisted that he wouldn't have anybody that was Dorothy Parkman's father even look at his eyes you'd have thought so, I guess. An'—why, he even wrote about it 'way back last Christmas—I mean, when he first told us about you. He said the doctor had a daughter, an' she was all right; but he didn't like her at all at first, 'cause her voice kept remindin' him of somebody he didn't want to be reminded of."

"Did he really write—THAT?"

"Them's the identifyin' words," avowed Susan. "So you'll jest have to keep it secret who you be, you see," she warned her.

"Yes, I—see," murmured the girl. All the pretty color had quite gone from her face now, leaving it a little white and strained-looking. "I'll try—to."

"Of course, when he gets back his sight he'll find out—that is, Miss Dorothy, he IS going to get it back, ain't he?" Susan's own face now had become a little white and strained-looking.

Miss Dorothy shook her head.

"I don't know, Susan; but I'm—afraid."

"Afraid! You don't mean he AIN'T goin' to?" Susan caught Miss Dorothy's arm in a vise-like grip.

"No, no, not that; but we aren't—SURE. And—and the symptoms aren't quite so good as they were," hurried on the girl a bit feverishly.

"But I thought he could see—light," faltered Susan.

"He could, at first, but it's been getting dimmer and dimmer, and now"—the girl stopped and wet her lips—"there's to be a second operation, you know. Father hopes to have it by Christmas, or before; but I know father is afraid—that is—he thinks—"

"He don't like the way things is goin'," cut in Susan grimly. "Ain't that about it?"

"I'm afraid it is," faltered Miss Dorothy, wetting her lips again. "And when I think of that boy—" She turned away her head, leaving her sentence unfinished.

"Well, we ain't goin' to think of it till it comes" declared Susan stoutly. "An' then—well, if it does come, we've all got to set to an' help him forget it. That's all."

"Yes, of—course," murmured the girl, turning away again.

And this time she turned quite away and went on down the street, leaving Susan by the gate alone.

"Nice girl, an' a mighty pretty one, too," whispered Susan, looking after the trim little figure in its scarlet cap and sweater. "An' she's got a good kind heart in her, too, a-carin' like that about that poor boy's bein'—"

Susan stopped short. A new look had come to her face—a look of wonder, questioning, and dawning delight. "Lan' sakes, why hain't I never thought of that before?" she muttered, her eyes still on the rapidly disappearing little red figure down the street. "Oh, 'course they're nothin' but babies now, but by an' by—! Still, if he ever found out she was Dorothy Parkman, an' of course he'd have to find it out if he married—Oh, lan' sakes, what fools some folks be!"

With which somewhat cryptic statement Susan turned and marched irritably into the house.

CHAPTER XVII

DANIEL BURTON TAKES THE PLUNGE

Dr. Stewart's second operation on Keith's eyes took place late in November. It was not a success. Far from increasing his vision, it lessened it. Only dimly now could he discern light at all.

In a letter to Daniel Burton, Dr. Stewart stated the case freely and frankly, yet he declared that he had not given up hope— yet. He had a plan which, with Mr. Burton's kind permission, he would carry out. He then went on to explain.

In Paris there was a noted specialist in whom he had great confidence. He wished very much that this man could see Keith. To take Keith over now, however, as war conditions were, would, of course, be difficult and hazardous. Besides, as he happened to know, this would not be necessary, for the great man was coming to this country some time in May. To bring Keith to his attention then would be a simple matter, and a chance well worth waiting for. Meanwhile, the boy was as comfortable where he was as he could be anywhere, and, moreover, there were certain treatments which should still be continued. With Daniel Burton's kind permission, therefore, the doctor would keep Keith where he was for the present, pending the arrival of the great specialist.

It was a bitter blow. For days after the letter came, Daniel Burton shut himself up in his studio refusing to see any one but Susan, and almost refusing to see her. Susan, indeed, heart-broken as she was herself, had no time to indulge her own grief, so busy was she trying to concoct something that would tempt her employer to break a fast that was becoming terrifying to her.

Then came Keith's letter. He wrote cheerfully, hopefully. He told of new games that he was playing, new things of interest that he was "seeing." He said nothing whatever about the operation. He did say that there was a big doctor coming from Paris, whom he was going to "see" in May, however. That was all.

When the doctor's letter had come, telling of the failure of the second operation, Susan had read it and accepted it with sternly controlled eyes that did not shed one tear. But when Keith's letter came, not even mentioning the operation, her self-control snapped, and she burst openly into tears.

"I don't care," she sobbed, in answer to Daniel Burton's amazed exclamation. "When I think of the way that blessed boy is holdin' up his head an' marchin' straight on; an' you an' me here—oh, lan' sakes, what's the use of TRYIN' to say it!" she despaired, turning and hurrying from the room.

In December Dr. Stewart came on again to take his daughter back for the holidays. He called at once to see Mr. Burton, and the two had a long conference in the studio, while Susan feverishly moved from room to room downstairs, taking up and setting down one object after another in the aimless fashion of one whose fingers are not controlled by the mind.

When the doctor had gone, Susan did not wait for Daniel Burton to seek her out. She went at once to the studio.

"No, he had nothing new to say about Keith," began the man, answering the agonized question in her eyes before her lips could frame the words.

"But didn't he say NOTHIN'?"

"Oh, yes, he said a great deal—but it was only a repetition of what he had said before in the letter." Daniel Burton spoke wearily, constrainedly. His face had grown a little white. "The doctor bought the big sofa in the hall downstairs, and the dropleaf table in the dining-room."

"Humph! But will he PAY anything for them things?"

"Yes, he will pay well for them. And—Susan."

"Yes, sir." Something in the man's face and voice put a curious note of respect into Susan's manner as sudden as it was unusual.

"I've been intending to tell you for some time. I—I shall want breakfast at seven o'clock to-morrow morning. I—I am going to work in McGuire's store."

"You are goin' to—what?" Susan's face was aghast.

"To work, I said," repeated Daniel Burton sharply. "I shall want breakfast at seven o'clock, Susan." He turned away plainly indicating that for him the matter was closed.

But for Susan the matter was not closed.

"Daniel Burton, you ain't goin' to demean yourself like that!" she gasped;—"an artistical gentleman like you! Why, I'd rather work my hands to the bones—"

"That will do, Susan. You may go."

And Susan went. There were times when Susan did go.

But not yet for Susan was the matter closed. Only an hour later Mrs. McGuire "ran over" with a letter from her John to read to Susan. But barely had she finished reading the letter aloud, when the real object of her visit was disclosed by the triumphant:

"Well, Susan Betts, I notice even an artist has to come down to bein' a 'common storekeeper' sometimes."

Susan drew herself up haughtily.

"Of course, Mis' McGuire, 't ain't for me to pretense that I don't know what you're inferrin' to. But jest let me tell you this: it don't make no difference how many potatoes an' molasses jugs an' kerosene cans Daniel Burton hands over the counter he won't never be jest a common storekeeper. He'll be THINKIN' flowers an' woods an' sunsets jest the same. Furthermore an' moreover, in my opinion it's a very honorary an' praiseful thing for him to do, to go out in the hedges an' byways an' earn money like that, when, if the world only knew enough to know a good thing when they see it, they'd be buy in' them pictures of his, an' not subjugate him to the mystification of earnin' his bread by the sweat of his forehead."

"Oh, good gracious me, Susan Betts, how you do run on, when you get started!" ejaculated Mrs. McGuire impatiently, yet laughingly. "An' I might have known what you'd say, too, if I'd stopped to think. Well, I must be goin', anyhow. I only came over to show you the letter from my John. I'm sure I wish't was him comin' back to his old place behind the counter instead of your Daniel Burton," she sighed. "I'd buy every picture he ever painted (if I had the money), if 't would only bring my John back, away from all those awful bombs an' shells an' shrapnel that he's always writin' about."

"Them be nice letters he writes, I'm free to confess," commented Susan graciously. "Not that they tell so much what he's doin', though; but I s'pose they're censured, anyhow—all them letters be."

Mrs. McGuire, her eyes dreamily fixed out the window, nodded her head slowly.

"Yes, I s'pose so; but there's a lot left—there's always a lot left. And everything he writes I can just see. It was always like that with my John. Let him go downtown an' come back—you'd think he'd been to the circus, the wonderful things he'd tell me he'd seen on the way. An' he'd set 'em out an' describe 'em until I could just see 'em myself! I'll never forget. One day he went to a fire. The old Babcock house burned, an' he saw it. He was twelve years old. I was sick in bed, an' he told me about it. I can see him now, standin' at the foot of the bed, his cheeks red, his eyes sparklin' an' his little hands flourishin' right an' left in his excitement. As he talked, I could just see that old house burn. I could hear the shouts of the men, the roar an' cracklin' of the flames, an' see 'em creepin', creepin', gainin', gainin'-! Oh, it was wonderful—an' there I was right in my own bed, all the time. It was just the way he told it. That's why I know he could have been a writer. He could make others see—everything. But now—that's all over now. He'll never be—anything. I can see him. I can see all that horrible battle-field with the reelin' men, the flames, the smoke, the burstin' shells, an', oh, God—my John! Will he ever, ever come back—to me?"

"There, there, Mis' McGuire, I jest wouldn't—" But Mrs. McGuire, with a shake of her head, and her eyes half covered with her hand, turned away and stumbled out of the kitchen.

Susan, looking after her, drew a long sigh.

> "Worry never climbed a hill,
> Worry never—

There's some times when it's frank impertinence to tell folks not to worry," she muttered severely to herself, attacking the piled-up dishes before her.

Daniel Burton went to work in McGuire's grocery store the next morning, after a particularly appetizing breakfast served to him by a silent, red-eyed, but very attentive Susan.

"An' 'twas for all the world like a lamb to the slaughter-house," Susan moaned to the law-student lodger when she met him on the stairs at eight o'clock that morning. "An' if you want to see a real slaughter-house, you jest come in here," she beckoned him, leading the way to the studio.

"But—but—that is—well—" stammered the young fellow, looking not a little startled as he followed her, with half-reluctant feet.

In the studio Susan flourished accusing arms.

"Look at that, an' that, an' that!" she cried. "Why, it's like jest any extraordinary common-sense room now, that anybody might have, with them pictures all put away, an' his easel hid behind the door, an' not a brush or a cube of paint in sight— an' him dolin' out vinegar an' molasses down to that old store. I tell you it made me sick, Mr. Jenkins, sick!"

"Yes, yes, that's so," murmured Mr. Jenkins, vaguely.

"Well, it did. Why, it worked me up so I jest sat right down an' made up a poem on it. I couldn't help it. An' it came easy, too—'most like the spontaneous combustion kind that I used to write, only I made it free verse. You know that's all the rage now. Like this," she finished, producing from somewhere about her person a half-sheet of note-paper.

"Alone an' dark
The studio
Waited:
Waited for the sun of day.
But when it rose,
Alas!
No lovely pictures greeted
The fiery gob.
Only their backs showed
White an' sorry an' some dusty.
No easel sprawled long legs
To trip
An' make you slip.
No cubes of pig-lent gray
Or black,
Nor any other color lent brightness
To this dank world.
An' he—the artist? The bright soul who
Bossed this ranch?
Alas!
Doomed to hide his bright talons
In smelly kegs of kerosene
An' molasses brown an' sticky.
Alas, that I should see an'
Know this
Day.

There, now, ain't that about the way 'tis?" she demanded feelingly.

"Er—yes, yes, it is. That's so." Mr. Jenkins was backing out of the room and looking toward the stairway. Mr. Jenkins had been a member of the Burton household long enough to have learned to take Susan at her own valuation, with no questions asked. "Yes, that's so," he repeated, as he plunged down the stairs.

To Daniel Burton himself Susan made no further protests or even comments—except the silent comment of eager service with some favorite dish for every meal. As Christmas drew near, and Daniel Burton's hours grew longer, Susan still made no audible comment; but she redoubled her efforts to make him comfortable the few hours left to him at home.

CHAPTER XVIII

"MISS STEWART"

It was just after Christmas that another letter came from Keith. It was addressed as usual to Susan. Keith had explained in his second letter that he was always going to write to Susan, so that she might read it to his father, thus saving him the disagreeableness of seeing how crooked and uneven some of his lines were. His father had remonstrated—feebly; but Keith still wrote to Susan.

Keith had been improving in his writing very rapidly, however, since those earliest letters, and most of his letters now were models of even lines and carefully formed characters. But this letter Susan saw at once was very different. It bore unmistakable marks of haste, agitation, and lack of care. It began abruptly, after the briefest of salutations:

Why didn't you tell me you knew Miss Stewart? She says she knows you real well, and father, too, and that she's been to the house lots of times, and that she's going back to Hinsdale next week, and that she is going to school there this year, and will graduate in June.

Oh, she didn't tell me all this at once, you bet your sweet life.

I had to worm it out of her little by little. But what I want to know is, why you folks didn't tell me anything about it—that you knew her, and all that? But you never said a word—not a word. Neither you nor dad. But she says she knows dad real well. Funny dad never mentioned it!

Miss Stewart sure is a peach of a girl all right and the best ever to me. She's always hunting up new games for me to play. She's taught me two this time, and she's read two books to me. There's a new fellow here named Henty, and we play a lot together. I am well, and getting along all right. Guess that's all for this time. Love to all.

KEITH

P.S. Now don't forget to tell me why you never said a thing that you knew Miss Stewart.

K.

"Well, now I guess the kettle is in the fire, all right!" ejaculated Susan, folding the letter with hands that shook a little.

"What do you mean?" asked Daniel Burton.

"Why, about that girl, of course. He'll find out now she's Dorothy Parkman. He can't help findin' it out!" "Well, what if he does?" demanded the man, a bit impatiently.

"'What if he does?'" repeated Susan, with lofty scorn. "I guess you'll find what 'tis when that boy does find out she's Dorothy Parkman, an' then won't have nothin' more to do with her, nor her father, nor her father's new doctor, nor anything that is hers."

"Nonsense, Susan, don't be silly," snapped the man, still more irritably. "'Nor her father, nor her father's new doctor, nor anything that is hers,' indeed! You sound for all the world as if you were chanting a catechism! What's the matter? Doesn't the boy like Miss Dorothy?"

"Why, Daniel Burton, you know he don't! I told you long ago all about it, when I explained how we'd got to give her father a resumed name, so Keith wouldn't know, an'—"

"Oh, THAT! What she said about not wanting to see blind people? Nonsense, Susan, that was years ago, when they were children! Why, Keith's a man, nearly. You're forgetting —he'll be eighteen next June, Susan."

"That's all right, Mr. Burton." Susan's lips snapped together grimly and her chin assumed its most defiant tilt. "I ain't sayin' he ain't. But there's some cases where age don't make a mite of difference, an' you'll find this is one of 'em. You mark my words, Daniel Burton. I have seen jest as big fools at eighteen, an' eighty, for that matter, as I have at eight. 'T ain't a matter of decree at all. Keith Burton got it into his head when he was first goin' blind that Dorothy Parkman would hate to look at him if ever he did get blind; an' he just vowed an' determined that if ever he did get that way, she shouldn't see him. Well, now he's blind. An' if you think he's forgot what Dorothy Parkman said, you'd oughter been with me when she came to see him with Mazie Sanborn one day, or even when they just called up to him on the piazza one mornin'."

"Well, well, very likely," conceded the man irritably; "but I still must remind you, Susan, that all this was some time ago. Keith's got more sense now." "Maybe—an' then again maybe not. However, we'll see—what we will see," she mumbled, as she left the room with a little defiant toss of her head.

Susan did not answer Keith's letter at once. Just how she was going to answer that particular question concerning their acquaintance with "Miss Stewart" she did not know, nor could she get any assistance from Daniel Burton on the subject.

"Why, tell him the truth, of course," was all that Daniel Burton would answer, with a shrug, in reply to her urgent appeals for aid in the matter. This, Susan, in utter horror, refused to do.

"But surely you don't expect to keep it secret forever who she is, do you?" demanded Daniel Burton scornfully one day.

"Of course I don't. But I'm going to keep it jest as long as I can," avowed Susan doggedly. "An' maybe I can keep it—till he gets his blessed eyes back. I shan't care if he does find out then."

"I don't think—we'll any of us—mind anything then, Susan," said the man softly, a little brokenly. And Susan, looking into his face, turned away suddenly, to hide her own.

That evening Susan heard that Dorothy Parkman was expected to arrive in Hinsdale in two days.

"I'll jest wait, then, an' intervene the young lady my own self," she mused, as she walked home from the post-office. "This tryin' to settle Dorothy Parkman's affairs without Dorothy Parkman is like havin' omelet with omelet left out," she finished, nodding to herself all in the dark, as she turned in at the Burton gateway.

Dorothy Parkman came two days later. As was usual now she came at once to the house. Susan on the watch, met her at the door, before she could touch the bell.

Eleanor H. Porter

"Come in, come in! My, but I'm glad to see you!" exclaimed Susan fervently, fairly pulling her visitor into the house. "Now tell me everything—every single thing."

"Why, there isn't much to tell, Susan. Mr. Keith is about the same, and—"

"No, no, I mean—about YOU" interrupted Susan, motioning the girl to a chair, and drawing her own chair nearer. "About your bein' in Hinsdale an' knowin' us, an' all that, an' his finding it out."

"Oh, THAT!" The color flew instantly into Miss Dorothy's cheeks. "Then he's—he's written you?"

"Written us! I should say he had! An' he wants to know why we hain't told him we know you. An', lan' sakes, Miss Dorothy, what can we tell him?"

"I—I don't know, Susan."

"But how'd you get in such a mess? How'd he find out to begin with?" demanded the woman.

Miss Dorothy drew a long sigh. "Oh, it was my fault, of course. I—forgot. Still, it's a wonder I hadn't forgotten before. You see, inadvertently, I happened to drop a word about Mr. Burton. 'Do you know my dad?' he burst out. Then he asked another and another question. Of course, I saw right away that I must turn it off as if I supposed he'd known it all the time. It wouldn't do to make a secret of it and act embarrassed because he'd found it out, for of course then he'd suspect something wrong right away."

"Yes, yes, I s'pose so," admitted Susan worriedly. "But, lan' sakes, look at us! What are we goin' to say? Now he wants to know why we hain't told him about knowin' you."

"I don't know, Susan, I don't know." The girl shook her head and caught her breath a bit convulsively. "Of course, when I first let it go that I was 'Miss Stewart,' I never realized where it was going to lead, nor how—how hard it might be to keep it up. I've been expecting every day he'd find out, from some one there. But he hasn't—yet. Of course, Aunt Hattie, who keeps house for father, is in the secret, and SHE'D never give it away. Most of the patients don't know much about me, anyway. You see, I've never been there much. They just know vaguely of 'the doctor's daughter,' and they just naturally call her 'Miss Stewart.'"

"Yes, yes, I see, I see," nodded Susan, again still worriedly. "But what I'm thinkin' of is US, Miss Dorothy. How are we goin' to get 'round not mentionin' you all this time, without his findin' out who you be an' demandin' a full exposition of the whole affair. Say, look a-here, would it be—be very bad if he DID find out you was Dorothy Parkman?"

"I'm afraid—it would be, Susan." The girl spoke slowly, a bit unsteadily. She had gone a little white at the question.

"Has he SAID anything?"

"Nothing, only he—When we were talking that day, and he was flinging out those questions one after another, about Hinsdale, and what I knew of it, he—he asked if I knew Dorothy Parkman."

"Miss Dorothy, he didn't!"

"But he did. It was awful, Susan. I felt like—like—"

"Of course you did," interposed Susan, her face all

sympathy, "a-sailin' under false premises like that, an' when you were perfectly innocuous, too, of any sinfulness, an' was jest doing it for his best good an' peace of mind. Lan' sakes, what a prediction to be in! What DID you say?"

"Why, I said yes, of course. I had to say yes. And I tried to turn it off right away, and not talk any more about it. But that was easy, anyway, for—for Mr. Keith himself dropped it. But I knew, by the way he looked, and said 'yes, I know her, too,' in that quiet, stern way of his, that—that I'd better not let him find out I was she—not if I wanted to—to stay in the room," she finished, laughing a little hysterically.

"Lan' sakes, you don't say!" frowned Susan.

"Yes; and so that's what makes me know that whatever you do, you mustn't let him know that I am Dorothy Parkman," cried the girl feverishly; "not now—not until he's seen the Paris doctor, for there's no knowing what he'd do. He'd be so angry, you see. He'd never forgive me, for on top of all the rest is the deceit—that I've been with him all these different times, and let him call me 'Miss Stewart.'"

"But how can we do that?" demanded Susan.

"Why, just turn it off lightly. Say, of course, you know me; and seem surprised that you never happened to mention it before. Tell him, oh, yes, I come quite often to tell you and Mr. Burton how he's getting along, and all that. Just make nothing of it—take it as a matter of course, not worth mentioning. See? Then go on and talk about something else. That'll fix it all right, I'm sure, Susan."

"Hm-m; maybe so, an' then again maybe not," observed Susan, with frowning doubt. "As I was tellin' Mr. Burton this mornin' we've got to be 'specially careful about Keith jest now. It's the most hypercritical time there can be—with him waitin' to see that big doctor, an' all—an' he mustn't be upset, no matter what happens, nor how many white lies we have to prognosticate here at home."

"I guess that's so, Susan." Miss Dorothy's eyes were twinkling now. "And, by the way, where is Mr. Burton? I haven't seen him yet."

"He ain't here."

"You don't mean he has gone out of town?" The girl had looked up in surprise at the crisp terseness of Susan's reply.

"Oh, no, he's—in Hinsdale."

"Painting any new pictures these days?" Miss Dorothy was on her feet to go. She asked the question plainly not for information, but to fill the embarrassing pause that Susan's second reply had brought to the conversation.

"No, he ain't," spoke up Susan with a vehemence as disconcerting as it was sudden. "He ain't paintin' nothin', an' he ain't drawin' nothin' neither—only molasses an' vinegar an' kerosene. He's clerkin' down to McGuire's grocery store, if you want to know. That's where he is."

"Why—SUSAN!"

"Yes, I know. You don't have to say nothin', Miss Dorothy. Besides, I wouldn't let you say it if you did. I won't let nobody say it but me. But I will say this much. When folks has set one foot in the cemetery, an' a lame one at that, an' can't see nor hear nor think straight, I don't think it's no hilarious offense to wish they'd hurry up an' get to where they could have all them handy facilities back again, an' leave their money to folks what has got their full complaint of senses, ready to enjoy life, if they get a chance. Oh, yes, I know you don't know what I'm talkin' about, an' perhaps it's jest as well you don't, Miss Dorothy. I hadn't oughter said it, anyhow. Well, I s'pose I've got to go write that letter to Keith now. Seein' as how you've come I can't put it off no longer. Goodness only knows, though, what I'm goin' to say," she sighed, as her visitor nodded back a wistful-eyed good-bye.

CHAPTER XIX

A MATTER OF LETTERS

Susan said afterward, in speaking of that spring, that "'twas nothin' but jest one serious of letters." And, indeed, life did seem to be mostly made up of letters.

At the sanatorium Keith was waiting for spring and the new doctor; and that the waiting was proving to be a little nerve-racking was proved by the infrequency of his letters home, and the shortness and uncommunicativeness of such as did come.

Letters to him from Hinsdale were longer and were invariably bright and cheery. Yet they did not really tell so much, after all. To be sure, they did contain frequent reference to "your Miss Stewart," and gave carefully casual accounts of what she did and said. In the very first letter Susan had hit upon the idea of always referring to the young lady as "your Miss Stewart."

"Then we won't be tellin' no lies," she had explained to Mr. Burton, "'cause she IS his 'Miss Stewart.' See? She certainly don't belong to no one else under that name—that's sure!"

But however communicative as regards "Miss Stewart" the

letters were, they were very far from that as regarded some other matters. For instance: neither in Daniel Burton's letters, nor in Susan's, was there any reference to the new clerk in McGuire's grocery store. So far as anything that Keith knew to the contrary, his father was still painting unsalable pictures in the Burton home-stead studio.

But even these were not all the letters that spring. There were the letters of John McGuire from far-away France—really wonderful letters—letters that brought to the little New England town the very breath of the battle-field itself, the smell of its smoke, the shrieks of its shells. And with Mr. Burton, with Susan, with the whole neighborhood indeed, Mrs. McGuire shared them. They were even printed occasionally in the town's weekly newspaper. And they were talked of everywhere, day in and day out. No wonder, then, that, to Susan, the spring seemed but a "serious of letters."

It was in May that the great Paris doctor was expected; but late in April came a letter from Dr. Stewart saying that, owing to war conditions, the doctor had been delayed. He would not reach this country now until July—which meant two more months of weary waiting for Keith and for Keith's friends at home.

It was just here that Susan's patience snapped.

"When you get yourself screwed up to stand jest so much, an' then they come along with jest a little more, somethin's got to break, I tell you. Well, I've broke."

Whether as a result of the "break" or not, Susan did not say, neither did she mention whether it was to assuage her own grief or to alleviate Keith's; but whatever it was, Susan wrote these verses and sent them to Keith:

BY THE DAY

When our back is nigh to breakin',
An' our strength is nearly gone,
An' along there comes the layin'
Of another burden on—

If we'll only jest remember,
No matter what's to pay,
That 'tisn't yet December,
An' we're livin' by the day.

'Most any one can stand it—
What jest TO-DAY has brought.
It's when we try to lump it,
An' take it by the lot!

Why, any back would double,
An' any legs'll bend,
If we pile on all the trouble
Meant to last us till the end!

So if we'll jest remember,
Half the woe from life we'll rob
If we'll only take it "by the day,"
An' not live it "by the job."

"Of course that "tisn't yet December' is poem license, and hain't really got much sense to it," wrote Susan in the letter she sent with the verses. "I put it in mostly to rhyme with 'remember.' (There simply wasn't a thing to rhyme with that word!) But, do you know, after I got it down I saw it really could mean somethin', after all—kind of diabolical-like for the end of life, you know, like December is the end of the year.

Eleanor H. Porter

"Well, anyhow, they done me lots of good, them verses did, an' I hope they will you."

In June Dorothy Parkman was graduated from the Hinsdale Academy. Both Mr. Burton and Susan attended the exercises, though not together. Then Susan sat down and wrote a glowing account of the affair to Keith, dilating upon the fine showing that "your Miss Stewart" made.

"It can't last forever, of course—this subtractin' Miss Stewart's name for Dorothy Parkman," she said to Mr. Burton, when she handed him the letter to mail. "But I'm jest bound an' determined it shall last till that there Paris doctor gets his hands on him. An' she ain't goin' back now to her father's for quite a spell—Miss Dorothy, I mean," further explained Susan. "I guess she don't want to take no chances herself of his findin' out—jest yet," declared Susan, with a sage wag of her head. "Anyhow, she's had an inspiration to go see a girl down to the beach, an' she's goin'. So we're safe for a while. But, oh, if July'd only hurry up an' come!"

And yet, when July came—

They were so glad, afterward, that Dr. Stewart wrote the letter that in a measure prepared them for the bad news. He wrote the day before the operation. He said that the great oculist was immensely interested in the case and eager to see what he could do—though he could hold out no sort of promise that he would be able to accomplish the desired results. Dr. Stewart warned them, therefore, not to expect anything—though, of course, they might hope. Hard on the heels of the letter came the telegram. The operation had been performed—and had failed, they feared. They could not tell surely, however, until the bandages were removed, which would be early in August. But even if it had failed, there was yet one more chance, the doctor wrote. He would say nothing about that, however, until he was obliged to.

In August he wrote about it. He was obliged to. The operation had been so near a failure that they might as well call it that. The Paris oculist, however, had not given up hope. There was just one man in the world who might accomplish the seemingly impossible and give back sight to Keith's eyes—at least a measure of sight, he said. This man lived in London. He had been singularly successful in several of the few similar cases known to the profession. Therefore, with their kind permission, the great Paris doctor would take Keith back with him to his brother oculist in London. He would like to take ship at once, as soon as arrangements could possibly be made. There would be delay enough, anyway, as it was. So far as any question of pay was concerned, the indebtedness would be on their side entirely if they were privileged to perform the operation, for each new case of this very rare malady added knowledge of untold value to the profession, hence to humanity in general. He begged, therefore, a prompt word of permission from Keith's father.

"Don't you give it, don't you give it!" chattered Susan, with white lips, when the proposition was made clear to her.

"Why, Susan, I thought you'd be willing to try anything, ANYTHING—for Keith's sake."

"An' so I would, sir, anything in season. But not this. Do you think I'd set that blessed boy afloat on top of them submarines an' gas-mines, an' to go to London for them German Zepherin's to rain down bombs an' shrapnel on his head, an' he not bein' able to see a thing to dodge 'em when he sees 'em comin'? Why, Daniel Burton, I'm ashamed of you—to think of it, for a minute!"

"There, there, Susan, that will do. You mean well, I know; but this is a matter that I shall have to settle for myself, for myself," he muttered with stern dignity, rising to his feet. Yet when he left the room a moment later, head and shoulders bowed, he looked so old and worn that Susan, gazing after him, put a spasmodic hand to her throat.

"An' I jest know I'm goin' to lose 'em both now," she choked as she turned away.

Keith went to London. Then came more weeks of weary, anxious waiting. Letters were not so regular now, nor so frequent. Definite news was hard to obtain. Yet in the end it came all too soon—and it was piteously definite.

Keith was coming home. The great London doctor, too, had—failed.

CHAPTER XX

WITH CHIN UP

Keith came in April. The day before he was expected, Susan, sweeping off the side porch, was accosted by Mrs. McGuire.

It was the first warm spring-like day, and Mrs. McGuire, bareheaded and coatless, had opened the back-yard gate and was picking her way across the spongy turf.

"My, but isn't this a great day, Susan!" she called, with an ecstatic, indrawn breath. "I only wish it was as nice under foot."

"Hain't you got no rubbers on?" Susan's disapproving eyes sought Mrs. McGuire's feet.

Mrs. McGuire laughed lightly.

"No. That's the one thing I leave off the first possible minute. Some way, I feel as if I was helpin' along the spring."

"Humph! Well, I should help along somethin' 'sides spring, I guess, if I did it. Besides, it strikes me rubbers ain't the only thing you're leavin' off." Susan's disapproving eyes had swept now to Mrs. McGuire's unprotected head and shoulders.

"Oh, I'm not cold. I love it. As if this glorious spring sunshine could do any one any harm! Susan, it's LIEUTENANT McGuire, now! I came over to tell you. My John's been promoted."

"Sho, you don't say! Ain't that wonderful, now?" Susan's broom stopped in midair,

"Not when you know my John!" The proud mother lifted her head a little. "'For bravery an' valiant service'—Lieutenant McGuire! Oh Susan, Susan, but I'm the proud woman this mornin'!"

"Yes, of course, of course, I ain't wonderin' you be!" Susan drew a long sigh and fell to sweeping again.

Mrs. McGuire, looking into Susan's face, came a step nearer. Her own face sobered.

"An' me braggin' like this, when you folks-! I know—you're thinkin' of that poor blind boy. An' it's just to-morrow that he comes, isn't it?"

Susan nodded dumbly.

"An' it's all ended now an' decided—he can't ever see, I s'pose," went on Mrs. McGuire. "I heard 'em talkin' down to the store last night. It seems terrible."

"Yes, it does." Susan was sweeping vigorously now, over and over again in the same place.

"I wonder how—he'll take it."

Susan stopped sweeping and turned with a jerk.

"Take it? He's got to take it, hain't he?" she demanded fiercely. "He's GOT TO! An' things you've got to do, you do. That's all. You'll see. Keith Burton ain't no quitter. He'll take it with his head up an' his shoulders braced. I know. You'll see. Don't I remember the look on his blessed face that day he went away, an' stood on them steps there, callin' back his cheery good-bye?"

"But, Susan, there was hope then, an' there isn't any now—an' you haven't seen him since. You forget that."

"No, I don't," retorted Susan doggedly. "I ain't forgettin' nothin'. 'But you'll see!"

"An' he's older. He realizes more. Why, he must be—How old is he, anyway?"

"He'll be nineteen next June."

"Almost a man. Poor boy, poor boy—an' him with all these years of black darkness ahead of him! I tell you, Susan, I never appreciated my eyes as I have since Keith lost his. Seems as though anybody that's got their eyes hadn't ought to complain of—anything. I was thinkin' this mornin', comin' over, how good it was just to SEE the blue sky an' the sunshine an' the little buds breakin' through their brown jackets. Why, Susan, I never realized how good just seein' was—till I thought of Keith, who can't never see again."

"Yes. Well, I've got to go in now, Mis' McGuire. Good-bye."

Words, manner, and tone of voice were discourtesy itself; but Mrs. McGuire, looking at Susan's quivering face, brimming eyes, and set lips, knew it for what it was and did not mistake it for—discourtesy. But because she knew Susan would prefer it so, she turned away with a light "Yes, so've I.

Good-bye!" which gave no sign that she had seen and understood.

Dr. Stewart came himself with Keith to Hinsdale and accompanied him to the house. It had been the doctor's own suggestion that neither the boy's father nor Susan should meet them at the train. Perhaps the doctor feared for that meeting. Naturally it would not be an easy one. Naturally too, he did not want to add one straw to Keith's already grievous burden. So he had written:

I will come to the house. As I am a little uncertain as to the train I can catch from Boston, do not try to meet me at the station.

"Jest as if we couldn't see through that subterranean!" Susan had muttered to herself over the dishes that morning. "I guess he knows what train he's goin' to take all right. He jest didn't want us to meet him an' make a scenic at the depot. I wonder if he thinks I would! Don't he think I knows anything?"

But, after all, it was very simple, very quiet, very ordinary. Dr. Stewart rang the bell and Susan went to the door. And there they stood: Keith, big and strong and handsome (Susan had forgotten that two years could transform a somewhat awkward boy into so fine and stalwart a youth); the doctor, pale, and with an apprehensive uncertainty in his eyes.

"Well, Susan, how are you?" Keith's voice was strong and steady, and the outstretched hand gripped hers with a clasp that hurt.

Then, in some way never quite clear to her, Susan found herself in the big living-room with Keith and the doctor and Daniel Burton, all shaking hands and all talking at once. They sat down then, and their sentences became less broken, less incoherent. But they said only ordinary things about the day, the weather, the journey home, John McGuire, the war, the President's message, the entry of the United States into the conflict. There was nothing whatever said about eyes that could see or eyes that could not see, or operations that failed.

And by and by the doctor got up and said that he must go. To be sure, the good-byes were a little hurriedly spoken, and the voices were at a little higher pitch than was usual; and when the doctor had gone, Keith and his father went at once upstairs to the studio and shut the door.

Susan went out into the kitchen then and took up her neglected work. She made a great clatter of pans and dishes, and she sang lustily at her "mad song," and at several others. But every now and then, between songs and rattles, she would stop and listen intently; and twice she climbed halfway up the back stairs and stood poised, her breath suspended, her anxious eyes on that closed studio door.

Yet supper that night was another very ordinary occurrence, with Keith and his father talking of the war and Susan waiting upon them with a cheerfulness that was almost obtrusive.

In her own room that night, however, Susan addressed an imaginary Keith, all in the dark.

"You're fine an' splendid, an' I love you for it, Keith, my boy," she choked; "but you don't fool your old Susan. Your chin is up, jest as I said 'twould be, an' you're marchin' straight ahead. But inside, your heart is breakin'. Do you think I don't KNOW? But we ain't goin' to let each other KNOW we know, Keith, my boy. Not much we ain't! An' I guess if you can march straight ahead with your chin up, the rest of us can, all right. We'll see!"

And Susan was singing again the next morning when she did her breakfast dishes.

At ten o'clock Keith came into the kitchen.

"Where's dad, Susan? He isn't in the studio and I've looked in every room in the house and I can't find him anywhere." Keith spoke with the aggrieved air of one who has been deprived of his just rights.

Susan's countenance changed. "Why, Keith, don't you—that is, your father—Didn't he tell you?" stammered Susan.

"Tell me what?"

"Why, that—that he was goin' to be away."

"No, he didn't. What do you mean? Away where? How long?"

"Why, er—working."

"Sketching?—in this storm? Nonsense, Susan! Besides, he'd have taken me. He always took me. Susan, what's the matter? Where IS dad?" A note of uncertainty, almost fear, had crept into the boy's voice. "You're keeping—SOMETHING from me."

Susan caught her breath and threw a swift look into Keith's unseeing eyes. Then she laughed, hysterically, a bit noisily.

"Keepin' somethin' from you? Why, sure we ain't, boy! Didn't I jest tell you? He's workin' down to McGuire's."

"WORKING! Down to MCGUIRE'S!" Keith plainly did not yet understand.

"Sure! An' he's got a real good position, too." Susan spoke jauntily, enthusiastically.

"But the McGuires never buy pictures," frowned Keith, "or want—" He stopped short. Face, voice, and manner underwent a complete change. "Susan, you don't mean that dad is CLERKING down there behind that grocery counter!"

Susan saw and recognized the utter horror and dismay in Keith's lace, and quailed before it. But she managed in some way to keep her voice still triumphant.

"Sure he is! An' he gets real good wages, too, an'—" But Keith with a low cry had gone.

Before the noon dinner, however, he appeared again at the kitchen door. His face was very white now.

"Susan, how long has dad been doing this?"

"Oh, quite a while. Funny, now! Hain't he ever told you?"

"No. But there seem to be quite a number of things that you people haven't told me."

Susan winced, but she still held her ground jauntily.

"Oh, yes, quite a while," she nodded cheerfully. "An' he gets-
"

"But doesn't he paint any more—at all?" interrupted the boy sharply.

"Why, no; no, I don't know that he does," tossed Susan airily. "An' of course, if he's found somethin' he likes better—"

"Susan, you don't have to talk like that to me" interposed Keith quietly. "I understand, of course. There are some things that can be seen without—eyes."

"Oh, but honest, Keith, he—" But once again Keith had gone and Susan found herself talking to empty air.

When Susan went into the dining-room that evening to wait at dinner, she went with fear and trepidation, and she looked apprehensively into the faces of the two men sitting opposite each other. But in the kitchen, a few minutes later, she muttered to herself:

"Pooh! I needn't have worried. They've got sense, both of 'em, an' they know that what's got to be has got to be. That's all. An' that it don't do no good to fuss. I needn't have worried."

But Susan did worry. She did not like the look on Keith's face. She did not like the nervous twitching of his hands. She did not like the exaggerated cheerfulness of his manner.

And Keith WAS cheerful. He played solitaire with his marked cards and whistled. He worked at his raised-picture puzzles and sang snatches of merry song. He talked with anybody who came near him—talked very fast and laughed a great deal. But behind the whistling and the singing and the laughter Susan detected a tense strain and nervousness that she did not like. And at times, when she knew Keith thought himself alone, there was an expression on his face that disturbed Susan not a little.

But because, outwardly, it was all "cheerfulness," Susan kept her peace; but she also kept her eyes on Keith.

CHAPTER XXI

THE LION

Keith had not been home a week before it was seen that Hinsdale was inclined to make a lion of the boy.

Women brought him jelly and fruit, and men clapped him on the shoulder and said, "How are you, my boy?" in voices that were not quite steady. Young girls brought him flowers, and asked Susan if they could not read or sing or do SOME-THING to amuse him. Children stood about the gate and stared, talking in awe-struck whispers, happy if they could catch a glimpse of his face at the window.

A part of this Susan succeeded in keeping from Keith—Susan had a well-founded belief that Keith would not care to be a lion. But a great deal of it came to his knowledge, of course, in spite of anything she could do. However, she told herself that she need not have worried, for if Keith had recognized it for what it was, he made no sign; and even Susan herself could find no fault with his behavior. He was cordial, cheery, almost gay, outwardly. But inwardly—

Susan was still keeping her eyes on Keith.

Mrs. McGuire came often to see Keith. She said she knew he

Eleanor H. Porter

would want to hear John's letters. And there were all the old ones, besides the new ones that came from time to time. She brought them all, and read them to him. She talked about the young soldier, too, a great deal, to the blind boy—She explained to Susan that she wanted to do everything she could to get him out of himself and interest him in the world outside; and that she didn't know any better way to do it than to tell him of these brave soldiers who were doing something so really worth while in the world.

"An' he's so interested—the dear boy!" she concluded, with a sigh. "An' so brave! I think he's the bravest thing I ever saw, Susan Betts."

"Yes, he is—brave," said Susan, a little shortly—so shortly that Mrs. McGuire opened her eyes a bit, and wondered why Susan's lips had snapped tight shut in that straight, hard line.

"But what ails the woman?" she muttered to herself, vexedly, as she crossed the back yard to her own door. "Wasn't she herself always braggin' about his bein' so brave? Humph! There's no such thing as pleasin' some folks, it seems!" finished Mrs. McGuire as she entered her own door.

But Mrs. McGuire was not the only frequent caller. There was Mazie Sanborn.

Mazie began by coming every two or three days with flowers and fudge. Then she brought the latest novel one day and suggested that she read it to Keith.

Susan was skeptical of this, even fearful. She had not forgotten Keith's frenzied avoidance of such callers in the old days. But to her surprise now Keith welcomed Mazie joyously—so joyously that Susan began to suspect that behind the joyousness lay an eagerness to welcome anything that would help him to forget himself.

She was the more suspicious of this during the days that followed, as she saw this same nervous eagerness displayed every time any one called at the house. Susan's joy then at Keith's gracious response to visitors' attentions changed to a vague uneasiness. Behind and beyond it all lay an intangible something upon which Susan could not place her finger, but which filled her heart with distrust. And so still she kept her eyes on Keith.

In June Dorothy Parkman came to Hinsdale. She came at once to see Susan. But she would only step inside the hall, and she spoke low and hurriedly, looking fearfully toward the closed doors beyond the stairway.

"I HAD to come—to see how he was," she began, a little breathlessly. "And I wanted to ask you if you thought I could do any good or—or be any help to him, either as Miss Stewart or Dorothy Parkman. Only I—I suppose I would HAVE to be Dorothy Parkman now. I couldn't keep the other up forever, of course. But I don't know how to tell—" She stopped, and looked again fearfully toward the closed doors. "Susan, how—how IS he?" she finished unsteadily.

"He's well—very well."

"He sees people—Mazie says he sees everybody now.

'Yes, oh, yes, he sees people."

'That's why I thought perhaps he wouldn't mind ME now—I mean the real me," faltered the girl wistfully. "Maybe." Susan's sigh and frown expressed doubt.

"But he's real brave," challenged the girl quickly. "Mazie

SAID he was."

"I know. Everybody says—he's brave." There was an odd constraint in Susan's voice, but the girl was too intent on her own problem to notice it.

"And that's why I hoped—about me, you know—that he wouldn't mind—now. And, of course, it can't make any difference—about his eyes, for he doesn't need father, or—or any one now." Her voice broke. "Oh, Susan, I want to help, some way, if I can! WOULD he see me, do you think?"

"He ought to. He sees everybody else."

"I know. Mazie says—"

"Does Mazie know about you?" interrupted Susan. "I mean, about your being 'Miss Stewart'?"

"A little, but not much. I told her once that he 'most always called me 'Miss Stewart,' but I never made anything of it, and I never told her how much I saw of him out home. Some way, I—" She stopped short, with a quick indrawing of her breath. In the doorway down the hall stood Keith.

"Susan, I thought I heard—WAS Miss Stewart here?" he demanded excitedly.

With only the briefest of hesitations and a half-despairing, half-relieved look into Susan's startled eyes, the young girl hurried forward.

"Indeed I'm here," she cried gayly, giving a warm clasp to his eagerly outstretched hand "How do you do? Susan was just saying—."

But Susan was gone with upflung hands and a look that said "No, you don't rake me into this thing, young lady!" as plainly as if she had spoken the words themselves.

In the living-room a minute later, Keith began eager questioning.

"When did you come?"

"Yesterday."

"And you came to see me the very next day! Weren't you good? You knew how I wanted to see you."

"Oh, but I didn't," she laughed a little embarrassedly. "You're at home now, and you have all your old friends, and—"

"But they're not you. There's not any one like you," cut in the youth fervently. "And now you're going to stay a long time, aren't you?"

"Y-yes, several weeks, probably."

"Good! And you'll come every day to see me?"

"W-well, as to that-"

"It's too much to ask, of course," broke off Keith contritely. "And, truly, I don't want to impose on you."

"No, no, it isn't that," protested the girl quickly. "It's only— There are so many—"

"But I told you there isn't anybody like you, Miss Stewart. There isn't any one here that UNDERSTANDS—like you. And it was you who first taught me to do—so many things."

His voice faltered.

He paused, wet his lips, then plunged on hurriedly. "Miss Stewart, I don't say this sort of thing very often. I never said it before—to anybody. But I want you to know that I understood and appreciated just what you were doing all those weeks for me out there at the sanatorium. And it was the WAY you did it, with never a word or a hint that I was different. You did things, and you made me do things, without reminding me all the time that I was blind. I shall never forget that first day when you told me dad would want to hear from me; and then, before I could say a word, you put that paper in my hands, and my fingers fell on those lines that I could feel. And how I blessed you for not TELLING me those lines were there! Don't you see? Everybody here, that comes to see me, TELLS me—the lines are there."

"Yes, I—know." The girl's voice was low, a little breathless.

"And that's why I need you so much. If anybody in the whole world can make me forget for a minute, you can. You will come?"

"Why, of course, I'll come, and be glad to. You know I will. And I'm so glad if I've helped—any!"

"You've helped more—than you'll ever know. But, come—look! I've got a dandy new game here." And Keith, very obviously to hide the shake in his voice and the emotion in his face, turned gayly to a little stand near him and picked up a square cardboard box.

Half an hour later, Dorothy Parkman, passing through the hall on her way to the outer door, was waylaid by Susan.

"Sh-h! Don't speak here, but come with me," she whispered,

leading the way through the diningroom. In the kitchen she stopped and turned eagerly. "Well, did you tell him?" she demanded.

Miss Dorothy shook her head, mutely, despairingly.

"You mean he don't know yet that you're Dorothy Parkman?"

"I mean just that."

"But, child alive, he'll find out—he can't help finding out—now."

"I know it. But I just couldn't tell him—I COULDN'T, Susan. I tried to do it two or three times. Indeed, I did. But the words just wouldn't come. And now I don't know when I can tell him."

"But he was tickled to death to see you. He showed it, Miss Dorothy."

"I know." A soft pink suffused the young girl's face. "But it was 'Miss Stewart' he was glad to see, not Dorothy Parkman. And, after the things he said—" She stopped and looked back over her shoulder toward the room she had just left.

"But, Miss Dorothy, don't you see? It'll be all right, now. You've SHOWN him that you don't mind being with blind folks a mite. So now he won't care a bit when he knows you are Dorothy Parkman."

But the girl shook her head again.

"Yes, I know. He might not mind that part, PERHAPS; but I know he'd mind the deceit all these long months, and it wouldn't be easy to—to make him understand. He'd never

Eleanor H. Porter

forgive it—I know he wouldn't—to think I'd taken advantage of his not being able to see."

"Nonsense! Of course he would."

"He wouldn't. You don't know. Just to-day he said something about—about some one who had tried to deceive him in a little thing, because he was blind; and I could see how bitter he was."

"But what ARE you goin' to do?"

"I don't know, Susan. It's harder than ever now," almost moaned the girl.

"You're COMIN' AGAIN?"

"Yes, oh, yes. I shall come as long as he'll let me. I know he wants me to. I know I HAVE helped a little. He spoke—beautifully about that to-day. But, whether, after he finds out—" Her voice choked into silence and she turned her head quite away.

"There, there, dear, don't you fret," Susan comforted her. "You jest go home and think no more about it.

When thinkin' won't mend it,
Then thinkin' won't end it.

So what's the use? When you get ready, you jest come again; an' you keep a-comin', too. It'll all work out right. You see if it don't."

"Thank you, Susan. Oh, I'll come as long as I can," sighed the girl, turning to go. "But I'm not so sure how it'll turn out," she finished with a wistful smile over her shoulder as she opened the door.

CHAPTER XXII

HOW COULD YOU, MAZIE?

As Miss Dorothy herself had said, it could not, of course, continue. She came once, and once again to see Keith; and in spite of her efforts to make her position clear to him, her secret still remained her own. Then, on the third visit, the dreaded disclosure came, naturally, and in the simplest, most unexpected way; yet in a way that would most certainly have been the last choice of Miss Dorothy herself could she have had aught to say about it.

The two, Keith and Dorothy, had had a wonderful hour over a book that Dorothy had brought to read. They had been sitting on the porch, and Dorothy had risen to go when there came a light tread on the front walk and Mazie Sanborn tripped up the porch steps.

"Well, Dorothy Parkman, is this where you were?" she cried gayly. "I was hunting all over the house for you half an hour ago."

"DOROTHY PARKMAN!" Keith was on his feet. His face had grown very white.

Dorothy, too, her eyes on Keith's face, had grown very

Eleanor H. Porter

white; yet she managed to give a light laugh, and her voice matched Mazie's own for gayety.

"Were you? Well, I was right here. But I'm going now."

"You! but—Miss Stewart!" Keith's colorless lips spoke the words just above his breath.

"Why, Keith Burton, what's the matter?" laughed Mazie. "You look as if you'd seen a ghost. I mean—oh, forgive that word, Keith," she broke off in light apology. "I'm always forgetting, and talking as if you could really SEE. But you looked so funny, and you brought out that 'Dorothy Parkman' with such a surprised air. Just as if you didn't ever call her that in the old school days, Keith Burton! Oh, Dorothy told me you called her 'Miss Stewart' a lot now; but—"

"Yes, I have called her 'Miss Stewart' quite a lot lately," interposed Keith, in a voice so quietly self-controlled that even Dorothy herself was almost deceived. But not quite. Dorothy saw the clenched muscles and white knuckles of his hands as he gripped the chair-back before him; and she knew too much to expect him to offer his hand in good-bye. So she backed away, and she still spoke lightly, inconsequently, though she knew her voice was shaking, as she made her adieus.

"Well, good-bye, I must be going now, sure. I'll be over to-morrow, though, to finish the book. Good-bye."

"Good-bye," said Keith.

And Dorothy wondered if Mazie noticed that he quite omitted a polite "Come again," and if Mazie saw that as he said the terse "Good-bye" he put both hands suddenly and resolutely behind his back. Dorothy saw it, and at home, long hours later she was still crying over it.

She went early to the Burtons' the next forenoon.

"I came to finish the book I was reading to Mr. Keith," she told Susan brightly, as her ring was answered. "I thought I'd come early before anybody else got here."

She would have stepped in, but Susan's ample figure still barred the way.

"Well, now, that's too bad!" Susan's voice expressed genuine concern and personal disappointment. "Ain't it a shame? Keith said he wa'n't feelin' nohow well this mornin', an' that he didn't want to see no one. An' under no circumstances not to let no one in to see him. But maybe if I told him't was you—"

"No, no, don't—don't do that!" cried the girl hurriedly. "I—I'll come again some other time."

On the street a minute later she whispered tremulously: "He did it on purpose, of course. He KNEW I would come this morning! But he can't keep it up forever! He'll HAVE to see me some time. And when he does—Oh, if only Mazie Sanborn hadn't blurted it out like that! Why didn't I tell him? Why didn't I tell him? But I will tell him. He can't keep this up forever."

When on a second and a third and a fourth morning, however, Dorothy had found Susan's figure barring the way, and had received the same distressed "He says he won't see no one, Miss Dorothy," from Susan's plainly troubled lips, Dorothy began to think Keith did mean to keep it up forever.

"But what IS it, Susan?" she faltered. "Is he sick, really sick?"

Eleanor H. Porter

"I don't know, Miss Dorothy," frowned Susan. "But I don't like the looks of it, anyhow. He says he ain't sick—not physicianly sick; but he jest don't want to talk an' see folks. An' he's been like that 'most a week now. An' I'm free to confess I don't like it."

"But what does he do—all day?" asked the girl.

"Nothin', that I can see," sighed Susan profoundly. "Oh, he plays that solitary some, an' putters a little with some of his raised books; but mostly he jest sits still an' thinks. An' I don't like it. If only his father was here. But with him gone peddlin' molasses, an' no one 'lowed into the house, there ain't anything for him to do but to think. An' 'tain't right nor good for him. I've watched him an' I know."

"But he used to see people, Susan."

"I know it. He saw everybody."

"Do you know why he won't—now?" asked the girl a little faintly.

"I hain't the faintest inception of an idea. It came as sudden as that," declared Susan, snapping her finger.

"Then he hasn't said anything special about not wanting to see—me?"

"Why, no. He—Do you mean—HAS he found out?" demanded Susan, interrupting herself excitedly.

"Yes. He found out last Monday afternoon. Mazie ran up on to the porch and called me by name right out. Oh, Susan, it was awful. I shall never forget the look on that boy's face as long as I live."

"Lan' sakes! MONDAY!" breathed Susan. "An' Tuesday he began refusin' to see folks. Then 'course that was it. But why won't he see other folks? They hain't anything to do with you."

"I don't know—unless he didn't want to tell you specially not to let me in, and so he said not to let anybody in."

"Was he awful mad?"

"It wasn't so much anger as it was grief and hurt and—oh, I can't express what it was. But I saw it; and I never shall forget it. You see, to have it blurted out to him like that without any warning—and of course he couldn't understand."

"But didn't you explain things—how 'twas, in the first place?"

She shook her head. "I couldn't—not with Mazie there. I said I'd come the next morning to—to finish the book. I thought he'd understand I was going to explain then. He probably did—and that's why he won't let me in. He doesn't want any explanations," sighed the girl tremulously.

"Well, he ought to want 'em," asserted Susan with vigor. "'Tain't fair nor right nor sensible for him to act like this, makin' a mountain out of an ant-hill. I declare, Miss Dorothy, he ought to be made to see you."

The girl flushed and drew back.

"Most certainly not, Susan! I—I am not in the habit of MAKING people see me, when they don't wish to. Do you suppose I'm going to beg and tease: 'PLEASE won't you let me see you?' Hardly! He need not worry. I shall not come again."

"Oh, Miss Dorothy!" remonstrated Susan.

"Why, of course I won't, Susan!" cried the girl. "Do you suppose I'm going to keep him from seeing other people just because he's afraid he'll have to let me in, too? Nonsense, Susan! Even you must admit I cannot allow that. You may tell Mr. Keith, please, that he may feel no further uneasiness. I shall not trouble him again."

"Oh, Miss Dorothy!" begged Susan agitatedly, once more.

But Miss Dorothy, with all the hurt dignity of her eighteen years, turned haughtily away, leaving Susan impotent and distressed, looking after her.

Two minutes later Susan sought Keith in the living-room. Her whole self spelt irate determination—but Keith could not see that. Keith, listless and idle-handed, sat in his favorite chair by the window.

"Dorothy Parkman jest rang the bell," began Susan, "an'-"

"But I said I'd see no one," interrupted Keith, instantly alert.

"That's what I told her, an' she's gone."

"Oh, all right." Keith relaxed into his old listlessness.

"An' she said to please tell you she'd trouble you no further, so you might let in the others now as soon as you please."

Keith sat erect in his chair with a jerk.

"What did she mean by that?"

"I guess you don't need me to tell you," observed Susan grimly.

With a shrug and an irritable gesture Keith settled back in his chair.

"I don't care to discuss it, Susan. I don't wish to see ANY one. We'll let it go at that, if you please," he said.

"But I don't please!" Susan was in the room now, close to Keith's chair. Her face was quivering with emotion. "Keith, won't you listen to reason? It ain't like you a mite to sit back like this an' refuse to see a nice little body like Dorothy Parkman, what's been so kind—"

"Susan!" Keith was sitting erect again. His face was white, and carried a stern anguish that Susan had never seen before. "I don't care to discuss Miss Parkman with you or with anybody else. Neither do I care to discuss the fact that I thoroughly understand, of course, that you, or she, or anybody else, can fool me into believing anything you please; and I can't—help myself."

"No, no, Keith, don't take it like that—please don't!"

"Is there any other way I CAN take it? Do you think 'Miss Stewart' could have made such a fool of me if I'd had EYES to see Dorothy Parkman?"

"But she was only tryin' to HELP you, an'—"

"I don't want to be 'helped'!" stormed the boy hotly. "Did it ever occur to you, Susan, that I might sometimes like to HELP somebody myself, instead of this everlastingly having somebody help me?"

"But you do help. You help me," asserted Susan feverishly, working her nervous fingers together. "An' you'd help me more if you'd only let folks in to see you, an'—"

Eleanor H. Porter

"All right, all right," interrupted Keith testily. "Let them in. Let everybody in. I don't care. What's the difference? But, please, PLEASE, Susan, stop talking any more about it all now."

And Susan stopped. There were times when Susan knew enough to stop, and this was one of them.

But she took him at his word, and when Mrs. McGuire came the next day with a letter from her John, Susan ushered her into the living-room where Keith was sitting alone. And Keith welcomed her with at least a good imitation of his old heartiness.

Mrs. McGuire said she had such a funny letter to read to-day. She knew he'd enjoy it, and Susan would, too, particularly the part that John had quoted from something that had been printed by the British soldiers in France and circulated among their comrades in the trenches and hospitals, and everywhere. John had written it off on a separate piece of paper, and this was it:

Don't worry: there's nothing to worry about.

You have two alternatives: either you are mobilized or you are not. If not, you have nothing to worry about.

If you are mobilized, you have two alternatives: you are in camp or at the front. If you are in camp, you have nothing to worry about.

If you are at the front, you have two alternatives: either you are on the fighting line or in reserve. If in reserve, you have nothing to worry about.

If you are on the fighting line, you have two alternatives:

either you fight or you don't. If you don't, you have nothing to worry about.

If you do, you have two alternatives: either you get hurt or you don't. If you don't, you have nothing to worry about.

If you are hurt, you have two alternatives: either you are slightly hurt or badly. If slightly, you have nothing to worry about.

If badly, you have two alternatives: either you recover or you don't. If you recover, you have nothing to worry about. If you don't, and have followed my advice clear through, you have done with worry forever.

Mrs. McGuire was in a gale of laughter by the time she had finished reading this; so, too, was Susan. Keith also was laughing, but his laughter did not have the really genuine ring to it—which fact did not escape Susan.

"Well, anyhow, he let Mis' McGuire in—an' that's somethin'," she muttered to herself, as Mrs. McGuire took her departure. "Besides, he talked to her real pleasant—an' that's more."

As the days passed, others came, also, and Keith talked with them. He even allowed Dorothy Parkman to be admitted one day.

Dorothy had not come until after long urging on the part of Susan and the assurance that Keith had said he would see her. Even then nothing would have persuaded her, she told Susan, except the great hope that she could say something, in some way, that would set her right in Keith's eyes.

So with fear and trembling and with a painful embarrassment

on her face, but with a great hope in her heart, she entered the room and came straight to Keith's side.

For a moment the exultation of a fancied success sent a warm glow all through her, for Keith had greeted her pleasantly and even extended his hand. But almost at once the glow faded and the great hope died in her heart, for she saw that even while she touched his hand, he was yet miles away from her.

He laughed and talked with her—oh, yes; but he laughed too much and talked too much. He gave her almost no chance to say anything herself. And what he said was so inconsequential and so far removed from anything intimately concerning themselves, that the girl found it utterly impossible to make the impassioned explanation which she had been saying over and over again all night to herself, and from which she had hoped so much.

Yet at the last, just before she bade him good-bye, she did manage to say something. But in her disappointment and excitement and embarrassment, her words were blurted out haltingly and ineffectually, and they were not at all the ones she had practiced over and over to herself in the long night watches; nor were they received as she had palpitatingly pictured that they would be, with Keith first stern and hurt, and then just dear and forgiving and UNDERSTANDING.

Keith was neither stern nor hurt. He still laughed pleasantly, and he tossed her whole labored explanation aside with a light: "Certainly—of course—to be sure—not at all! You did quite right, I assure you!" And then he remarked that it was a warm day, wasn't it? And Dorothy found herself hurrying down the Burton front walk with burning cheeks and a chagrined helplessness that left her furious and with an ineffably cheap feeling—yet not able to put her finger on any discourteous flaw in Keith's punctilious politeness.

"I wish I'd never said a word—not a word," she muttered hotly to herself as she hurried down the street. "I wonder if he thinks—I'll ever open my head to him about it again. Well, he needn't—worry! But—oh, Keith, Keith, how could you?" she choked brokenly. Then abruptly she turned down a side street, lest Mazie Sanborn, coming toward her, should see the big tears that were rolling down her cheeks.

CHAPTER XXIII

JOHN McGUIRE

So imperative was the knock at the kitchen door at six o'clock that July morning that Susan almost fell down the back stairs in her haste to obey the summons.

"Lan' sakes, Mis' McGuire, what a start you did give—why, Mis' McGuire, what is it?" she interrupted herself, aghast, as Mrs. McGuire, white-faced and wild-eyed, swept past her and began to pace up and down the kitchen floor, moaning frenziedly:

"It's come—it's come—I knew't would come. Oh, what shall I do? What shall I do?"

"What's come?"

"Oh, John, John, my boy, my boy!"

"You don't mean he's—dead?"

"No, no, worse than that, worse than that!" moaned the woman, wringing her hands. "Oh, what shall I do, what shall I do?"

With a firm grasp Susan caught the twisting fingers and gently but resolutely forced their owner into a chair.

"Do? You'll jest calm yourself right down an' tell me all about it, Mis' McGuire. This rampagin' 'round the kitchen like this don't do no sort of good, an' it's awful on your nerves. An' furthermore an' moreover, no matter what't is that ails your John, it can't be worse'n death; for while there's life there's hope, you know."

"But it is, it is, I tell you," sobbed Mrs. McGuire still swaying her body back and forth. "Susan, my boy is— BLIND." With the utterance of the dread word Mrs. McGuire stiffened suddenly into rigid horror, her eyes staring straight into Susan's.

"MIS' MCGUIRE!" breathed Susan in dismay; then hopefully, "But maybe 'twas a mistake."

The woman shook her head. She went back to her swaying from side to side.

"No, 'twas a dispatch. It came this mornin'. Just now. Mr. McGuire was gone, an' there wasn't anybody there but the children, an' they're asleep. That's why I came over. I HAD to. I had to talk to some one!"

"Of course, you did! An' you shall, you poor lamb. You shall tell me all about it. What was it? What happened?"

"I don't know. I just know he's blind, an' that he's comin' home. He's on his way now. My John—blind! Oh, Susan, what shall I do, what shall I do?"

"Then he probably ain't sick, or hurt anywheres else, if he's on his way home—leastways, he ain't hurt bad. You can be

Eleanor H. Porter

glad for that, Mis' McGuire."

"I don't know, I don't know. Maybe he is. It didn't say. It just said blinded," chattered Mrs. McGuire feverishly. "They get them home just as soon as they can when they're blinded. We were readin' about it only yesterday in the paper—how they did send 'em home right away. Oh, how little I thought that my son John would be one of 'em—my John!"

"But your John ain't the only one, Mis' McGuire. There's other Johns, too. Look at our Keith here."

"I know, I know."

"An' I wonder how he'll take this—about your John?"

"HE'LL know what it means," choked Mrs. McGuire.

"He sure will—an' he'll feel bad. I know that. He ain't hisself, anyway, these days."

"He ain't?" Mrs. McGuire asked the question abstractedly, her mind plainly on her own trouble; but Susan, intent on HER trouble, did not need even the question to spur her tongue.

"No, he ain't. Oh, he's brave an' cheerful. He's awful cheerful, even cheerfuler than he was a month ago. He's too cheerful, Mis' McGuire. There's somethin' back of it I don't like. He—"

But Mrs. McGuire was not listening. Wringing her hands she had sprung to her feet and was pacing the floor again, moaning: "Oh, what shall I do, what shall I do?" A minute later, only weeping afresh at Susan's every effort to comfort her, she stumbled out of the kitchen and hurried across the yard to her own door.

Watching her from the window, Susan drew a long sigh.

"I wonder how he WILL take—But, lan' sakes, this ain't gettin' my breakfast," she ejaculated with a hurried glance at the clock on the little shelf over the stove.

There was nothing, apparently, to distinguish breakfast that morning from a dozen other breakfasts that had gone before. Keith and his father talked cheerfully of various matters, and Susan waited upon them with her usual briskness. If Susan was more silent than usual, and if her eyes sought Keith's face more frequently than was her habit, no one, apparently, noticed it. Susan did fancy, however, that she saw a new tenseness in Keith's face, a new nervousness in his manner; but that, perhaps, was because she was watching him so closely, and because he was so constantly in her mind, owing to her apprehension as to how he would take the news of John McGuire's blindness.

From the very first Susan had determined not to tell her news until after Mr. Burton had left the house. She could not have explained it even to herself, but she had a feeling that it would be better to tell Keith when he was alone. She planned, also, to tell him casually, as it were, in the midst of other conversation—not as if it were the one thing on her mind. In accordance with this, therefore, she forced herself to finish her dishes and to set her kitchen in order before she sought Keith in the living-room.

But Keith was not in the living-room; neither was he on the porch or anywhere in the yard.

With a troubled frown on her face Susan climbed the stairs to the second floor. Keith's room was silent, and empty, so far as human presence was concerned. So, too, was the studio, and every other room on that floor.

At the front of the attic stairs Susan hesitated. The troubled frown on her face deepened as she glanced up the steep, narrow stairway.

She did not like to have Keith go off by himself to the attic, and already now twice before she had found him up there, poking in the drawers of an old desk that had been his father's. He had shut the drawers quickly and had laughingly turned aside her questions when she had asked him what in the world he was doing up there. And he had got up immediately and had gone downstairs with her. But she had not liked the look on his face. And to-day, as she hesitated at the foot of the stairs, she was remembering that look. But for only a moment. Resolutely then she lifted her chin, ran up the stairs, and opened the attic door.

Over at the desk by the window there was a swift move-ment—but not so swift that Susan did not see the revolver pushed under some loose papers.

"Is that you, Susan?" asked Keith sharply. "Yes, honey. I jest came up to get somethin'."

Susan's face was white like paper, and her hands were cold and shaking, but her voice, except for a certain breathless-ness, was cheerfully steady. With more or less noise and with a running fire of inconsequent comment, she rummaged among the trunks and boxes, gradually working her way to, ward the desk where Keith still sat.

At the desk, with a sudden swift movement, she thrust the papers to one side and dropped her hand on the revolver. At the same moment Keith's arm shot out and his hand fell, covering hers.

She saw his young face flush and harden and his mouth set into stern lines.

"Susan, you'll be good enough, please, to take your hand off that," he said then sharply.

There was a moment's tense silence. Susan's eyes, agonized and pleading, were on his face. But Keith could not see that. He could only hear her words a moment later—light words, with a hidden laugh in them, yet spoken with that same curious breathlessness.

"Faith, honey, an' how can I, with your own hand holdin' mine so tight?"

Keith removed his hand instantly. His set face darkened.

"This is not a joke, Susan, and I shall have to depend on your honor to let that revolver stay where it is. Unfortunately I am unable to SEE whether I am obeyed or not."

It was Susan's turn to flush. She drew back at once, leaving the weapon uncovered on the desk between them.

"I'm not takin' the pistol, Keith." The laugh was all gone from Susan's voice now. So, too, was the breathlessness. The voice was steady, grave, but very gentle. "We take matches an' pizen an' knives away from CHILDREN—not from grown men, Keith. The pistol is right where you can reach it—if you want it."

She saw the fingers of Keith's hand twitch and tighten. Otherwise there was no answer. After a moment she went on speaking.

"But let me say jest this: 'tain't like you to be a—quitter, Keith." She saw him wince, but she did not wait for him to speak. "An' after you've done this thing, there ain't any one in the world goin' to be so sorry as you'll be. You mark my words."

It was like a sharp knife cutting a taut cord. The tense muscles relaxed and Keith gave a sudden laugh. True, it was a short laugh, and a bitter one; but it was a laugh.

"You forget, Susan. If—if I carried that out I wouldn't be in the world—to care."

"Shucks! You'd be in some world, Keith Burton, an' you know it. An' you'd feel nice lookin' down on the mess you'd made of THIS world, wouldn't you?"

"Well, if I was LOOKING, I'd be SEEING, wouldn't I?" cut in the youth grimly. "Don't forget, Susan, that I'd be SEEING, please."

"Seein' ain't everything, Keith Burton. Jest remember that. There is some things you'd rather be blind than see. An' that's one of 'em. Besides, seein' ain't the only sensible you've got, an' there's such a lot of things you can do, an'—"

"Oh, yes, I know," interrupted Keith fiercely, flinging out both his hands. "I can feel a book, and eat my dinner, and I can hear the shouts of the people cheering the boys that go marching by my door. But I'm tired of it all. I tell you I can't stand it—I CAN'T, Susan. Yes, I know that's a cheap way out of it," he went on, after a choking pause, with a wave of his hand toward the revolver on the desk;" and a cowardly one, too. I know all that. And maybe I wouldn't have—have done it to-day, even if you hadn't come. I found it last week, and it—fascinated me. It seemed such an easy way out of it.

Since then I've been up here two or three times just to—to feel of it. Somehow I liked to know it was here, and that, if—if I just couldn't stand things another minute—

"But—I've tried to be decent, honest I have. But I'm tired of being amused and 'tended to like a ten-year-old boy. I don't want flowers and jellies and candies brought in to me. I don't want to read and play solitaire and checkers week in and week out. I want to be over there, doing a man's work. Look at Ted, and Tom, and Jack Green, and John McGuire!"

"John McGuire!" It was a faltering cry from Susan, but Keith did not even hear.

"What are they doing, and what am I doing? Yet you people expect me to sit here contented with a dice-box and a deck of playing-cards, and be GLAD I can do that much. Oh, well, I suppose I ought to be. But when I sit here alone day after day and think and think—"

"But, Keith, we don't want you to do that," interposed Susan feverishly. "Now there's Miss Dorothy—if you'd only let her—"

"But I tell you I don't want to be babied and pitied and 'tended to by young women who are SORRY for me. *I* want to do the helping part of the time. And if I see a girl I—I could care for, I want to be able to ask her like a man to marry me; and then if she says 'yes,' I want to be able to take care of her myself—not have her take care of me and marry me out of pity and feed me fudge and flowers! And there's—dad."

Keith's voice broke and stopped. Susan, watching his impassioned face, wet her lips and swallowed convulsively. Then Keith began again.

"Susan, do you know the one big thing that drives me up here every time, in spite of myself? It's the thought of—dad. How do you suppose I feel to think of dad peddling peas and beans and potatoes down to McGuire's grocery store?—dad!"

Susan lifted her head defiantly.

"Well, now look a-here, Keith Burton, let me tell you that peddlin' peas an' beans an' potatoes is jest as honorary as paintin' pictures, an'—"

"I'm not saying it isn't," cut in the boy incisively. "I'm merely saying that, as I happen to know, he prefers to paint pictures—and I prefer to have him. And he'd be doing it this minute—if it wasn't for his having to support me, and you know it, Susan."

"Well, what of it? It don't hurt him any."

"It hurts me, Susan. And when I think of all the things he hoped—of me. I was going to be Jerry and Ned and myself; and I was going to make him so proud, Susan, so proud! I was going to make up to him all that he had lost. All day under the trees up on the hill, I used to lie and dream of what I was going to be some day—the great pictures I was going to paint—for dad. The great fame that was going to come to me—for dad. The money I was going to earn—for dad: I saw dad, old and white-haired, leaning on me. I saw the old house restored—all the locks and keys and sagging blinds, the cracked ceilings and tattered wallpaper—all made fresh and new. And dad so proud and happy in it all—so proud and happy that perhaps he'd think I really had made up for Jerry and Ned, and his own lost hopes.

"And, now, look at me! Useless, worse than useless—all my

life a burden to him and to everybody else. Susan, I can't stand it. I CAN'T. That's why I want to end it all. It would be so simple—such an easy way—out."

"Yes, 'twould—for quitters. Quitters always take easy ways out. But you ain't no quitter, Keith Burton. Besides, 't wouldn't end it. You know that. 'Twould jest be shuttin' the door of this room an' openin' the one to the next. You've had a good Christian bringin' up, Keith Burton, an' you know as well as I do that your eternal, immoral soul ain't goin' to be snuffled out of existence by no pistol shot, no matter how many times you pull the jigger."

Keith laughed—and with the laugh his tense muscles relaxed.

"All right, Susan," he shrugged a little grimly. "I'll concede your point. You made it—perhaps better than you know. But—well, it isn't so pleasant always to be the hook, you know," he finished bitterly.

"The—hook?" frowned Susan.

Keith laughed again grimly.

"Perhaps you've forgotten—but I haven't. I heard you talking to Mrs. McGuire one day. You said that everybody was either a hook or an eye, and that more than half the folks were hooks hanging on to somebody else. And that's why some eyes had more than their share of hooks hanging on to them. You see—I remembered. I knew then, when you said it, that I was a hook, and—"

"Keith Burton, I never thought of you when I said that," interrupted Susan agitatedly.

"Perhaps not; but *I* did. Why, Susan, of course I'm a hook— an old, bent, rusty hook. But I can hang on—oh, yes, I can hang on—to anybody that will let me! But, Susan, don't you see?—sometimes it seems as if I'd give the whole world if just for once I could feel that I—that some one was hanging on to me! that I was of some use somewhere."

"An' so you're goin' to be, honey. I know you be," urged Susan eagerly. "Just remember all them fellers that wrote books an' give lecturing an'—"

"Oh, yes, I know," interposed Keith, with a faint smile. "You were a good old soul, Susan, to read me all those charming tales, and I understood of course, what you were doing it for. You wanted me to go and do likewise. But I couldn't write a book to save my soul, Susan, and my voice would stick in my throat at the second word of a 'lecturing.'"

"But there'll be somethin', Keith, I know there'll be somethin'. God never locked up the doors of your eyes without givin' you the key to some other door. It's jest that you hain't found it yet."

"Perhaps. I certainly haven't found it—that's sure," retorted the lad bitterly. "And just why He saw fit to send me this blindness—"

"We don't have to know," interposed Susan quickly; "an' questionin' about it don't settle nothin', anyhow. If we've got it, we've got it, an' if it's somethin' we can't possibly help, the only questionin' worth anything then is how are we goin' to stand it. You see, there's more'n one way of standin' things."

"Yes, I know there is." Keith stirred restlessly in his seat.

"An' some ways is better than others."

"There, there, Susan, I know just what you're going to say, and it's all very true, of course," cried Keith, stirring still more restlessly. "But you see T don't happen to feel like hearing it just now. Oh, yes, I know I've got lots to be thankful for. I can hear, and feel, and taste, and walk; and I should be glad for all of them. And I am, of course. I should declare that all's well with the world, and that both sides of the street are sunny, and that there isn't any shadow anywhere. There, you see! I know all that you would say, Susan, and I've said it, so as to save you the trouble."

"Humph!" commented Susan, bridling a little; then suddenly, she gave a sly chuckle. "That's all very well an' good, Master Keith Burton, but there's one more thing I would have said if I was doin' the sayin'!"

"Well?"

"About that both sides of the street bein' sunny—it seems to me that the man what says, yes, he knows one side is shady an' troublous, but that he thinks it'll be healthier an' happier for him an' everybody else 'round him if he walks on the sunny side, an' then WALKS THERE—it seems to me he's got the spots all knocked off that feller what says there AIN'T no shady side!"

Keith gave a low laugh—a laugh more nearly normal than Susan had heard him give for several days.

"All right, Susan, I'll accept your amendment and—we'll let it go that one side is shady, and that I'm supposed to determinedly pick the sunny side. Anything more?"

"M-more?"

"That you came up to say to me—yes. You know I have just

saved you the trouble of saying part of it."

"Oh!" Susan laughed light-heartedly. (This was Keith—her Keith that she knew.) "No that's all I—" She stopped short in dismay! All the color and lightness disappeared from her face, leaving it suddenly white and drawn. "That is," she faltered, "there was somethin' else—I was goin' to say, about—about John McGuire. He—"

"I don't care to hear it." Keith had frozen instantly into frigid aloofness. Stern lines had come to his boyish mouth.

"But—but, Keith, Mrs. McGuire came over to-"

"To read another of those precious letters, of course," cut in Keith angrily, "but I tell you I don't want to hear it. Do you suppose a caged bird likes to hear of the woods and fields and tree-tops while he's tied to a three-inch swing between two gilt bars? Well, hardly! There's lots that I do have to stand, Susan, but I don't have to stand that."

Susan caught her breath with a half sob.

"But, Keith, I wasn't going to tell you of—of woods an' fields an' tree-tops this time. You see—now he's in a cage himself."

"What do you mean?"

"He's coming home. He's—blind."

Keith leaped from his chair.

"BLIND? JOHN McGUIRE?"

"Yes."

"Oh-h-h!" Long years of past suffering and of future woe filled the short little word to bursting, as Keith dropped back into his chair. For a moment he sat silent, his whole self held rigid. Then, unsteadily he asked the question:

"What—happened?"

"They don't know. It was a dispatch that came this mornin'. He was blinded, an' is on his way home. That's all."

"That's—enough."

"Yes, I knew you'd—understand."

"Yes, I do—understand."

Susan hesitated. Keith still sat, with his unseeing gaze straight ahead, his body tense and motionless. On the desk within reach lay the revolver. Cautiously Susan half extended her hand toward it, then drew it back. She glanced again at Keith's absorbed face, then turned and made her way quietly down the stairs.

At the bottom of the attic flight she glanced back. "He won't touch it now, I'm sure," she breathed. "An', anyhow, we only take knives an' pizen away from children—not grown men!"

CHAPTER XXIV

AS SUSAN SAW IT

It was the town talk, of course—the home-coming of John McGuire. Men gathered on street corners and women clustered about back-yard fences and church doorways. Children besieged their parents with breathless questions, and repeated to each other in awe-struck whispers what they had heard. Everywhere was horror, sympathy, and interested speculation as to "how he'd take it."

Where explicit information was so lacking, imagination and surmise eagerly supplied the details; and Mrs. McGuire's news of the blinding of John McGuire was not three days old before a full account of the tragedy from beginning to end was flying from tongue to tongue—an account that would have surprised no one so greatly as it would have surprised John McGuire himself.

To Susan, Dorothy Parkman came one day with this story.

"Well, 't ain't true," disavowed Susan succinctly when the lurid details had been breathlessly repeated to her.

"You mean—he isn't blind?" demanded the young girl.

"Oh, yes, he's blind, all right, poor boy! But it's the rest I mean—about his killin' twenty-eight Germans single-handed, an' bein' all shot to pieces hisself, an' benighted for bravery."

"But what did happen?"

"We don't know. We just know he's blind an' comin' home. Mis' McGuire had two letters yesterday from John, but—"

"From John—himself?"

"Yes; but they was both writ long before the apostrophe, an' 'course they didn't say nothin' about it. He was well an' happy, he said. She had had only one letter before these for a long time. An' now to have—this!"

"Yes, I know. It's terrible. How does—Mr. Keith take it?"

Susan opened wide her eyes.

"Why, you've seen him—you see him yesterday yourself, Miss Dorothy."

"Oh, I saw him—in a way, but not the real him, Susan. He's miles away now, always."

"You mean he ain't civil an' polite?" demanded Susan.

"Oh, he's very civil—too civil, Susan. Every time I go I say I won't go again. Then, when I get to thinking of him sitting there alone all day, and of how he used to like to have me read to him and play with him, I—I just have to go and see if he won't be the same as he used to be. But he never is."

"I know." Susan shook her head mournfully. "An' he ain't the same, Miss Dorothy. He don't ever whistle nor sing now, nor play solitary, nor any of them things he used to do. Oh, when folks comes in he braces back an' talks an' laughs. YOU know that. But in the exclusion of his own home here he jest sits an' thinks an' thinks an' thinks. An', Miss Dorothy, I've found out now what he's thinkin' of."

"Yes?"

"It's John McGuire an' them other soldiers what's comin' back blind from the war. An' he talks an' talks about 'em, an' mourns an' takes on something dreadful. He says HE knows what it means, an' that nobody can know what hain't had it happen to 'em. An' he broods an' broods over it."

"I can—imagine it." The girl said it with a little catch in her voice.

"An'—an' there's somethin' else I want to tell you about. I've got to tell somebody. I want to know if you think I done right. An' you're the only one I can tell. I've thought it all out. Daniel Burton is too near, an' Mis' McGuire an' all them others is too far. You ain't a relation, an' yet you care. You do care, don't you?—about Mr. Keith?"

"Why, of—of course. I care a great deal, Susan." Miss Dorothy spoke very lightly, very impersonally; but there was a sudden flame of color in her face. Susan, however, was not noticing this. Furtively she was glancing one way and another over her shoulder.

"Yes. Well, the other day he—he tried to—that is, well, I—I found him with a pistol in his hand, an'—"

"Susan!" The girl had gone very white.

"Oh, he didn't do it. Well, that ain't a very sensitive state-ment, is it? For if he had done it, he wouldn't be alive now, would he?" broke off Susan, with a faint smile. "But what I mean is, he didn't do it, an' I don't think he's goin' to do it."

"But, oh, Susan," faltered the girl, "you didn't leave that—that awful thing with him, did you? Didn't you take it—away?"

"No." Susan's mouth set grimly. "An' that's what I wanted to ask you about—if I did right, you know."

"Oh, no, no, Susan! I'm afraid," shuddered the girl. "Can't you—get it away—now?"

"Maybe. I know where 'tis. I was up there yesterday an' see it. 'T was in the desk drawer in the attic, jest where it used to be."

"Then get it, Susan, get it. Oh, please get it," begged the girl. "I'm afraid to have it there—a single minute."

"But, Miss Dorothy, stop; wait jest a minute. Think. How's he goin' to get self-defiance an' make a strong man of hisself if we take things away from him like he was a little baby?"

"I know, Susan; but if he SHOULD be tempted—"

"He won't. He ain't no more. I'm sure of that. I talked with him. Besides, I hain't caught him up there once since that day last week. Oh, I'm free to confess I HAVE watched him," admitted Susan defensively, with a faint smile.

"But what did happen that day you—you found him?"

"Oh, he had it, handlin' it, an' when he heard me, he jumped a little, an' hid it under some papers. My, Miss Dorothy, 'twas awful. I was that scared an' frightened I thought I couldn't move. But I knew I'd got to, an' I knew I'd got to move RIGHT, too, or I'd spoil everything. This wa'n't no ten-cent melodydrama down to the movies, but I had a humane soul there before me, an' I knew maybe it's whole internal salvation might depend on what I said an' did."

"But what DID you say?"

"I don't know. I only know that somehow, when it was over, I had a feelin' that he wouldn't never do that thing again. That somehow the MAN in him was on top, an' would stay on top. An' I'm more sure than ever of it now. He ain't thinkin' of hisself these days. It's John McGuire and them others. An' ain't it better that he let that pistol alone of his own free will an' accordance, an' know he was a man an' no baby, than if I'd taken it away from him?"

"I suppose—it was, Susan; but I don't think I'd have been strong enough—to make him strong."

"Yes, you would, if you'd been there. I reckon we're all goin' to learn to do a lot of things we never did before, now that the war has come."

"Yes, I know." A quivering pain swept across the young girl's face.

"Somehow, the war never seemed real to me before. 'T was jest somethin' 'way off—a lot of Dagoes an' Dutchmen, like the men what dug up the McGuires' frozen water-pipes last spring, fightin'. Not our kind of folks what talked English. Even when I read the papers, an' the awful things they did over there—it didn't seem as if 't was folks on our earth. It was like somethin' you read about in them old histronic days, or somethin' happenin' up on the moon, or on that plantation of Mars. Oh, of course, I knew John McGuire had gone; but somehow I never thought of him as fightin'—not with guns an' bloody gore, in spite of them letters of his. Some way, in my mind's eyes I always see him marchin' with flags flyin' an' folks cheerin'; an' I thought the war'd be over, anyhow, by the time he got there.

"But, now—! Why, now they're all gone—our own Teddy Somers, an' Tom Spencer, an' little Jacky Green that I used to hold on my knee. Some of 'em in France, an' some of 'em in them army canteens down to Ayer an' Texas an' everywhere. An' poor Tom's died already of pneumonia right here in our own land. An' now poor John McGuire! I tell you, Miss Dorothy, it brings it right home now to your own heart, where it hurts."

"It certainly does, Susan."

"An' let me tell you. What do you s'pose, more 'n anything else, made me see how really big it all is?"

"I don't know, Susan,"

"Well, I'll tell you. 'Twas because I couldn't write a poem on it."

"Sure enough, Susan! I don't believe I've heard you make a rhyme to-day," smiled Miss Dorothy.

Susan sighed and shook her head.

"Yes, I know. I don't make 'em much now. Somehow they don't sing all the time in my heart, an' burst out natural-like, as they used to. I think them days when I tried so hard to sell my poems, an' couldn't, kinder took the jest out of poetizin' for me. Somehow, when you find out somethin' is invaluable to other folks, it gets so it's invaluable to you, I s'pose. Still, even now, when I set right down to it, I can 'most always write 'em right off 'most as quick as I used to. But I couldn't on this war. I tried it. But it jest wouldn't do. I begun it:

Oh, woe is me, said the bayonet,
Oh, woe is me, said the sword.

Then the whole awful frightfulness of it an' the bigness of it seemed to swallow me up, an' I felt like a little pigment overtopped an' surrounded by great tall mountains of horror that were tumblin' down one after another on my head, an' buryin' me down so far an' deep that I couldn't say anything, only to moan, 'Oh, Lord, how long, oh, Lord, how long?' An' I knew then't was too big for me. I didn't try to write no more."

"I can see how you couldn't," faltered the girl, as she turned away. "I'm afraid—we're all going to find it—too big for us,"

CHAPTER XXV

KEITH TO THE RESCUE

John McGuire had not been home twenty-four hours before it was known that he "took it powerful hard."

To Keith Susan told what she had learned.

"They say he utterly refuses to see any one outside the family; an' that he'd rather not see even his own folks—that he's always askin' 'em to let him alone."

"Is he ill or wounded otherwise?" asked Keith.

"No, he ain't hurt outwardly or infernally, except his eyes, an' he says that's the worst of it, one woman told me. He's as sound as a nut, an' good for a hundred years yet. If he'd only been smashed up good an' solid, so's he'd have some hope of dyin' pretty quick, he wouldn't mind it, he says. But to live along like this!—oh, he's in an awful state of mind, everybody says."

"I can—imagine it," sighed Keith. And by the way he turned away Susan knew that he did not care to talk any more.

An hour later Mrs. McGuire hurried into Susan's kitchen.

Mrs. McGuire was looking thin and worn these days. From her half-buttoned shoes to her half-combed hair she was showing the results of strain and anxiety. With a long sigh she dropped into one of the kitchen chairs.

"Well, Mis' McGuire, if you ain't the stranger!" Susan greeted her cordially.

"Yes, I know," sighed Mrs. McGuire. "But, you see, I can't leave—him." As she spoke she looked anxiously through the window toward her own door. "Mr. McGuire's with him, now, so I got away."

"But there's Bess an' Harry," began Susan,

"We don't leave him with the children, ever," interposed Mrs. McGuire, with another hurried glance through the window. "We—don't dare to. You see, once we found—we found him with his father's old pistol. Oh, Susan, it—it was awful!"

"Yes, it—must have been." Susan, after one swift glance into her visitor's face, had turned her back suddenly. She was busy now with the dampers of her kitchen stove.

"Of course we took it right away," went on Mrs. McGuire, "an' put it where he'll never get it again. But we're always afraid there'll be somethin' somewhere that he WILL get hold of. You see, he's SO despondent—in such a terrible state!"

"Yes, I know," nodded Susan. Susan had abandoned her dampers, and had turned right about face again. "If only he'd see folks now."

"Yes, an' that's what I came over to talk to you about," cried

Mrs. McGuire eagerly. "We haven't been able to get him to see anybody—not anybody. But I've been wonderin' if he wouldn't see Keith, if we could work it right. You see he says he just won't be stared at; an' Keith, poor boy, COULDN'T stare, an' John knows it. Oh, Susan, do you suppose we could manage it?"

"Why, of course. I'll tell him right away, an' he'll go over; I know he'll go!" exclaimed Susan, all interest at once.

"Oh, but that wouldn't do at all!" cried Mrs. McGuire. "Don't you see? John refuses, absolutely refuses, to see any one; an' he wouldn't see Keith, if I should ASK him to. But he's interested in Keith—I KNOW he's that, for once, when I was talkin' to Mr. McGuire about Keith, John broke in an' asked two or three questions, an' he's NEVER done that before, about anybody. An' so I was pretty sure it was because Keith was blind, you know, like himself."

"Yes, I see, I see."

"An' if I can only manage it so they'll meet without John's knowin' they're goin' to, I believe he'll get to talkin' with him before he knows it; an' that it'll do him a world of good. Anyway, somethin's got to be done, Susan—it's GOT to be—to get him out of this awful state he's in."

"Well, we'll do it. I know we can do it some way."

"You think Keith'll do his part?" Mrs. McGuire's eyes were anxious.

"I'm sure he will—when he understands."

"Then listen," proposed Mrs. McGuire eagerly. "I'll get my John out on to the back porch to-morrow mornin'. That's the only place outdoors I CAN get him—he can't be seen from the street there, you know. I'll get him there as near ten o'clock as I can. You be on the watch, an' as soon as I get him all nicely fixed, you get Keith to come out into your yard an' stroll over to the fence an' speak to him, an' then come up on to the porch an' sit down, just naturally. He can do that all right, can't he? It's just wonderful—the way he gets around everywhere, with that little cane of his!"

"Yes, oh, yes."

"Well, I thought he could. An' tell him to keep right on talkin' every minute so my John won't have a chance to get up an' go into the house. Of course, I shall be there myself, at first. We never leave him alone, you know. But as soon as Keith comes, I shall go. They'll get along better by themselves, I'm sure—only, of course, I shall be where I can keep watch out of the window. Now do you understand?"

"Yes, an' we can do it. I know we can do it."

"All right, then. I'm not so sure we can, but we'll try it, anyway," sighed Mrs. McGuire, rising to her feet, the old worry back on her face. "Well, I must be goin'. Mr. McGuire'll have a fit. He's as nervous as a witch when he's left alone with John. There! What did I tell you?" she broke off, with an expressive gesture and glance, as a careworn-looking man appeared in the doorway of the house across the two back yards, and peered anxiously over at the Burtons' kitchen door. "Now, don't forget—ten o'clock to-morrow mornin'."

"I won't forget," promised Susan cheerfully, "Now, do you go home an' set easy, Mis' McGuire, an' don't you fret no more. It's comin' out all right—all right, I tell you," she reiterated, as Mrs. McGuire hurried through the doorway.

But when Mrs. McGuire was gone Susan drew a dubious sigh; and her cheery smile had turned to a questioning frown as she went in search of Keith. Very evidently Susan was far from feeling quite so sure about Keith's cooperation as she would have Mrs. McGuire think.

Keith was in the living-room, his head bowed in his two hands, his elbows on the table before him. At the first sound of Susan's steps he lifted his head with a jerk.

"I was lookin' for you," began Susan the moment she had crossed the threshold. Susan had learned that Keith hated above all things to have to speak first, or to ask, "Who is it?" "Mis' McGuire's jest been here."

"Yes, I heard her voice," returned the boy indifferently.

"She was tellin' about her John."

"How is he getting along?"

"He's in a bad way. Oh, he's real well physicianally, but he's in a bad way in his mind."

"Well, you don't wonder, do you?"

"Oh, no, 'course not. Still, well, for one thing, he don't like to see folks."

"Strange! Now, I'd think he'd just dote on seeing folks, wouldn't you?"

Susan caught the full force of the sarcasm, but superbly she ignored it.

"Well, I don't know—maybe; but, anyhow, he don't, an' Mis'

McGuire's that worried she don't know what to do. You see, she found him once with his daddy's pistol"—Susan was talking very fast now—"an' 'course that worked her up somethin' terrible. I'm afraid he hain't got much backbone. They don't dare to leave him alone a minute—not a minute. An' Mis' McGuire, she was wonderin' if—if you couldn't help 'em out some way."

"*I?*" The short ejaculation was full of amazement.

"Yes. That's what she come over for this mornin'."

"I? They forget." Keith fell back bitterly. "John McGuire might get hold of a dozen revolvers, and I wouldn't know it."

"Oh, 'twa'n't that. They didn't want you to WATCH him. They wanted you to—Well, it's jest this. Mis' McGuire thought as how if she could get her John out on the back porch, an' you happened to be in our back yard, an' should go over an' speak to him, maybe you'd get to talkin' with him, an' go up an' sit down. She thought maybe 'twould get him out of hisself that way. You see, he won't talk to—to most folks. He don't like to be stared at." (Susan threw a furtive glance into Keith's face, then looked quickly away.) "But she thought maybe he WOULD talk to you."

"Yes, I—see." Keith drew in his breath with a little catch.

"An' so she said there wa'n't anybody anywhere that could help so much as you—if you would."

"Why, of course, if I really could HELP—"

Susan did not need to look into Keith's face to catch the longing and heart-hunger and dawning hope in the word left suspended on his lips. She felt her own throat tighten; but in a moment she managed to speak with steady cheerfulness.

"Well, you can. You can help a whole lot. I'm sure you can. An' Mis' McGuire is, too. An' what's more, you're the only one what can help 'em, in this case. So we'll keep watch to-morrow mornin', an' when he comes out on the porch—well, we'll see what we will see." And Susan, just as if her own heart was not singing a triumphant echo of the song she knew was in his, turned away with an elaborate air of indifference.

Yet, when to-morrow came, and when Keith went out into the yard in response to the presence of John McGuire on his back porch, the result was most disappointing—to Susan. To Keith it did not seem to be so much so. But perhaps Keith had not expected quite what Susan had expected. At all events, Keith came back to the house with a glow on his face and a springiness in his step that Susan had not seen there for months. Yet all that had happened was that Keith had called out from the gate a pleasant "Good-morning!" to the blinded soldier, and had followed it with an inconsequential word or two about the weather. John McGuire had answered a crisp, cold something, and had risen at once to go into the house. Keith, at the first sound of his feet on the porch floor, had turned with a cheery "Well, I must be going back to the house." Whereupon John McGuire had sat down again, and Mrs. McGuire, who at Keith's first words, had started to her feet, dropped back into her chair.

Apparently not much accomplished, certainly; yet there was the glow on Keith's face and the springiness in Keith's step; and when he reached the kitchen, he said this to Susan:

"The next time John McGuire is on the back porch, please let me know."

And Susan let him know, both then and at subsequent times.

It was a pretty game and one well worth the watching. Certainly Susan and Mrs. McGuire thought it so. On the one side were persistence and perseverance and infinite tact. On the other were a distrustful antagonism and a palpable longing for an understanding companionship.

At first the intercourse between the two blind youths consisted of a mere word or two tossed by Keith to the other who gave a still shorter word in reply. And even this was not every day, for John McGuire was not out on the porch every day. But as the month passed, he came more and more frequently, and one evening Mrs. McGuire confided to Susan the fact that John seemed actually to fret now if a storm kept him indoors.

"An' he listens for Keith to come along the fence—I know he does," she still further declared. "Oh, I know he doesn't let him say much yet, but he hasn't jumped up to go into the house once since those first two or three times, an' that's somethin'. An' what's more, he let Keith stay a whole minute at the gate talkin' yesterday!" she finished in triumph.

"Yes, an' the best of it is," chimed in Susan, "it's helpin' Keith Burton hisself jest as much as 'tis John McGuire. Why, he ain't the same boy since he's took to tryin' to get your John to talkin'. An' he asks me a dozen times a mornin' if John's out on the porch yet. An' when he IS out there, he don't lose no time in goin' out hisself."

Yet it was the very next morning that Keith, after eagerly asking if John McGuire were on the back porch, did not go out. Instead he settled back in his chair and picked up one of his embossed books.

Susan frowned in amazed wonder, and opened her lips as if to speak. But after a glance at Keith's apparently absorbed face, she turned and went back to her work in the kitchen. Twice during the next ten minutes, however, she invented an excuse to pass again through the living-room, where Keith sat. Yet, though she said a pointed something each time about John McGuire on the back porch, Keith did not respond save with an indifferent word or two. And, greatly to her indignation, he was still sitting in his chair with his book when at noon John McGuire, on the porch across the back yard, rose from his seat and went into the house.

Susan was still more indignant when, the next morning, the same programme was repeated—except for the fact that Susan's reminders of John McGuire's presence on the back porch were even more pointed than they had been on the day before. Again the third morning it was the same. Susan resolved then to speak. She said to herself that "patience had ceased to be virtuous," and she lay awake half that night rehearsing a series of arguments and pleadings which she meant to present the next morning. She was the more incited to this owing to Mrs. McGuire's distracted reproaches the evening before.

"Why, John has asked for him, actually ASKED for him," Mrs. McGuire had wept. "An' it is cruel, the cruelest thing I ever saw, to get that poor boy all worked up to the point of really WANTIN' to talk with him, an' then stay away three whole days like this!"

On the fourth morning, therefore, when John McGuire appeared on the back porch, Susan went into the Burton living-room with the avowed determination of getting Keith out of the house and into the back yard, or of telling him exactly what she thought of him.

She had all of her elaborate scheming for nothing, however, for at her first terse announcement that John McGuire was on the back porch, Keith sprang to his feet with a cheery:

"So? Well, I guess I'll go out myself."

And Susan was left staring at him with open eyes and mouth—yet not too dazed to run to the open window and watch what happened.

And this is what Susan saw—and heard. Keith, with his almost uncannily skillful stick to guide him, sauntered down the path and called a cheery greeting to John McGuire—a John McGuire who, in his eagerness to respond, leaned away forward in his chair with a sudden flame of color in his face.

Keith still sauntered toward the dividing fence, pausing only to feel with his fingers and pick the one belated rose from the bush at the gate. He pushed the gate open then, still talking cheerfully, and the next moment Susan was holding her breath, for Keith had gone straight up the walk and up the steps, and had dropped himself into the vacant chair beside John McGuire—and John McGuire, after a faint start as if to rise, had fallen back in his seat, and had turned his face uncertainly, fearfully, yet with infinite longing, toward the blind youth at his side.

Susan looked then at Mrs. McGuire. Mrs. McGuire, too, was plainly holding her breath suspended. On her face, too, were uncertainty, fearfulness, and infinite longing. For a moment she watched the two boys intently. Then she rose and with cautious steps made her way into the house. After supper that night she came over and told Susan all about it. Her face was beaming.

"Did you see them?" she began breathlessly. "Wasn't it

wonderful? A whole half-hour those two blessed boys sat there an' talked; an' John laughed twice, actually laughed."

"Yes, I know," nodded Susan, her own face no less beaming.

"An' to think how just last night I was scoldin' an' blamin' Keith because he didn't come over these last three days. An' I never saw at all what he was up to."

"Up to?" frowned Susan.

"Yes, yes! Don't you see? He did it on purpose—stayed away three whole days, so John would miss him an' WANT him. An' John DID miss him. Why, he listened for him all the time. I could just SEE he was listenin'. An' that's what made me so angry, because Keith didn't come. The idea!— My boy wantin' somebody, an' that somebody not there!

"But I know now. I understand. An' I love him for it. He did it to make him want him. An' it worked. Why, if he'd come before, every day, just as usual, John wouldn't have talked with him. I know he wouldn't. But now—oh, Susan, it was wonderful, wonderful! I watched 'em from the window. I HAD to watch. I was afraid—still. An' of course I heard some things. An', oh, Susan, it was wonderful, the way that boy understood."

"You mean—Keith?"

"Yes. You see, first John began to talk just as he talks to us—ravin' because he's so strong an' well, an' likely to live to be a hundred; an' of how he'll look, one of these days, with his little tin cup held out for pennies an' his sign, 'Please Help the Blind,' an' of what he's got to look forward to all his life. Oh, Susan, it—it's enough to break the heart of a stone, when he talks like that."

Eleanor H. Porter

Susan drew in her breath.

"Don't you s'pose I know? Well, I guess I do! But what did Keith say to him?"

"Nothin'. An' that was the first wonderful thing. You see, we—we always talk an' try to comfort him when he talks like that. But Keith didn't. He just let him talk, with nothin' but just a sympathetic word now an' then. But it wasn't long before I noticed a wonderful thing was happenin'. Keith was beginnin' to talk—not about that awful tin cup an' the pennies an' the sign, but about other things; first about the rose in his hand. An' pretty quick John was talkin' about it, too. He had the rose an' was smellin' of it. Then Keith had a new knife, an' he passed that over, an' pretty quick I saw that John had that little link puzzle of Keith's, an' was havin' a great time tryin' to straighten it out. That's the first time I heard him laugh.

"I began to realize then what Keith was doin'. He was fillin' John's mind full of somethin' else beside himself, for just a minute, an' was showin' him that there were things he could call by name, like the rose an' the knife an' the puzzle, even if he couldn't SEE 'em. Oh, Keith didn't SAY anything like that to him—trust him for that. But before John knew it, he was DOIN' it—callin' things by name, I mean.

"An' Keith is comin' again to-morrow. John TOLD me so. An' if you could have seen his face when he said it! Oh, Susan, isn't it wonderful?" she finished fervently, as she turned to go.

"It is, indeed—wonderful," murmured Susan. But Susan's eyes were out the window on Keith's face—Keith and his father were coming up the walk talking; and on Keith's face was a light Susan had never seen there before.

CHAPTER XXVI

MAZIE AGAIN

It came to be the accepted thing almost at once, then, that Keith Burton and John McGuire should spend their mornings together on the McGuires' back porch. In less than a fortnight young McGuire even crossed the yard arm in arm with Keith to the Burtons' back porch and sat there one morning. After that it was only a question as to which porch it should be. That it would be one of them was a foregone conclusion.

Sometimes the two boys talked together. Sometimes they worked on one of Keith's raised picture puzzles. Sometimes Keith read aloud from one of his books. Whatever they did, their doing it was the source of great interest to the entire neighborhood. Not only did Mrs. McGuire and Susan breathlessly watch from their respective kitchens, but friends and neighbors fabricated excuses to come to the two houses in order to see for themselves; and children gathered along the divisional fence and gazed with round eyes of wonder. But they gazed silently. Everybody gazed silently. Even the children seemed to understand that the one unpardonable sin was to let the blind boys on the porch know that they were the objects of any sort of interest.

One day Mazie Sanborn came. She brought a new book for

Eleanor H. Porter

Mrs. McGuire to read—an attention she certainly had never before bestowed on John McGuire's mother. She talked one half-minute about the book—and five minutes about the beautiful new friendship between the two blind young men. She insisted on going into the kitchen where she could see the two boys on the porch. Then, before Mrs. McGuire could divine her purpose and stop her, she had slipped through the door and out on to the porch itself.

"How do you do, gentlemen," she began blithely. "I just—"

But the terrified Mrs. McGuire had her by the arm and was pulling her back into the kitchen before she could finish her sentence.

On the porch the two boys had leaped to their feet, John McGuire, in particular, looking distressed and angry.

"Who was that? Is anybody—there?" he demanded.

"No, dear, not now." In the doorway Mrs. McGuire was trying to nod assurance to the boys and frown banishment to Mazie Sanborn at one and the same moment.

"But there was—some one," insisted her son sharply.

"Just some one that brought a book to me, dearie, an' she's gone now." Frantically Mrs. McGuire was motioning Mazie to make her assertion the truth.

John McGuire sat down then. So, too, did Keith. But all the rest of the morning John was nervously alert for all sounds. And his ears were frequently turned toward the kitchen door. He began to talk again, too, bitterly, of the little tin cup for the pennies and the sign "Pity the Poor Blind." He lost all interest in Keith's books and puzzles, and when he was not railing at the tragedy of his fate, he was sitting in gloomy silence.

Keith told Susan that afternoon that if Mrs. McGuire did not keep people away from that porch when he was out there with John, he would not answer for the consequences. Susan told Mrs. McGuire, and Mrs. McGuire told Mazie Sanborn, at the same time returning the loaned book—all of which did not tend to smooth Miss Mazie's already ruffled feelings.

To Dorothy Mazie expressed her mind on the matter.

"I don't care! I'll never go there again—never!" she declared angrily; "nor speak to Mrs. McGuire, nor that precious son of hers, nor Keith Burton, either. So there!"

"Oh, Mazie, but poor Keith isn't to blame," remonstrated Dorothy earnestly, the color flaming into her face.

"He is, too. He's just as bad as John McGuire. He jumped up and looked just as cross as John McGuire did when I went out on to that porch. And he doesn't ever really want to see us. You know he doesn't. He just stands us because he thinks he's got to be polite."

"But, Mazie, dear, he's so sensitive, and he feels his affliction keenly, and—"

"Oh, yes, that's right—stand up for him! I knew you would," snapped Mazie crossly. "And everybody knows it, too—running after him the way you do."

"RUNNING AFTER HIM!" Dorothy's face was scarlet now.

"Yes, running after him," reiterated the other incisively; "and you always have—trotting over there all the time with books

Eleanor H. Porter

and puzzles and candy and flowers. And—"

"For shame, Mazie!" interrupted Dorothy, with hot indignation. "As if trying to help that poor blind boy to while away a few hours of his time were RUNNING AFTER HIM."

"But he doesn't WANT you to while away an hour or two of his time. And I should think you'd see he didn't. You could if you weren't so dead in love with him, and—"

"Mazie!" gasped Dorothy, aghast.

"Well, it's so. Anybody can see that—the way you color up every time his name is mentioned, and the way you look at him, with your heart in your eyes, and—"

"Mazie Sanborn!" gasped Dorothy again. Her face was not scarlet now. It had gone dead white. She was on her feet, horrified, dismayed, and very angry.

"Well, I don't care. It's so. Everybody knows it. And when a fellow shows so plainly that he'd rather be let alone, how you can keep thrusting yourself—"

But Dorothy had gone. With a proud lifting of her head, and a sharp "Nonsense, Mazie, you are wild! We'll not discuss it any longer, please," she had turned and left the room.

But she remembered. She must have remembered, for she did not go near the Burton homestead for a week. Neither did the next week nor the next see her there. Furthermore, though the little stand in her room had shown two new picture puzzles and a new game especially designed for the blind, it displayed them no longer after those remarks of Mazie Sanborn's. Not that Keith had them, however. Indeed, no. They were buried deep under a pile of clothing in the farther corner of Dorothy's bottom bureau drawer.

At the Burton homestead Susan wondered a little at her absence. She even said to Keith one day:

"Why, where's Dorothy? We haven't see her for two weeks."

"I don't know, I'm sure."

The way Keith's lips came together over the last word caused Susan to throw a keen glance into his face.

"Now, Keith, I hope you two haven't been quarreling again," she frowned anxiously.

"'Again'! Nonsense, Susan, we never did quarrel. Don't be silly." The youth shifted his position uneasily.

"I'm thinkin' tain't always me that's silly," observed Susan, with another keen glance. "That girl was gettin' so she come over jest natural-like again, every little while, bringin' in one thing or another, if 'twas nothin' more'n a funny story to make us laugh. An' what I want to know is why she stopped right off short like this, for—"

"Nonsense!" tossed Keith again, with a lift of his chin. Then, with an attempt at lightness that was very near a failure, he laughed: "I reckon we don't want her to come if she doesn't want to, do we, Susan?"

"Humph!" was Susan's only comment—outwardly. Inwardly she was vowing to see that young woman and have it out with her, once for all.

But Susan did not see her nor have it out with her; for, as it happened, something occurred that night so all-absorbing and exciting that even the unexplained absence of Dorothy Parkman became as nothing beside it.

With the abrupt suddenness that sometimes makes the long-waited-for event a real shock, came the news of the death of the poor old woman whose frail hand had held the wealth that Susan had coveted for Daniel Burton and his son.

The two men left the next morning on the four-hundred-mile journey that would take them to the town where Nancy Holworthy had lived.

Scarcely had they left the house before Susan began preparations for their home-coming, as befitted their new estate. Her first move was to get out all the best silver and china. She was busy cleaning it when Mrs. McGuire came in at the kitchen door.

"What's the matter?" she began breathlessly.

"Where's Keith? John's been askin' for him all the mornin'. Is Mr. Burton sick? They just telephoned from the store that Mr. Burton had sent word that he wouldn't be down for a few days. He isn't sick, is he?—or Keith? I couldn't make out quite all they said; but there was somethin' about Keith. They ain't either of 'em sick, are they?"

"Oh, no, they're both well—very well, thank you." There was an air, half elation, half superiority, about Susan that was vaguely irritating to Mrs. McGuire.

"Well, you needn't be so secret about it, Susan," she began a little haughtily. But Susan tossed her head with a light laugh.

"Secret! I guess 't won't be no secret long. Mr. Daniel Burton an' Master Keith have gone away, Mis' McGuire."

"Away! You mean—a—a vacation?" frowned Mrs. McGuire doubtfully.

Susan laughed again, still with that irritating air of superiority.

"Well, hardly. This ain't no pleasure exertion, Mis' McGuire. Still, on the other hand, Daniel Burton wouldn't be half humane if he didn't get some pleasure out of it, though he wouldn't so demean himself as to show it, of course. Mis' Nancy Holworthy is dead, Mis' McGuire. We had the signification last night."

"Not—you don't mean THE Nancy Holworthy—the one that's got the money!" The excited interest in Mrs. McGuire's face and voice was as great as even Susan herself could have desired.

Susan obviously swelled with the glory of the occasion, though she still spoke with cold loftiness.

"The one and the same, Mis' McGuire."

"My stars an' stockin's, you don't say! An' they've gone to the funeral?"

"They have."

"An' they'll get the money now, I s'pose."

"They will."

"But are you sure? You know sometimes when folks expect the money they don't get it. It's been willed away to some one else."

"Yes, I know. But't won't be here," spoke Susan with decision. "Mis' Holworthy couldn't if she'd wanted to. It's all foreordained an' fixed beforehand. Daniel Burton was to get jest the annual while she lived, an' then the whole in a plump sum when she died. Well, she's dead, an' now he gets it. An' a right tidy little sum it is, too."

"Was she awful rich, Susan?"

"More'n a hundred thousand. A hundred an' fifty, I've heard say."

"My gracious me! An' to think of Daniel Burton havin' a hundred and fifty thousand dollars! What in the world will he do with it?"

Susan's chin came up superbly.

"Well, I can tell you one thing he'll do, Mis' McGuire. He'll stop peddlin' peas an' beans over that counter down there, an' retire to a life of ease an' laxity with his paint-brushes, as he ought to. An' he'll have somethin' fit to eat an' wear, an' Keith will, too. An' furthermore an' likewise you'll see SOME difference in this place, or my name ain't Susan Betts. Them two men have got an awful lot to live up to, an' I mean they shall understand it right away."

"Which explains this array of china an' silver, I take it," observed Mrs. McGuire dryly.

"Eh? What?" frowned Susan doubtfully; then her face cleared. "Yes, that's jest it. They've got to have things now fitted up to their new estation. We shall get more, too. We need some new teaspoons an' forks. An' I want 'em to get some of them bunion spoons."

"BUNION spoons!"

"Yes—when you eat soup out of them two-handled cups, you know. Or maybe you don't know," she corrected herself, at the odd expression that had come to Mrs. McGuire's face. "But I do. Mrs. Professor Hinkley used to have 'em. They're awful pretty an' stylish, too. And we've got to have a lot of other things—new china, an' some cut-glass, an'—"

"Well, it strikes me," interrupted Mrs. McGuire severely, "that Daniel Burton had better be puttin' his money into Liberty Bonds an' Red Cross work, instead of silver spoons an' cut-glass, in these war-times. An'—"

"My lan', Mis' McGuire!" With the sudden exclamation Susan had dropped the spoon she was polishing. Her eyes, wild and incredulous, were staring straight into the startled eyes of the woman opposite. "Do you know? Since that yeller telegram came last night tellin' us Nancy Holworthy was dead, I hain't even once thought of—the war."

"Well, I guess you would think of it—if you had my John right before you all the time." With a bitter sigh Mrs. McGuire had relaxed in her chair. "You wouldn't need anything else."

"Humph! I don't need anything else with Daniel Burton 'round."

"What do you mean?"

"Why, I mean that that man don't do nothin' but read war an' talk war every minute he's in the house. An' what with them wheatless days an' meatless days, he fairly EATS war. You heard my poem on them meatless, wheatless days, didn't you?"

Mrs. McGuire shook her head listlessly. Her somber eyes were on the lonely figure of her son on the porch across the two back yards.

"You didn't? Well, I'll say it to you, then. 'Tain't much; still, it's kind of good, in a way. I hain't written hardly anything lately; but I did write this:

We've a wheatless day,
An' a meatless day,
An' a tasteless, wasteless,
      sweetless day.

But with never a pause,
For the good of the cause,
We'd even consent to an
      eatless day.

"An' we would, too, of course."

"An' as far as that's concerned, there's a good many other kinds of 'less days that I'm thinkin' wouldn't hurt none of us. How about a fretless day an' a worryless day? Wouldn't they be great? An' only think what a talkless day'd mean in some households I could mention. Oh, of course, present comp'ny always accentuated," she hastened to add with a sly chuckle, as Mrs. McGuire stirred into sudden resentment."

"Humph!" subsided Mrs. McGuire, still a little resentfully.

"An' I'm free to confess that there's some kinds of 'less days that we've already got plenty of," went on Susan, after a moment's thoughtful pause. "There is folks that take quite enough workless days, an' laughless days, an' pityless days, an' thankless days. My lan', there ain't no end to them kind, as any one can see. An' there was them heatless days last winter—I guess no one was hankerin' for more of THEM. Oh, 'course I understand that that was just preservation of coal, an' that 'twas necessary, an' all that. An' that's another thing, too—this preservation business. I'd like to add a few things to that, an' make 'em preserve in fault-findin', an' crossness, an' backbitin', an' gossip, as well as in coal, an' sugar, an' wheat, an' beef."

Mrs. McGuire gave a short laugh.

"My goodness, Susan Betts, if you ain't the limit, an' no mistake! I s'pose you mean CONservation."

"Heh? What's that? Well, CONservation, then. What's the difference, anyway?" she scoffed a bit testily. Then, abruptly, her face changed. "But, there! this ain't settlin' what I'm going to do with Daniel Burton," she finished with a profound sigh.

"Do with him?" puzzled Mrs. McGuire.

"Yes." Susan picked up the silver spoon and began indifferently to polish it. "'Tain't no use for me to be doin' all this. Daniel Burton won't know whether he's eatin' with a silver spoon or one made of pewter. No more will he retire to a life of ease an' laxity with his paint-brushes—unless they declarate peace to-morrow mornin'."

"You don't mean—he'll stay in the store?"

Susan made a despairing gesture.

"Goodness only knows what he'll do—I don't. I know what

he does now. He's as uneasy as a fish out o' water, an' he roams the house from one end to the other every night, after he reads the paper. He's got one of them war maps on his wall, an' he keeps changin' the pins an' flags, an' I hear him mutterin' under his breath. You see, he has to keep it from Keith all he can, for Keith hisself feels so bad 'cause he can't be up an' doin'; an' if he thought he was keepin' his father back from helpin', I don't know what the poor boy would do. But I think if 'twa'n't for Keith, Daniel Burton would try to enlist an' go over. Oh, of course, he's beyond the malicious age, so far as bein' drafted is concerned, an' you wouldn't naturally think such a mild-tempered-lookin' man would go in much for killin'. But this war's stirred him up somethin' awful."

"Well, who wouldn't it?"

"Oh, I know that; an' I ain't sayin' as how it shouldn't. But that don't make it no easier for Daniel Burton to keep his feelin's hid from his son, particularly when it's that son that's made him have the feelin's, partly. There ain't no doubt but that one of the things that's made Daniel Burton so fidgety an' uneasy, an' ready to jest fling hisself into that ravin' conflict over there is his unhappiness an' disappointment over Keith. He had such big plans for that boy!"

"Yes, I know. We all have big plans for—our boys." Mrs. McGuire choked and turned away.

"An' girls, too, for that matter," hurried on Susan, with a quick glance into the other's face. "An' speakin' of girls, did you see Hattie Turner on the street last night?"

Dumbly Mrs. McGuire answered with a shake of her head. Her eyes had gone back to her son's face across the yard.

"Well, I did. Her Charlie's at Camp Devens, you know. They say he's invited to more places every Sunday than he can possibly accept; an' that he's petted an' praised an' made of everywhere he goes, an' tended right up to so's he won't get lonesome, or attend unquestionable entertainments. Well, that's all right an' good, of course, an' as it should be. But I wish somebody'd take up Charlie Turner's wife an' invite her to Sunday dinners an' take her to ride, an' see that she didn't attend unquestionable entertainments."

"Why, Susan Betts, what an idea!" protested Mrs. McGuire, suddenly sitting erect in her chair. "Hattie Turner isn't fightin' for her country."

"No, but her husband is," retorted Susan crisply. "An' she's fightin' for her honor an' her future peace an' happiness, an' she's doin' it all alone. She's pretty as a picture, an' nothin' but a child when he married her four months ago, an' we've took away her natural pervider an' entertainer, an' left her nothin' but her freedom for a ballast wheel. An' I say I wish some of the patriotic people who are jest showerin' every Charlie Turner with attentions would please sprinkle jest a few on Charlie's wife, to help keep her straight an' sweet an' honest for Charlie when he comes back."

"Hm-m, maybe," murmured Mrs. McGuire, rising wearily to her feet; "but there ain't many that thinks of that."

"There'll be more think of it by an' by—when it's too late," observed Susan succinctly, as she, too, rose from her chair.

CHAPTER XXVII

FOR THE SAKE OF JOHN

In due course Daniel Burton and his son Keith returned from the funeral of their kinswoman, Mrs. Nancy Holworthy.

The town, aware now of the stupendous change that had come to the fortunes of the Burton family, stared, gossiped, shook wise heads of prophecy, then passed on to the next sensation—which happened to be the return of four soldiers from across the seas; three crippled, one blinded.

At the Burton homestead the changes did not seem so stupendous, after all. True, Daniel Burton had abandoned the peddling of peas and beans across the counter, and had, at the earnest solicitation of his son, got out his easel and placed a fresh canvas upon it; but he obviously worked half-heartedly, and he still roamed the house after reading the evening paper, and spent even more time before the great war map on his studio wall.

True, also, disgruntled tradesmen no longer rang peremptory peals on the doorbell, and the postman's load of bills on the first of the month was perceptibly decreased. The dinner-table, too, bore evidence that a scanty purse no longer controlled the larder, but no new china or cut-glass graced the board, and Susan's longed-for bouillon spoons had never materialized. Locks and doors and sagging blinds had received prompt attention, and already the house was being prepared for a new coat of paint; but no startling alterations or improvements were promised by the evidence, and Keith was still to be seen almost daily on the McGuire back porch, as before, or on his own, with John McGuire.

It is no wonder, surely, that very soon the town ceased to stare and gossip, or even to shake wise heads of prophecy.

Nancy Holworthy's death was two months in the past when one day Keith came home from John McGuire's back porch in very evident excitement and agitation.

"Why, Keith, what's the matter? What IS the matter?" demanded Susan concernedly.

"Nothing. That is, I—I did not know I acted as if anything was the matter," stammered the youth.

"Well, you do. Now, tell me, what is it?"

"Nothing, nothing, Susan. Nothing you can help." Keith was pacing back and forth and up and down the living-room, not even using his cane to define the familiar limits of his pathway. Suddenly he turned and stopped short, his whole body quivering with emotion. "Susan, I can't! I can't—stand it," he moaned.

"I know, Keith. But, what is it—now?"

"John McGuire. He's been telling me how it is—over there. Why, Susan, I could see it—SEE it, I tell you, and, oh, I did so want to be there to help. He told me how they held it—the little clump of trees that meant so much to US, and how one

Eleanor H. Porter

by one they fell—those brave fellows with him. I could see it. I could hear it. I could hear the horrid din of the guns and shells, and the crash of falling trees about us; and the shouts and groans of the men at our side. And they needed men—more men—to take the place of those that had fallen. Even one man counted there—counted for, oh, so much!—for at the last there was just one man left—John McGuire. And to hear him tell it—it was wonderful, wonderful!"

"I know, I know," nodded Susan. "It was like his letters—you could SEE things. He MADE you see 'em. An' that's what he always did—made you see things—even when he was a little boy. His mother told me. He wanted to write, you know. He was goin' to be a writer, before—this happened. An' now—" The sentence trailed off into the silence unfinished.

"And to think of all that to-day being wasted on a blind baby tied to a picture puzzle," moaned Keith, resuming his nervous pacing of the room. "If only a man—a real man could have heard him—one that could go and do a man's work—! Why, Susan, that story, as he told it, would make a stone fight. I never heard anything like it. I never supposed there could be anything like that battle. He never talked like this, until to-day. Oh, he's told me a little, from time to time. But to-day, to-day, he just poured out his heart to me—ME!—and there are so many who need just that message to stir them from their smug complacency—men who could fight, and win: men who WOULD fight, and win, if only they could see and hear and know, as I saw and heard and knew this afternoon. And there it was, wasted, WASTED, worse than wasted on—me!"

Chokingly Keith turned away, but with a sudden cry Susan caught his arm.

"No, no, Keith, it wasn't wasted—you mustn't let it be wasted," she panted. "Listen! You want others to hear it—what you heard—don't you?"

"Why, y-yes, Susan; but—"

"Then make 'em hear it," she interrupted. "You can—you can!"

"How?"

"Make him write it down, jest as he talks. He can—he wants to. He's always wanted to. Then publish it in a book, so everybody can see it and hear it, as you did."

"Oh, Susan, if we only could!" A dawning hope had come into Keith Burton's face, but almost at once it faded into gray disappointment. "We couldn't do it, though, Susan. He couldn't do it. You know he can't write at all. He's only begun to practice a little bit. He'd never get it down, with the fire and the vim in it, learning to write as he'd have to. What do you suppose Lincoln's Gettysburg Speech would have been if he'd had to stop to learn how to spell and to write each word before he could put it down?"

"I know, I know," nodded Susan. "It's that way with me in my poetry. I jest HAVE to get right ahead while the fuse burns, an' spell 'em somehow, anyhow, so's to get 'em down while I'm in the fit of it. He couldn't do it. I can see that now. But, Keith, couldn't YOU do it?—take it down, I mean, as he talked, like a stylographer?"

Keith shook his head.

"I wish I could. But I couldn't, I know I couldn't. I couldn't begin to do it fast enough to keep up with him, and 't would

Eleanor H. Porter

spoil it all to have to ask him to slow down. When a man's got a couple of Huns coming straight for him, and he knows he's got to get 'em both at once, you can't very well sing out: 'Here, wait—wait a minute till I get that last sentence down!'"

"I know, I know," nodded Susan again. She paused, drew a long sigh, and turned her eyes out the window. Up the walk was coming Daniel Burton. His step was slow, his head was bowed. He looked like anything but the happy possessor of new wealth. Susan frowned as she watched him.

"I wish your father—" she began. Suddenly she stopped. A new light had leaped to her eyes. "Keith, Keith," she cried eagerly. "I have it! Your father—he could do it—I know he could!"

"Do what?"

"Take down John McGuire's story. Couldn't he do it?"

"Why, y-yes, he could, I think," hesitated Keith doubtfully. "He doesn't know shorthand, but he—he's got eyes" (Keith's voice broke a little) "and he could SEE what he was doing, and he could take down enough of it so he could patch it up afterwards, I'm sure. But Susan, John McGuire wouldn't TELL it to HIM. Don't you see? He won't even see anybody but me, and he didn't talk like this even to me until to-day. How's dad going to hear it to write it down? Tell me that?"

"But he could overhear it, Keith. No, no, don't look like that," she protested hurriedly, as Keith began to frown. "Jest listen a minute. It would be jest as easy. He could be over on the grass right close, where he could hear every word; an' you could get John to talkin', an' as soon as he got really started on a story your father could begin to write, an' John wouldn't know a thing about it; an'—"

"Yes, you're quite right—John wouldn't know a thing about it," broke in Keith, with a passion so sudden and bitter that Susan fell back in dismay.

"Why, Keith!" she exclaimed, her startled eyes on his quivering face.

"I wonder if you think I'd do it!" he demanded. "I wonder if you really think I'd cheat that poor fellow into talking to me just because he hadn't eyes to see that I wasn't the only one in his audience!"

"But, Keith, he wouldn't mind; he wouldn't mind a bit," urged Susan, "if he didn't know an'—"

"Oh, no, he wouldn't mind being cheated and deceived and made a fool of, just because he couldn't see!"

"No, he wouldn't mind," persisted Susan stoutly. "It wouldn't be a mean listenin', nor sneak listenin'. It wouldn't be listenin' to things he didn't want us to hear. He'd be glad, after it was all done, an'—"

"Would he!" choked Keith, still more bitterly. "Maybe you think *I* was glad after it was all done, and I found I'd been fooled and cheated into thinking the girl that was reading and talking to me and playing games with me was a girl I had never known before—a girl who was what she pretended to be, a new friend doing it all because she wanted to, because she liked to."

"But, Keith, I'm sure that Dorothy liked—"

"There, there, Susan," interposed Keith, with quickly uplifted hand. "We'll not discuss it, please, Yes, I know, I began the subject myself, and it was my fault; but when I heard you say John McGuire would be glad when he found out how we'd lied to his poor blind eyes, I—I just couldn't hold it in. I had to say something. But never mind that now, Susan; only you'll—you'll have to understand I mean what I say. There's no letting dad copy that story on the sly."

"But there's a way, there must be a way," argued Susan feverishly. "Only think what it would mean to that boy if we could get him started to writin' books—what he's wanted to do all his life. Oh, Keith, why, he'd even forget his eyes then."

"It would—help some." Keith drew in his breath and held it a moment suspended. "And he'd even be helping us to win out—over there; for if we could get that story of his on paper as he told it to me, the fellow that reads it wouldn't need any recruiting station to send him over there. If there was only a way that father could—"

"There is, an' we'll find it," interposed Susan eagerly. "I know we will. An' Keith, it's goin' to be 'most as good for him as it is for John McGuire. He's nervous as a witch since he quit his job."

"I know." A swift cloud crossed the boy's face. "But 'twasn't giving up his job that's made him nervous, Susan, as you and I both know very well. However, we'll see. And you may be sure if there is a way I'll find it, Susan," he finished a bit wearily, as he turned to go upstairs.

CHAPTER XXVIII

THE WAY

Keith was still looking for "the way," when October came, bringing crisp days and chilly winds. When not too cold, the boys still sat out of doors. When it was too cold, John McGuire did not appear at all on his back porch, and Keith did not have the courage to make a bold advance to the McGuire door and ask admittance. There came a day, however, when a cold east wind came up after they were well established in their porch chairs for the morning. They were on the Burton porch this time, and Keith suddenly determined to take the bull by the horns.

"Brrr! but it's cold this morning," he shivered blithely. "What say you? Let's go in. Come on." And without waiting for acquiescence, he caught John McGuire's arm in his own and half pulled him to his feet. Before John McGuire knew then quite what was happening, he found himself in the house.

"No, no!—that is, I—I think I'd better be going home," he stammered.

But Keith Burton did not seem even to hear.

"Say, just try your hand at this puzzle," he was saying gayly.

Eleanor H. Porter

"I gave it up, and I'll bet you'll have to," he finished, thrusting a pasteboard box into his visitor's hands and nicely adjudging the distance a small table must be pushed in order to bring it conveniently in front of John McGuire's chair.

The quick tightening of John McGuire's lips and the proud lifting of his chin told that Keith's challenge had been accepted even before the laconic answer came.

"Oh, you do, do you? Well, we'll see whether I'll have to give it up or not."

John McGuire loved picture puzzles, as Keith Burton well knew.

It was easy after that. Keith took it so unhesitatingly for granted that they were to go indoors when it was cold that John McGuire found it difficult to object; and it was not long before the two boys were going back and forth between the two houses with almost as much ease as if their feet had been guided by the eye instead of by the tap of a slender stick.

John McGuire was learning a great deal from Keith these days, though it is doubtful if he realized it. It is doubtful, also, if he realized how constantly he was being made to talk of the war and of his experience in it. But Keith realized it. Keith was not looking for "the way" now. He believed he had found it; and there came a day when he deemed the time had come to try to carry it out.

They were in his own home living-room. It had been a wonderful story that John McGuire had told that day of a daring excursion into No Man's Land, and what came of it. Upstairs in the studio Daniel Burton was sitting alone, as Keith knew. Keith drew a long breath and made the plunge. Springing to his feet he turned toward the door that led into the hall.

"McGuire, that was a bully story—a corking good story. I want dad to hear it. Wait, I'll get him." And he was out of the room with the door fast closed behind him before John McGuire could so much as draw a breath.

Upstairs, Daniel Burton, already in the secret, heard Keith's eager summons and came at once. For some days he had been expecting just such an urgent call from Keith's lips. He knew too much to delay. He was down the stairs and at Keith's side in an incredibly short time. Then together they pushed open the door and entered the living-room.

John McGuire was on his feet. Very plainly he was intending to go home, and at once. But Daniel Burton paid no attention to that. He came straight toward him and took his hand.

"I call this mighty good of you, McGuire," he said. "My boy here has been raving about your stories of the war until I'm fairly green with envy. Now I'm to hear a bit of them myself, he says. I wish you would tell me some of your experiences, my lad. You know a chance like this is a real god-send to us poor stay-at-homes. Now fire away! I'm ready."

But John McGuire was not ready. True, he sat down—but not until after a confused "No, no, I must go home—that is, really, they're not worth repeating—those stories." And he would not talk at all—at first.

Daniel Burton talked, however. He talked of wars in general and of the Civil War in particular; and he told the stories of Antietam and Gettysburg as they had been told to him by his father. Then from Gettysburg he jumped to Flanders, and talked of aeroplanes, and gas-masks, and tanks, and trenches, and dugouts.

Little by little then John McGuire began to talk—sometimes a whole sentence, sometimes only a word or two. But there was no fire, no enthusiasm, no impetuous rush of words that brought the very din of battle to their ears. And not once did Daniel Burton thrust his fingers into his pocket for his pencil and notebook. Yet, when it was all over, and John McGuire had gone home, Keith dropped into his chair with a happy sigh.

"It wasn't much, dad, I know," he admitted, "but it was something. It was a beginning, and a beginning is something—with John McGuire."

And it was something; for the next time Daniel Burton entered the room, John McGuire did not even start from his chair. He gave a faint smile of welcome, too, and he talked sooner, and talked more—though there was little of war talk; and for the second time Daniel Burton did not reach for his pencil.

But the third time he did. A question, a comment, a chance word—neither Keith nor his father could have told afterward what started it. They knew only that a sudden light as of a flame leaped into John McGuire's face—and he was back in the trenches of France and carrying them with him.

At the second sentence Daniel Burton's fingers were in his pocket, and at the third his pencil was racing over the paper at breakneck speed. There was no pause then, no time for thought, no time for careful forming of words and letters. There was only the breakneck race between a bit of lead and an impassioned tongue; and when it was all over, there were only a well-nigh hopeless-looking mass of hieroglyphics in Daniel Burton's notebook—and the sweat of spent excitement on the brows of two youths and a man.

"Gee! we got it that time!" breathed Keith, after John McGuire had gone home.

"Yes; only I was wondering if I had really—got it," murmured Daniel Burton, eyeing a bit ruefully the confused mass of words and letters in his notebook. "Still, I reckon I can dig it out all right—if I do it right away," he finished confidently. And he did dig it out before he slept that night.

If Daniel Burton and his son Keith thought the thing was done, and it was going to be easy sailing thereafter, they found themselves greatly mistaken. John McGuire scarcely said five sentences about the war the next time they were together, though Daniel Burton had his pencil poised expectantly from the start. He said only a little more the next time, and the next; and Daniel Burton pocketed his pencil in despair. Then came a day when a chance word about a new air raid reported in the morning paper acted like a match to gunpowder, and sent John McGuire off into a rapid-fire story that whipped Daniel Burton's pencil from his pocket and set it to racing again at breakneck speed to keep up with him.

It was easier after that. Still, every day it was like a game of hide-and-seek, with Daniel Burton and his pencil ever in pursuit, and with now and then a casual comment or a tactful question to lure the hiding story out into the open. Little by little, as the frank comradeship of Daniel Burton won its way, John McGuire was led to talk more and more freely; and by Christmas the eager scribe was in possession of a very complete record of John McGuire's war experiences, dating even from the early days of his enlistment.

Day by day, as he had taken down the rough notes, Daniel Burton had followed it up with a careful untangling and copying before he had had a chance to forget, or to lose the wonderful glow born of the impassioned telling. Then, from time to time he had sorted the notes and arranged them in proper sequence, until now he had a complete story, logical and well-rounded.

It was on Christmas Day that he read the manuscript to Keith. At its conclusion Keith drew a long, tremulous breath.

"Dad, it's wonderful!" he exclaimed. "How did you do it?"

"You know. You heard yourself."

"Yes; but to copy it like that—! Why, I could hear him tell it as you read it, dad. I could HEAR him."

"Could you, really? I'm glad. That makes me know I've succeeded. Now for a publisher!"

"You wouldn't publish it without his—knowing?"

"Certainly not. But I'm going to let a publisher see it, before he knows."

"Y-yes, perhaps."

"Why, Keith, I'd have to do that. Do you suppose I'd run the risk of its being turned down, and then have to tell that boy that he couldn't have the book, after all?"

"No, no, I suppose not. But—it isn't going to be turned down, dad. Such a wonderful thing can't be turned down."

"Hm-m; perhaps not." Daniel Burton's lips came together a bit grimly. "But—there ARE wonderful things that won't sell, you know. However," he finished with brisk cheerfulness, "this isn't one of my pictures, nor a bit of Susan's free verse; so there's some hope, I guess. Anyhow, we'll see—but we won't tell John until we do see."

"All right. I suppose that would be best," sighed Keith, still a little doubtfully.

They had not long to wait, after all. In a remarkably short time came back word from the publishers. Most emphatically they wanted the book, and they wanted it right away. Moreover, the royalty they offered was so good that it sent Daniel Burton down the stairs two steps at a time like a boy, in his eagerness to reach Keith with the good news.

"And now for John!" he cried excitedly, as soon as Keith's joyous exclamations over the news were uttered. "Come, let's go across now."

"But, dad, how—how are you going to tell him?" Keith was holding back a little.

"Tell him! I'm just going to tell him," laughed the man. "That's easy."

"I know; but—but—" Keith wet his lips and started again. "You see, dad, he didn't know we were taking notes of his stories. He couldn't see us. We—we took advantage of—"

But Daniel Burton would not even listen.

"Shucks and nonsense, Keith!" he cried. Then a little grimly he added: "I only wish somebody'd take advantage like that of me, and sell a picture or two when I'm not looking. Come, we're keeping John waiting." And he took firm hold of his son's arm.

Yet in the McGuire living-room, in the presence of John McGuire himself, he talked fully five minutes of nothing in particular, before he said:

"Well, John, I've got some good news for you."

"GOOD news?"

"That's what I'd call it. I—er—hear you're going to have a book out in the spring."

"I'm going to—WHAT?"

"Have a book out—war stories. They were too good to keep to ourselves, John, so I jotted them down as you told them, and last week I sent them off to a publisher."

"A—a real publisher?" The boy's voice shook. Every trace of color had drained from his face.

"You bet your life—and one of the biggest in the country." Daniel Burton's own voice was shaking. He had turned his eyes away from John McGuire's face.

"And they'll—print it?"

"Just as soon as ever you'll sign the contract. And, by the way, that contract happens to be a mighty good one, for a first book, my boy."

John McGuire drew a long breath. The color was slowly coming back to his face.

"But I can't seem to quite—believe it," he faltered.

"Nonsense! Simplest thing in the world," insisted Daniel Burton brusquely. "They saw the stories, liked them, and are going to publish them. That's all."

"All! ALL!" The blind boy was on his feet, his face working with emotion. "When all my life I've dreamed and dreamed and longed for—" He stopped short and sat down. He had the embarrassed air the habitually reserved person usually displays when caught red-handed making a "scene." He gave a confused laugh. "I was only thinking—what a way. You see—I'd always wanted to be a writer, but I'd given it up long ago. I had my living to earn, and I knew I couldn't earn it—that way—not at first. I used to say I'd give anything if I could write a book; and I was just wondering if—if I'd been willing then to have given—my eyes!"

CHAPTER XXIX

DOROTHY TRIES HER HAND

It was on a mild day early in February that Susan met Dorothy Parkman on the street. She stopped her at once.

"Well, if I ain't glad to see you!" she cried. "I didn't know you'd got back."

"I haven't been back long, Susan."

"You hain't been over to see us once, Miss Dorothy," Susan reproached her.

"I—I have been very busy." Miss Dorothy seemed ill at ease, and anxious to get away.

"An' you didn't come for a long, long time when you was here last fall." Susan had laid a detaining hand on the girl's arm now.

"Didn't I?" Miss Dorothy smiled brightly. "Well, perhaps I didn't. But you didn't need me, anyway. I've heard all about it—the splendid work Mr. Burton and his son have done for John McGuire. And I'm so glad."

"Oh, yes, that's all right." Susan spoke without enthusiasm.

"And the book is going to be published?"

"Yes, oh, yes." Susan still spoke with a preoccupied frown.

"Why, Susan, what's the matter? I thought you'd be glad."

Susan drew a long sigh.

"I am glad, Miss Dorothy. I'm awful glad—for John McGuire. They say it's wonderful, the change in him already. He's so proud an' happy to think he's done it—not sinfully proud, you understand, but just humbly proud an' glad. An' his ma says he's writin' other things now—poems an' stories, an' he's as happy as a lark all day. An' I'm awful glad. But it's Keith hisself that I'm thinkin' of. You see, only yesterday I found him—cryin'."

"Crying!" Miss Dorothy seemed to have forgotten all about her haste to get away. She had Susan's arm in HER grasp now. She had pulled her to one side, too, where they could have a little sheltered place to talk, in the angle of two store windows.

"Yes, cryin'. You see, 't was like this," hurried on Susan. "Mis' McGuire was over, an' I'd been readin' a new poem to her an' him. 'T was a real pretty one, too, if I do say it as shouldn't—the best I ever done; all about how fame an' beauty an' pleasure didn't count nothin' beside workin'. I got the idea out of something I found in a magazine. 'T was jest grand; an' it give me the perspiration right away to turn it into a poem. An' I did. An' 't was that I was readin'. I'd jest got it done that mornin'."

"Yes, yes," nodded Miss Dorothy. "I see."

Eleanor H. Porter

"Well, I never thought of its meanin' anything to Keith, or of his takin' it nohow wrong; but after Mis' McGuire had gone home (she came out an' set with me a spell first in the kitchen) I heard a queer little noise in the settin'-room, an' I went an' looked in. Keith was at the table, his arms flung straight out in front of him, an' his head bowed down. An', Miss Dorothy, he was cryin' like a baby."

"Oh, Susan, what did you do? What did you say?"

"Say? Nothin'!" Susan's eyes flashed her scorn. "Do you s'pose I'd let that poor lamb know I see him cryin'? Well, I guess not! I backed out as soft as a feather bed, an' I didn't go near that settin'-room for an hour, nor let any one else. I was a regular dragon-fly guardin' it. Well, by an' by Keith comes out. His face was white an' strained-lookin'. But he was smiling, an' he handed out my poem—I'd left it on the table when I come out with Mis' McGuire. 'I found this paper on the table, Susan. It's your poem, isn't it?' he says real cheerful-like. Then he turns kind of quick an' leaves the room without another word.

"Well, I didn't know then that't was the poem he'd been cryin' over. I didn't know—till this mornin'. Then somethin' he said made me see right off."

"Why, Susan, what was it?"

"It was somethin' about—work. But first you wouldn't understand it, unless you see the poem. An' I can show it to you, 'cause I've got it right here. I'm tryin' to memorialize it, so I keep it with me all the time, an' repeat one line over an' over till I get it. It's right here in my bag. You'll find it's the best I've wrote, Miss Dorothy; I'm sure you will," she went on a bit wistfully. "You see I used a lot of the words that was in the magazine—not that I pleasurized it any, of course.

Mine's different, 'cause mine is poetry an' theirs is prosy. There! I guess maybe you can read it, even if't is my writin'," she finished, taking a sheet of note-paper from her bag and carefully spreading it out for Miss Dorothy to read.

And this is what Dorothy read:

CONTENTMENT

Wealth
I asked for the earth—but when in my hands
It shriveled and crumbled away;
And the green of its trees and the blue of its skies
Changed to a somber gray.

Beauty
I asked for the moon—but the shimmering thing
Was only reflected gold,
And vanished away at my glance and touch,
And was then but a tale that is told.

Pleasure
I asked for the stars—and lots of them came,
And twinkled and danced for me;
But the whirling lights soon wearied my gaze—
I squenched their flame in the sea.

Fame
I asked for the sun!—but the fiery ball,
Brought down from its home on high,
Scorched and blistered my finger tips,
As I swirled it back to the sky.

Labor
I asked for a hoe, and I set me to work,
And my red blood danced as I went:

Eleanor H. Porter

At night I rested, and looking back,
I counted my day well spent.

"But, Susan, I don't see," began Miss Dorothy, lifting puzzled eyes from the last line of the poem, "I don't see what there is about that to make Mr. Keith—cry."

"No, I didn't, till this mornin'; an' then—Well, Keith came out into the kitchen an' begun one of them tramps of his up an' down the room. It always drives me nearly crazy when he does that, but I can't say anything, of course. I did begin this mornin' to talk about John McGuire an' how fine it was he'd got somethin' he could do. I thought't would take the poor boy's mind off hisself, if I could get him talkin' about John McGuire—he's been SO interested in John all winter! An' so glad he could help him. You know he's always so wanted to HELP somebody hisself instead of always havin' somebody helpin' him. But, dear me, instead of its bein' a quieter now for him, it was a regular stirrup.

"'That's just it, that's just it, Susan,' he moans. 'You've got to have work or you die. There's nothin' in the whole world like work—YOUR WORK! John McGuire's got his work, an' I'm glad of it. But where's mine? Where's mine, I tell you?'

"An' I told him he'd jest been havin' his work, helpin' John McGuire. You know it was wonderful, perfectly wonderful, Miss Dorothy, the way them two men got hold of John McGuire. You know John wouldn't speak to anybody, not anybody, till Keith an' his father found some way to get on the inside of his shell. An' Keith's been so happy all winter doin' it; an' his father, too. So I tried to remind him that he'd been doin' his work.

"But it didn't do no good. Keith said that was all very well, an' he was glad, of course; but that was only a little bit of a thing, an' 't was all past an' gone, an' John didn't need 'em any more, an' there wasn't anything left for him now at all. Oh, Miss Dorothy, he talked awfully. I never heard him run on so. An' I knew, from a lot of it that he said, that he was thinkin' of that poem—he wouldn't ask for wealth or beauty or fame, or anything, an' that there didn't anything count but labor. You see?"

"Yes, I—see." Miss Dorothy's voice was very low. Her face was turned quite away, yet Susan was very sure that there were tears in her eyes.

"An' his father!—he's 'most as bad as Keith," sighed Susan. "They're both as nervous as witches, what with the war an' all, an' they not bein' able to do anything. Oh, they do give money—lots of it—Liberty Bonds an' Red Cross, an' drives, of course. You knew they'd got it now—their money, didn't you, Miss Dorothy?"

"Yes, I had heard so."

"Not that it seems to do 'em any particular good," complained Susan wistfully. "Oh, of course things ain't so— so ambiguous as they was, an' we have more to eat an' wear, an' don't have to worry about bills. But they ain't any happier, as I can see. If only Keith could find somethin'—"

"Yes, I know," sighed Miss Dorothy again, as she turned slowly away. "I wish he—could."

"Well, come to see us, won't you?" urged Susan anxiously. "That'll help some—it'll help a lot."

But Miss Dorothy did not seem to have heard. At least she did not answer. Yet not twenty-four hours later she was ringing the Burtons' doorbell.

"No, no—not there! I want to see YOU," she panted a little breathlessly, when Susan would have led the way to the living-room.

"But Keith would be so glad—" begged Susan.

"No, no! I particularly don't want him to know I am here," insisted Dorothy.

And without further ado, but with rebellious lips and eyes, Susan led the way to the kitchen.

"Susan, I have a scheme, I think, that may help out Mr. Keith," began the young girl abruptly. "I'll have to begin by telling you something of what I've seen during these last two or three months, while I've been away. A Mr. Wilson, an old college friend of my father's, has been taking a lot of interest in the blind—especially since the war. He got to thinking of the blinded soldiers and wishing he could help them. He had seen some of them in Canada, and talked with them. What he thought of first for them was brooms, and basket-weaving and chair-caning, same as everybody does. But he found they had a perfect horror of those things. They said nobody bought such things except out of pity—they'd rather have the machine-made kind. And these men didn't want things bought of them out of pity. You see, they were big, well, strong, young fellows, like John McGuire here; and they were groping around, trying to find a way to live all those long years of darkness that they knew were ahead of them. They didn't have any especial talent. But they wanted to work,—do something that was necessary—not be charity folks, as they called it."

"I know," responded Susan sympathetically.

"Well, this Mr. Wilson is at the head of a big electrical

machinery manufacturing company near Chicago, like Mr. Sanborn's here, you know. And suddenly one day it came to him that he had the very thing right in his own shop—a necessary kind of work that the blind could be taught to do."

"My lan', what was it? Think of blind folks goin' to work in a big shop like Tom Sanborn's!"

"I know it. But there was something. It was wrapping the coils of wire with tape. Mr. Wilson said they used hundreds of thousands of these coils all the time, and they had to be wrapped to insulate them. It was this work that he believed the blind could learn to do. Anyhow, he determined to try it. And try it he did. He sent for those soldiers he had talked with in Canada, and he took two or three of father's patients, and opened a little winding-room with a good electrical engineer in charge. And, do you know? it was wonderful, the way those poor fellows took hold of that work! Why, they got really skillful in no time, and they learned to do it swiftly, too."

"My lan'!" breathed Susan again.

"They did. He took me in to see them one day. It was just a big room on the ground floor of an office building. He didn't put them in his shop. He said he wanted to keep them separate, for the present, anyway. It had two or three long tables, and the superintendent moved up and down the room overseeing their work, and helping where it was necessary. There was a new man that morning, and it was perfectly wonderful how he took hold of it. And they were all so happy, laughing and talking, and having the best time ever; but they sobered up real earnest when Mr. Wilson introduced one or two of them to me. One man in particular—he was one of the soldiers, a splendid, great, blond fellow six feet tall, and only twenty-one—told me what this work meant to them; how glad they were to feel of real use in the world. Then his face flushed, and his shoulders straightened a bit. 'And we're even helping a little to win the war,' he said, 'for these coils we are winding now are for some armatures to go in some big motors that are going to be used in making munitions. So you see, we are helping—a little.' Bless his heart! He didn't know how much he was helping every one, just by his big, brave courage.

"Well, Susan, all this gave me an idea, after what you said yesterday about Mr. Keith. And I wondered—why couldn't he wind coils, too? And maybe he'd get others to do it also. So I went to Mr. Sanborn, and he's perfectly willing to let us give it a trial. He's pleased and interested, and says he will furnish everything for the experiment, including a first-class engineer to superintend; only he can't spend any time over it himself, and we'll have to get somebody else to take charge and make arrangements, about the place, and the starting of it, and all that. And, Susan, now comes my second idea. Could we—do you suppose we could get Mr. Daniel Burton to take charge of it?"

"Oh, Miss Dorothy, if we only could!"

"It would be so fine for Mr. Keith, and for all the others. I've been hearing everywhere how wonderfully he got hold of John McGuire."

"He did, he did," cried Susan, "an' he was like a different man all the time he was doin' it. He hain't had no use for his paintin' lately, an' he's been so uneasy. I'm sure he'll do it, if you ask him."

"Good! Then I will. Is—is he at home to-day?"

"Yes, he's upstairs. I'll call him." Susan sprang to her feet with alacrity.

"But, Susan, just a minute!" Miss Dorothy had put out a detaining hand. "Is—is Mr. Keith here, too?"

"Yes, both of 'em. Keith is in the settin'-room an' I'll call his father down. 'T won't take but jest a minute." Susan was plainly chafing at the detaining hand.

"No, no, Susan!" Miss Dorothy, too, had sprung to her feet. "If—if Mr. Keith is here I'll wait. I want to see Mr. Daniel Burton first—er—alone: to—to tell him about it, you know," she added hastily, as Susan began to frown her disappointment.

"But I don't see why," argued Susan, her disapproving eyes on the girl's flushed cheeks. "I should think you'd want to talk it up with both of 'em."

"Yes, yes, of course; but not—not at first," stammered Miss Dorothy, plainly growing more and more embarrassed as she tried to appear less so. "I would rather—er—that is, I think it would be better to ask Mr. Daniel Burton first, and then after we get it well started let him tell his son. So I'll come to-morrow in the morning—at ten. Mr. Keith is with Mr. John McGuire, then, isn't he? And over at his house? I heard he was."

"Yes, he is, most generally."

"Then I'll come then. If—if you'll tell Mr. Daniel Burton, please," hurried on Miss Dorothy, "and ask him to see me. And please, PLEASE keep it from Mr. Keith, Susan. Truly, I don't want him to know a thing about it till his father and I have—have got it all fixed up," she finished.

"But, Miss Dorothy, I know that Keith would want—"

"Susan!" With an imperiousness quite foreign to her usual manner, Miss Dorothy cut in sharply. "If you don't promise to speak only to Mr. Daniel Burton about this matter I shall not come at all."

"Oh, lan' sakes! Well, well, have it your own way," snapped Susan.

"You promise?"

"Yes, I promise." Susan's lips obeyed, but her eyes were still mutinous.

"Good! Thank you, Susan. Then I'll come to-morrow at ten," nodded Miss Dorothy, once again her smiling, gracious self, as she turned to leave the room.

CHAPTER XXX

DANIEL BURTON'S "JOB"

Dorothy came at ten, or, to be strictly accurate, at five minutes past ten. The additional five minutes had been consumed by her going out of her way around the block so that she might see if Keith were visible in one of the McGuires' windows. He was visible—and when she went up the Burton walk at five minutes past ten, her step was confident and her face eager; and there was about her manner none of the furtive, nervous questioning that had marked her coming the day before.

"Good-morning, Susan," she began cheerily, as Susan answered her ring. "Did Mr. Burton say he would see me?"

"He did. And Mr. Keith is over to the McGuires' all safe, so you don't have to worry about him." Susan's eyes were still mutinous, her voice still coldly disapproving.

"Yes, I know he is," nodded Miss Dorothy with a bright smile.

"Oh, you do!"

"Yes. Well, that is—er—I—" Under Susan's uncompromising

frigidity Miss Dorothy's stammering tongue came to a painful pause.

"Humph!" vouchsafed Susan. "Well, come in, an' I'll tell Mr. DANIEL Burton you're here."

That the emphasis on "Daniel" was not lost was shown by the sudden broad smile that chased away the confusion on Miss Dorothy's face, as Susan led the way to the living-room. Two minutes later Daniel Burton, thinner, paler, and more worn-looking than Dorothy had ever seen him before, entered the room and held out a cordial hand.

"Good-morning, Miss Dorothy. I'm glad to see you," he said. "What is it,—Red Cross, Y.M.C.A., Smileage Books?" The whimsical smile on his lips only served to emphasize the somber pain in his eyes.

"Not any of them. Then Susan didn't tell you?"

"Not a word. Sit down, please."

"Thank you. Then I shall have to begin at the beginning," sighed the girl a little constrainedly as she took the chair he offered her. "I—I have a certain project that I want to carry out, Mr. Burton, and I—I want your help."

"Why, of course—certainly. I shall be glad to, I know." Daniel Burton's hand had already reached for his check-book. "Any project of yours, Miss Dorothy—! How much do you want?"

But Miss Dorothy lifted her hand, palm outward.

"Thank you, Mr. Burton; but not any—in money, just yet. Oh, it'll take money, probably, to get it started, before it's on a self-supporting basis, I suppose. But it isn't money I want to-day, Mr. Burton. It—it's yourself."

The man gave a short, dry laugh, not untinged with bitterness.

"I'm afraid I can't endorse either your taste or your judgment there, Miss Dorothy. You've come for a poor stick. I can't imagine myself as being much benefit to any sort of project. However, I shall be glad to hear about it, of course. What is it?"

And Miss Dorothy told him. With her eyes shining, and her voice quivering with eagerness, she told the story as she had told it to Susan the afternoon before, but with even greater elaboration of detail.

"And so now, Mr. Burton, you—you will help, won't you?" she begged, in closing.

"Help! But my dear girl, how?"

"Take charge. Be the head and shoulders, the backbone of the whole thing. Oh, yes, I know it's a whole lot to ask," she hurried on, as she saw the dawning dismay and refusal in his face. "But I thought, for the sake of the cause—"

"The cause!" The man's voice was bitter as he interrupted her. "I'd crawl to France on my hands and knees if that would do any good! But, my dear young lady, I'm an ignoramus, and worse than an ignoramus, when it comes to machinery. I'll venture to wager that I wouldn't know the tape from the coils—or whatever they are."

"Oh, we'd have an engineer for that part, of course," interposed the girl eagerly. "And we want your son, too."

"You want Keith! Pray, do you expect him to teach how to wind coils?"

"No—no—not exactly;—though I think he will be teaching before he realizes it. I want him to learn to wind them himself, and thus get others to learn. You don't understand, Mr. Burton. I want you and Mr. Keith to—to do just what you did for John McGuire—arouse interest and enthusiasm and get them to do it. Don't you see?"

"But that was Keith, not I, in the case of John McGuire."

"It was you at the last," corrected the girl gently. "Mr. Burton, John McGuire wouldn't have any book out this spring if it weren't for you and—your eyes."

"Hm-m, perhaps not. Still there'd have been a way, probably. But even if I grant that—all you say in the case of John McGuire—that isn't winding armatures, or whatever they are."

"Mr. Burton, you aren't going to refuse," pleaded the girl.

"What else can I do? Miss Dorothy, you don't want to stamp this project of yours a FAILURE from the start, do you?" Words, voice, manner, and gesture were unmistakable. All the longing and heartache and bitterness of years of fruitless effort and final disappointment pulsated through that one word FAILURE.

For a moment nobody spoke. Daniel Burton had got to his feet and crossed the room to the window. The girl, watching him with compassionate eyes as he stood looking out, had caught her breath with a little choking sigh. Suddenly she lifted her head resolutely.

"Mr. Burton, you've got one gift that—that I don't believe you realize at all that you possess. Like John McGuire you can make folks SEE what you are talking about. Perhaps it's because you can paint pictures with a brush. Or—or perhaps it's because you've got such a wonderful command of words."(Miss Dorothy stumbled a little precipitately into this sentence—she had not failed to see the disdainful movement of the man's head and shoulders at the mention of his pictures.) "Whatever it is," she hurried on, "you've got it. I saw it first years ago, with—with your son, when I used to see him at father's. He would sit and talk to me by the hour about the woods and fields and mountains, the sunsets and the flowers back home; and little by little I found out that they were the pictures you drew for him—on the canvas of his soul. You've done it again now for John McGuire. Do you suppose you could have caught those wonderful stories of his with your pencil, if you hadn't been able to help him visualize them for himself—you and Keith together with your wonderful enthusiasm and interest?

"I know you couldn't. And that's what I want you now for—you and your son. Because he is blind, and knows, and understands, as no seeing person can know and understand, they will trust him; they will follow where he leads. But behind him has got to be YOU. You've got to be the eyes for—for them all; not to teach the work—we'll have others for that. Any good mechanic will do for that part. But it's the other part of it—the soul of the thing. These men, lots of them, are but little more than boys—big, strong, strapping fellows with the whole of life before them. And they are—blind. Whichever way they turn a big black curtain shuts them in. And it's those four black curtains that I want you to paint. I want you to give them something to look at, something to think of, something to live for. And you can do it. And when you have done it, you'll find they're the best and—and the biggest pictures you ever painted." Her voice

Eleanor H. Porter

broke with the last word and choked into silence.

Over at the window the man stood motionless. One minute, two minutes passed. Then a bit abruptly he turned, crossed the room to the girl's side, and held out his hand.

"Miss Dorothy, I—I'll take the job," he said.

He spoke lightly, and he smiled as he said the words; but neither the smile nor the lightness of his manner quite hid the shake in his voice nor the moisture in his eyes.

"Thank you, Mr. Burton. I was sure you would," cried the girl.

"And now for Keith! He's over to the McGuires'. I'll get him!" exclaimed the man boyishly.

But Miss Dorothy was instantly on her feet.

"No, no, please," she begged a little breathlessly. "I'd rather you didn't—now. I—I think we'd better get it a little farther along before we tell him. There's a whole lot to do, you know—getting the room and the materials and the superintendent, and all that; and there isn't a thing he can do—yet."

"All right. Very good. Perhaps that would be better," nodded the man. "But, let me tell you, I already have some workers for your project."

"You mean Jack Green, here in town?"

"No. Oh, we'd want him, of course; but it's some others—a couple of boys from Hillsboro. I had a letter yesterday from the father of one of the boys, asking what to do with his son.

He thought because of—of Keith, that I could help him. It was a pitiful letter. The man was heart-broken and utterly at sea. His boy—only nineteen—had come home blind, and well-nigh crazed with the tragedy of it. And the father didn't know which way to turn. That's why he had appealed to me. You see, on account of Keith—"

"Yes, I understand," said the girl gently, as the man left his sentence unfinished.

"I've had others, too—several of them—in the last few weeks. If you'll wait I'll get the letters." He was already halfway to the door. "It may take a minute or two to look them up; but—they'll be worth it, I think."

"Of course they will," she cried eagerly. "They'll be just exactly what we want, and I'm not in a bit of a hurry," she finished, dropping back in her chair as the door closed behind him.

Alone, she looked about the room, her eyes wistful, brimming with unshed tears. Over by the window was Keith's chair, before it the table, with a half-completed picture puzzle spread upon it. Near the table was a set of shelves containing other picture puzzles, games, and books—all, as the girl well knew, especially designed and constructed for eyes that could not see.

She had risen to her feet and half started to cross the room toward the table when the door to the side hall opened and Keith Burton entered the room.

With a half-stifled gasp the girl stepped back to her chair. The blind boy stopped instantly, his face turned toward her.

"Is that—you, Susan?"

The girl wet her lips, but no words came.

"Who's there, please?" He spoke sharply this time. As everybody knew—who knew Keith—the one thing that angered him more than anything else was the attempted deception as to one's presence in the room.

Miss Dorothy gave a confused little laugh, and put her hand to her throat.

"Why, Keith, it's only I! Don't look so—"

"You?" For one brief moment his face lighted up as with a hidden flame; then instantly it changed. It became like the gray of ashes after the flame is spent. "Why didn't you speak, then?" he questioned. "It did no good to keep quiet. You mustn't forget that I have ears—if I haven't eyes."

"Nonsense, Keith!" She laughed again confusedly, though her own face had paled a little. "I did speak as soon as I caught my breath;—popping in on a body like that!"

"But I didn't know—you were here," stammered the young fellow uncertainly. "Nobody called me. I beg your pardon if—" He came to a helpless pause.

"Not a bit of it! You needn't. It wasn't necessary at all." The girl tossed off the words with a lightness so forced that it was almost flippancy. "You see, I didn't come to see you at all. It was your father."

"My father!"

"Certainly."

"But—but does he know?"

The girl laughed merrily—too merrily for sincerity.

"Know? Indeed he does. We've just been having a lovely talk. He's gone upstairs for some letters. He's coming right back—right back."

"Oh-h!" Was it an indefinable something in her voice, or was it the repetition of the last two words? Whatever it was that caused it, Keith turned away with a jerk, walked with the swift sureness of long familiarity straight to the set of shelves and took down a book. "Then I'll not disturb you any further—as long as you're not needing me," he said tersely. "I only came for this." And with barely a touch of his cane to the floor and door-casing, he strode from the room.

The pity of it—that he could not have seen Dorothy Parkman's eyes looking after him!

CHAPTER XXXI

WHAT SUSAN DID NOT SEE

There was apparently no limit to Daniel Burton's enthusiastic cooperation with Dorothy Parkman on the matter of establishing a workroom for the blind. He set to work with her at once. The very next morning after her initial visit, he went with her to Mazie Sanborn's father, and together they formulated the first necessary plans.

Thomas Sanborn was generous, and cordially enthusiastic, though his words and manner carried the crisp terseness of the busy man whose time is money. At the end of five minutes he summoned one David Patch to the office, and introduced him to Miss Dorothy and Daniel Burton as one of his most expert engineers.

"And now I'll turn the whole thing over to you," he declared briskly, with his finger already on the button that would summon his stenographer for dictation. "Just step into that room there and stay as long as you like. Whatever Patch says I'll back up. You'll find him thoroughly capable and trustworthy. And now good luck to you," he finished, throwing wide the door of the adjoining room.

The next moment Miss Dorothy and Daniel Burton found

themselves alone with the keen-eyed, alert little man who had been introduced as David Patch. And David Patch did, indeed, appear to be very capable. He evidently understood his business, and he gave interested attention to Miss Dorothy's story of what she had seen, and of what she wished now to try to do. He took them then for a tour of the great shop, especially to the department where the busy fingers were winding with tape the thousands of wire coils.

Miss Dorothy's eyes sparkled with excitement, and she fairly clapped her hands in her delight, while Daniel Burton said that even he could see the possibilities of that kind of work for their purpose.

At the end of a long hour of talking and planning, Miss Dorothy and Daniel Burton started for home. But even then Daniel Burton had yet more to say, for at his gate, which was on Miss Dorothy's way home, he begged her to come in for a moment.

"I had another letter to-day about a blind soldier—this time from Baltimore. I want to show it to you. You see, so many write to me, on account of my own boy. You will come in, just a minute?"

"Why, yes, of course I—will." The pause, and the half-stifled word that finished the sentence came as the tall figure of Keith Burton turned the corner of the piazza and walked toward the steps.

"Hullo! Dad?" Keith's voice was questioning.

"Yes; and—"

"And Dorothy Parkman," broke in the girl with a haste so precipitate as to make her almost choke.

"Miss Parkman?" Once again, for a moment, Keith's face lighted as with a flame. "Come up. Come around on the south side," he cried eagerly. "I've been sunning myself there. You'd think it was May instead of March."

"No, she can't go and sun herself with you," interposed Daniel Burton with mock severity. "She's coming with me into the house. I want to show her something."

"Well, I—I like that," retorted the youth. He spoke jauntily, and gave a short little laugh. But the light had died from his face and a slow red had crept to his forehead.

"Well, she can't. She's coming with me," reiterated the man. "Now run back to your sun bath. If you're good maybe we'll be out pretty soon," he laughed back at his son, as he opened the house door for his guest. "That's right—you didn't want him to know, yet, did you?" he added, looking a bit anxiously into the girl's somewhat flushed face as he closed the hall door.

"Quite right. No, I don't want him to know yet. There's so much to be done to get started, and he'd want to help. And he couldn't help about that part; and't would only fret him and make him unhappy."

"My idea exactly," nodded the man. "When we get the room, and the goods there, we'll want to tell him then."

"Of course, you'll tell him then," cried the girl.

"Yes, indeed, of course we will!" exclaimed the man, very evidently not noticing the change in the pronoun. "Now, if you'll wait a minute I'll get that letter, then we'll go out to Keith on the piazza."

It was a short letter, and one quickly read; and very soon they were out on the piazza again. But Miss Dorothy said "No, no!" very hastily when he urged her to go around on the other side; and she added, "I really must go home now," as she hurried down the steps. Daniel Burton went then around the corner of the piazza to explain her absence to his son Keith. But he need not have hurried. His son Keith was not there.

For all the good progress that was made on that first day, things seemed to move a bit slowly after that. To begin with, the matter of selecting a suitable room gave no little difficulty. The right room in the right location seemed not to be had; and Daniel Burton even suggested that they use some room in his own house. But after a little thought he gave up this idea as being neither practical nor desirable.

Meanwhile he was in daily communication with Dorothy Parkman, and the two spent hours together, thrashing out the different problems one by one as they arose, sometimes at her home, more frequently at his; for "home" to Dorothy in Hinsdale meant the Sanborn house, where Mazie was always in evidence—and Daniel Burton did not care for Mazie. Especially he did not care for her advice and assistance on the problems that were puzzling him now.

To be sure, at his own home there was Keith; but he contrived to avoid Keith on most occasions. Besides, Keith himself seemed quite inclined to keep out of the way (particularly if he heard the voice of Dorothy Parkman), which did not disturb Daniel Burton in the least, under the circumstances. Until they got ready to tell Keith, he was rather glad that he did keep so conveniently out of the way. And as Dorothy seemed always glad to avoid seeing Keith or talking to him, there was really very little trouble on that score; and they could have their consultations in peace and quietness.

Eleanor H. Porter

And there were so many of them—those consultations! When at last the room was found, there were the furnishings to select, and the final plans to be made for the real work to be done. David Patch proved himself to be invaluable then. As if by magic a long table appeared, and the coils and the tape, and all the various paraphernalia of a properly equipped winding-room marched smoothly into place. Meanwhile three soldiers and one civilian stood ready and eager to be taught, needing only the word of command to begin.

"And now we'll tell Keith," said Daniel Burton.

"Yes; now you must tell Keith," said Miss Dorothy.

"To-morrow at nine."

"To-morrow at nine," bowed Miss Dorothy.

"I'll bring him down and we'll show him."

"And I do so hope he'll like it."

"Of course, he'll like it!" cried Daniel Burton. "You wait and see."

But she did not see. She was not there to see.

Promptly at nine o'clock Daniel Burton appeared at the winding-room with Keith. But Dorothy Parkman was nowhere in sight. He waited ten, fifteen minutes; then he told Keith the story of the room, and of what they hoped to do there, fuming meanwhile within himself because he had to tell it alone.

But it was not lack of interest that kept Miss Dorothy away. It could not have been; for that very afternoon she sought

Daniel Burton out and asked eagerly what his son had said, and how he had taken it. And her eyes shone and her breath quickened at the story Daniel Burton told; and so eager was she to know every little word that had fallen from Keith's lips that she kept Daniel Burton repeating over and over each minute detail.

Yet the next day when Keith and four other blind youths began work in earnest, she never once went near Keith's chair, though she went often to the others, dropping here and there a word of encouragement or a touch of aiding fingers. When night came, however, and she found an opportunity for a few words alone with Daniel Burton, she told him that, in her opinion, Keith had done the best work of the five, and that it was perfectly marvelous the way he was taking hold. And again her eyes sparkled and her breath quickened; and she spent the entire ten minutes talking about Keith to his father. Yet the next day, when the work began again, she still went to the back of every chair but Keith's.

Things happened very rapidly after that. It was not a week before the first long table in the big room was filled with eager workers, and the second one had to be added to take care of the newcomers.

The project was already the talk of the town, and not the least excited and interested of the observers was John McGuire's mother. When the news came of the second table's being added to the equipment of the place, she hurried over to Susan's kitchen without delay—though with the latest poem of her son's as the ostensible excuse.

"It's 'The Stumbling-Block,'" she announced. "He just got it done yesterday, an' I copied it for you. I think it's the best yet," she beamed, handing over a folded paper. "It's kind of long, so don't stop to read it now. Say, is it true? Have they had to put in another table at that blind windin'-room?"

"They have."

"Well, if that ain't the greatest! I think it's just grand. They took my John down there to see the place yesterday. Do you know? That boy is a different bein' since his book an' his writin'. An' he's learnin' to do such a lot of things for himself, an' he's so happy in it! An' he doesn't mind seein' anybody now. An' it's all owin' to your wonderful Keith an' his father. I wouldn't ever have believed it of them."

Susan's chin came up a bit.

"I would. I KNEW. An' I always told you that Daniel Burton was a superlative man in every way, an' his son's jest like him. Only you wouldn't believe me."

"Nobody'd believe you," maintained Mrs. McGuire spiritedly. "Nobody'd believe such a thing could be as my John bein' changed like that—an' all those others down to the windin'-room, too. They say it's perfectly marvelous what Keith an' his father are doin' with those men an' boys. Aren't they awful happy over it—Keith an' his father, I mean?"

"Daniel Burton is. Why, he's like a different man, Mis' McGuire. You'd know that, jest to see him walk, an' hear him speak. An' I don't hear nothin' more about his longin' to get over there. I guess he thinks he's got work enough to do right here. An' he hardly ever touches his war maps these days."

"But ain't Keith happy, too?"

"Y-yes, an' no," hesitated Susan, her face clouding a little. "Oh, he's gone into it heart an' soul; an' while he's workin' on somethin' he's all right. But when it's all quiet, an' he's settin' alone, I don't like the look on his face. But I know he's glad to be helpin' down there; an' I know it's helpin' him, too."

"It's helpin' everybody—not forgettin' Miss Dorothy Parkman," added Mrs. McGuire, with a smile and a shrug, as she rose to go. "But, then, of course, we all know what she's after."

"After! What do you mean?"

"Susan Betts!" With a jerk Mrs. McGuire faced about. "It ain't possible, with eyes in your head, that you hain't seen!"

"Seen what?"

"Well, my lan'! With that girl throwin' herself at Daniel Burton's head for the last six weeks, an' you calmly set there an' ask 'seen what?'!"

"Daniel Burton—Dorothy Parkman!" There was no mistaking Susan's dumfounded amazement.

"Yes, Daniel Burton an' Dorothy Parkman. Oh, I used to think it was Keith; but when the money came to old Daniel I guess she thought he wasn't so old, after all. Besides, Keith, with his handicap—you couldn't blame the girl, after all, I s'pose."

"Daniel Burton an' Dorothy Parkman!" repeated Susan, this time with the faintness of stupefaction.

"Why, Susan, you must've seen it—her runnin' in here every day, walkin' home with him, an' talk, talk, talkin' to him every chance she gets!"

"But, they—they've been makin' plans for—for the work,"

murmured Susan.

"Work! Well, I guess it no need to've taken quite so many consultations for just the work. Besides, she never thought of such a scheme as this before the money came, did she? Not much she did! Oh, come, Susan, wake up! She'll be walkin' off with him right under your nose if you don't look out," finished Mrs. McGuire with a sly laugh, as she took her departure.

Left alone, Susan sat for some time absorbed in thought, a deep frown on her face; then with a sigh and a shrug, as if throwing off an incomprehensible burden, she opened the paper Mrs. McGuire had left with her.

Once, twice, three times she read the verses; then with a low chuckle she folded up the paper, tucked it into her apron pocket, and rose to her feet. A minute later she had attacked the pile of dishes in the sink, and was singing lustily:

"I've taken my worries, an' taken my woes,
I have, I have,
An' shut 'em up where nobody knows,
I have, I have.
I chucked 'em down, that's what I did,
An' now I'm sittin' upon the lid,
An' we'll all feel gay when Johnny comes marchin' home.
I'm sittin' upon the lid, I am,
Hurrah! Hurrah!
I'm tryin' to be a little lamb,
Hurrah! Hurrah!
But I'm feelin' more like a great big slam
Than a nice little peaceful woolly lamb,
But we'll all feel gay when Johnny comes marchin' home."

CHAPTER XXXII

THE KEY

There was no work at the winding-room Saturday afternoons, and it was on Saturday afternoon that Susan found Keith sitting idle-handed in his chair by the window in the living-room.

As was her custom she spoke the moment she entered the room—but not before she had noted the listless attitude and wistful face of the youth over by the window.

"Keith, I've been thinkin'."

"Bad practice, Susan—sometimes," he laughed whimsically.

"Not this time."

"Poetry?"

She shook her head.

"No. I ain't poetizin' so much these days, though I did write one yesterday—about the ways of the world. I'm goin' to read it to you, too, by an' by. But that's jest a common poem about common, every-day folks. An' this thing I was thinkin' about was—was diff'rent."

"And so you couldn't put this into a poem—eh?"

Susan shook her head again and sighed.

"No. An' it's been that way lots o' times lately, 'specially since I seen John McGuire's poems—so fine an' bumtious! Oh, I have the perspiration to write, lots o' times, an' I yield up to it an' write. But somehow, when it's done, I hain't said a mite what I want to, an' I hain't said it the way I want to, either. I think maybe havin' so many of 'em disinclined by them editors has made me kinder fearsome."

"I'm afraid it has, Susan," he smiled.

"Now, this afternoon, what I was thinkin' about—once I'd've made a poem of that easy; but to-day I didn't even try. I KNEW I couldn't do it. An', say, Keith, it was you I was thinkin' about."

"Heavens, Susan! A poem out of me? No wonder your muse balked! I'm afraid you'd find even—er—perspiration wouldn't make a poem out of me."

"Keith, do you remember?" Susan was still earnest and preoccupied. "I told you once that it didn't make no diff'rence if God had closed the door of your eyes. He'd open up another room to you sometime, an' give you the key to unlock the door. An' he has. An' now you've got it—that key."

"I've got it—the key!"

"Yes. It's that work down there—helpin' them blind men an' boys to get hold of their souls again. Oh, Keith, don't you see? An' it's such a big, wide room that God has given you, an' it's all yours. There ain't no one that can help them poor blind soldiers like you can. An' you couldn't 'a' done it if the door of your eyes hadn't been shut first. That was what give you the key to this big, beautiful room of helpin' our boys what's come back to us, blinded, an' half-crazed with despair an' discouragement. Oh, if I only could make you see it the way I do! But I can't say it—the right way. There's such a big, beautiful idea there, if only I could make you see it. That's why I wanted to write the poem."

"I can see it, Susan—without the poem." Keith was not smiling now. His face was turned away and his voice had grown a bit unsteady. "And I'm glad you showed it to me. It's going to help me a whole lot if—if I'll just keep remembering that key, I think."

Susan threw a quick look into Keith's averted face, then promptly she reached for the folded paper in her apron pocket.

There were times when Susan was wise beyond her station as to when the subject should be changed.

"An' now I'm goin' to read you the poem I did write," she announced briskly—"about every-day folks—diff'rent kinds of folks. Six of 'em. It shows that there ain't any one anywhere that's really satisfied with their lot, when you come right down to it, whether they've got eyes or not."

And she began to read:

THE WAY OF THE WORLD

A beggar girl on the curbstone sat,
All ragged an' hungry-eyed.
Across the street came Peggy McGee;

The beggar girl saw an' sighed.

"I wish'd I was rich—as rich as she,
For she has got things to eat;
An' clo's an' shoes, an' a place to live,
An' she don't beg in the street."

When Peggy McGee the corner turned,
SHE climbed to her garret high
From there she gazed through curtainless panes
At hangin's of lace near by.

"Ah, me!" sighed Peggy. "If I had those
An' rugs like hers on the floor,
It seems to me that I'd never ask
For nothin' at all no more."

* * * * *

From out those curtains that selfsame day,
Looked a face all sour an' thin.
"I hate to live on this horrid street,
In the children's yellin' din!

"An' where's the good of my nice new things,
When nobody'll see or know?
I really think that I ought to be
A-livin' in Rich Man's Row."

A carriage came from "Rich Man's Row,"
An' rumbled by to the park.
A lady sat on the carriage seat;
"Oh, dear," said she, "what an ark!

"If only this coach could show some style,
My clothes, so shabby, would pass.

Now there's an auto quite my kind—
But 'tisn't my own—alas!"

The "auto" carried a millionaire,
Whose brow was knotted an' stern.
"A million is nowhere, now," thought he,
"That's somethin' we all must learn.

"It's millions MANY one has to have,
To be in the swim at all.
This tryin' to live when one is so poor
Is really all folderol!"

* * * * *

A man of millions was just behind;
The beggar was passin' by.
Business at beggin' was good that day,
An' the girl was eatin' pie.

The rich man looked, an' he groaned aloud,
An' swore with his gouty pain.
"I'd give my millions, an' more beside,
Could I eat like that again!"

"Now, ain't that jest like folks?" Susan demanded, as she finished the last verse.

Keith laughed.

"I suspect it is, Susan. And—and, by the way, I shouldn't wonder if this were quite the right time to show that I'm no different from other folks. You see, I, too,—er—am going to make a change—in living."

"A change in living! What do you mean?"

"Oh, not now—not quite yet. But you see I'VE been doing some thinking, too. I've been thinking that if father—that is, WHEN father and Miss Parkman are married—that—"

But Susan interrupted with a groan.

"My sakes, Keith, have you seen it, too?"

Keith laughed embarrassedly.

"To be sure I have! You don't have to have eyes to see that, do you, Susan?"

"Oh, good lan', I don't know," frowned Susan irritably. "I didn't s'pose—"

She did not finish her sentence, and after a moment's silence Keith began again to speak.

"I've been talking a little to David Patch—the superintendent, you know. We're going to take the whole house where we are, for our work, pretty quick, and when we do, Patch and his wife will come there to live upstairs; and they'll take me to board. I asked them. Then I'll be right there handy all the time, you see, which will be a fine arrangement all around."

"A fine arrangement, indeed—with you 'way off down there, an' livin' with David Patch!"

"But, Susan," argued Keith, a bit wearily, "I couldn't be living here, you know."

"I should like to know why not."

"Because I—couldn't." He had grown very white now.

"Besides, I—I think they would be happier without me here; and I know—I should be." His voice was low and almost indistinct, but Susan heard—and understood. "The very fact that once I—I thought—that I was foolish enough to think— But, of course, as soon as I remembered my blindness—And to tie a beautiful young girl down to—" He stopped short and pulled himself up. "Susan, are you still there?"

"I'm right here, Keith." Susan spoke constrainedly.

He gave an embarrassed laugh. A painful red had suffused his face.

"I'm afraid I got to talking—and forgetting that I wasn't— alone," he stumbled on hurriedly. "I—I meant to go on to say that I hoped they'd be very happy. Dad deserves it; and—and if they'd only hurry up and get it over with, it—it would be easier—for me. Not that it matters, of course. Dad has had an awful lot to put up with me already, as it is, you know—the trouble, the care, and the disappointment. You see, I—I was going to make up to him for all he had lost. I was going to be Jerry and Ned and myself, all in a bunch. And now to turn out to be nothing—and worse than nothing—"

"Keith Burton, you stop!" It was the old imperious Susan back again. "You stop right where you be. An' don't you never let me hear you say another word about your bein' a disappointment. Jerry an' Ned, indeed! I wonder if you think a dozen Jerrys an' Neds could do what you've done! An' no matter what they done, they couldn't have done a bigger, splendider thing than you've done in triumphating over your blindness the way you've done, nor one that would make your father prouder of you! An' let me tell you another thing, Keith Burton. No matter what you done—no matter how many big pictures you painted, or big books you wrote, or how much money you made for your dad; there ain't anything you could've done that would do him so much solid good as what you have done."

"Why, Susan, are you wild? I haven't done a thing, not a thing for dad."

"Yes, you have. You've done the biggest thing of all by NEEDIN' him."

"Needing him!"

"Yes. Keith Burton, look at your father now. Look at the splendid work he's doin'. You know as well as I do that he used to be a thoroughly insufficient, uncapacious man (though I wouldn't let anybody else say it!), putterin' over a mess of pictures that wouldn't sell for a nickel. An' that he used to run from anything an' everything that was unpropitious an' disagreeable, like he was bein' chased. Well, then you was took blind. An' what happened?

"You know what happened. He came right up an' toed the mark like a man an' a gentleman. An' he's toed it ever since. An' I can tell you that the pictures he's paintin' now with his tongue for them poor blind boys to see is bigger an' better than any pictures he could have painted with—with his pigmy paints if he worked on 'em for a thousand years. An' it's YOU that's done it for him, jest by needin' him. So there!"

And before Keith could so much as open his lips, Susan was gone, slamming the door behind her.

CHAPTER XXXIII

AND ALL ON ACCOUNT OF SUSAN

Not one wink did Susan Betts sleep that night. To Susan her world was tumbling about her ears in one dizzy whirl of destruction.

Daniel Burton and Dorothy Parkman married and living there, and her beloved blind boy banished to a home with one David Patch? Unthinkable! And yet—

Well, if it had got to be, it had got to be, she supposed—the marriage. But they might at least be decent about it. As for keeping that poor blind boy harrowed up all the time and prolonging the agony—well, at least she could do something about THAT, thank goodness! And she would, too.

When there was anything that Susan could do—particularly in the line of righting a wrong—she lost no time in doing it. Within two days, therefore, she made her opportunity, and grasped it. A little peremptorily she informed Miss Dorothy Parkman that she would like to speak to her, please, in the kitchen. Then, tall, and cold, and very stern, she faced her.

"Of course, I understand, Miss Dorothy, I'm bustlin' in where I hain't no business to. An' I hain't no excuse to offer except my boy, Keith. It's for him I'm askin' you to do it."

"To do—what, Susan?" She had changed color slightly, as she asked the question.

"Not let it be seen so plain—the love-makin'."

"Seen! Love-making!" gasped the girl.

"Well, the talkin' to him, then, an' whisperin', an' consultin's, an' runnin' here every day, an'—"

"I beg your pardon, Susan," interrupted the girl incisively. She had grown very white. "I am tempted to make no sort of reply to such an absurd accusation; but I'm going to say, however, that you must be laboring under some mistake. I do not come here to see Mr. Keith Burton, and I've scarcely exchanged a dozen words with him for months."

"I'm talkin' about Mr. Daniel, not Keith, an'—"

"Mr. DANIEL Burton!"

"Of course! Who else?" Susan was nettled now, and showed it. "I don't s'pose you'll deny runnin' here to see him, an' talkin' to him, an'—"

"No, no, wait!—wait! Don't say any more, PLEASE!" The girl was half laughing, half crying, and her face was going from white to red and back to white again. "Am I to understand that I am actually being accused of—of running after Mr. Daniel Burton?—of—of love-making toward HIM?" she choked incoherently.

"Why, y-yes; that is—er—"

"Oh, this is too much, too much! First Keith, and now—" She broke off hysterically. "To think that—Oh, Susan, how could you, how could you!" And this time she dropped into a chair and covered her face with her hands. But she was laughing. Very plainly she was laughing.

Susan frowned, stared, and frowned again.

"Then you ain't in love with—" Suddenly her face cleared, and broke into a broad smile. "Well, my lan', if that ain't the best joke ever! Of course, you ain't in love with him! I don't believe I ever more 'n half believed it, anyway. Now it'll be dead easy, an' all right, too."

"But—but what does it all mean?" stammered the girl.

"Why, it's jest that—that everybody thought you was after him, an't would be a match—you bein' together so much. But even then I wouldn't have said a thing if it hadn't been for Keith."

"Keith!"

"Yes—poor boy, he—an' it WAS hard for him, seein' you two together like this, an' thinkin' you cared for each other. An' he'd got his plans all made how when you was married he'd go an' live with David Patch."

"David Patch! But—why?"

"Why, don't you see? 'T wouldn't be very easy to see you married to another man, would it?—an' lovin' you all the time hisself, an'—"

"LOVING ME!"

Eleanor H. Porter

"That's what I said." Susan's lips came sharply together and her keen eyes swept the girl's face.

"But, I—I think you must be mistaken—again," faltered the girl, growing rosy.

"I ain't. I've always suspicioned it, an' now I know it."

"But, he—he's acted as if he didn't care for me at all—as if he hated me."

"That's because he cared so much."

"Nonsense, Susan!"

"'T ain't nonsense. It's sense. As I told you, I've always suspicioned it, an' last Saturday, when I heard him talk, I knew. He as good as owned it up, anyhow."

"But why didn't he—he tell me?" stammered the girl, growing still more rosy.

"Because he was blind."

"As if I'd minded—" She stopped abruptly and turned away her face.

Susan drew a resolute breath and squared her shoulders.

"Then why don't you do somethin'?" she demanded.

"Do something?"

"Yes, to—to show him that you don't mind."

"Oh, Susan, I—I couldn't do—that."

"All right. Settle back, then, an' do nothin'; an' he'll settle back an' do nothin', an' there'll be a pretty pair of you, eatin' your hearts out with love for each other, an' passin' each other by with converted faces an' highbrow chins; an' all because you're afraid of offendin' Mis' Grundy, who don't care no more about you than two sticks. But I s'pose you'd both rather be miserable than brace up an' defy the properties an' live long an' be happy ever after."

"But if I could be sure he—cared," spoke the girl, in a faint little voice.

"You would have been, if you'd seen him Saturday, as I did."

"And if—"

"If—if—if!" interrupted Susan impatiently. "An' there that poor blind boy sets an' thinks an' thinks an' thinks, an' longs for some one that loves him to smooth his pillow an' rumple his hair, an'—"

"Susan, I'm going to do it. I'M GOING TO DO IT!" vowed the girl, springing to her feet, her eyes like stars, her cheeks like twin roses.

"Do what?" demanded Susan.

"I don't know. But, I'm going to do SOMETHING. Anyhow, whatever I do I know I'm going to—to defy the 'properties,'" she babbled deliriously, as she hurried from the room, looking very much as if she were trying to hide from herself.

Four days later, Keith, in his favorite chair, sat on the south piazza. It was an April day, but it was like June, and the window behind him was wide open into the living-room. He did not hear Dorothy Parkman's light step up the walk. He did not know that she had paused at sight of him sitting there, and had put her hand to her throat, and then that she had almost run, light-footed, into the house, again very much as if she were trying to run away from herself. But he did hear her voice two minutes later, speaking just inside the window.

At the first sentence he tried to rise, then with a despairing gesture as if realizing that flight would be worse than to remain where he was, he sat back in his chair. And this is what he heard Dorothy Parkman say:

"No, no, Mr. Burton, please—I—I can't marry you. You'll have to understand. No—don't speak, don't say anything, please. There's nothing you could say that—that would make a bit of difference. It's just that I—I don't love you and I do—love somebody else—Keith, your son—yes, you have guessed it. Oh, yes, I know we don't seem to be much to each other, now. But—but whether we ever are, or not, there can't ever be—any one else. And I think—he cares. It's just that— that his pride won't let him speak. As if his dear eyes didn't make me love him—

"But I mustn't say all this—to you. It's just that—that I wanted you to surely—understand. And—and I must go, now. I—must—go!"

And she went. She went hurriedly, a little noisily. She shut one door, and another; then, out on the piazza, she came face to face with Keith Burton.

"Dorothy, oh, Dorothy—I heard!"

And then it was well, indeed, that the Japanese screen on the front piazza was down, for Keith stood with his arms outstretched, and Dorothy, with an ineffably contented little indrawn breath, walked straight into them. And with that light on his face, she would have walked into them had he been standing in the middle of the sidewalk outside.

To Dorothy at that moment nobody in all the world counted for a feather's weight except the man who was holding her close, with his lips to hers.

Later, a little later, when they sat side by side on the piazza settee, and when coherence and logic had become attributes to their conversation, Keith sighed, with a little catch in his voice:

"The only thing I regret about this—all this—the only thing that makes me feel cheap and mean, is that I've won where dad lost out. Poor old dad!"

There was the briefest of pauses, then a small, subdued voice said:

"I—I suspect, Keith, confession is good for the soul."

"Well?" he demanded in evident mystification.

"Anyhow, I—I'll have to do it. Your father wasn't there at all."

"But I heard you speaking to him, my dear."

She shook her head, and stole a look into his face, then caught her breath with a little choking sob of heartache because he could not see the love she knew was in her eyes. But the heartache only nerved her to say the words that almost refused to come. "He—he wasn't there," she repeated, fencing for time.

"But who was there? I heard you call him by name, 'Mr. Burton,' clearly, distinctly. I know I did."

"But—but he wasn't there. Nobody was there. I—I was just talking to myself."

"You mean—practicing what you were going to say?" questioned Keith doubtfully. "And that—that he doesn't know yet that you are going to refuse him?"

"N-no—er—well, yes. That is, I mean, it's true. He—he doesn't know I am going to refuse him." There was a hint of smothered laughter in the girl's voice.

"Dorothy!" The arm about her waist perceptibly loosened and almost fell away. "Why, I don't feel now that—that you half belong to me, yet. And—and think of poor dad!"

The girl caught her breath and stole another look into his face.

"But, Keith, you—you don't understand. He—he hasn't proposed to me yet. That is, I mean," she amended hastily, "he—he isn't going to propose to me—ever."

"But he was. He—cares. And now he'll have to know about—us."

"But he wasn't—he doesn't. You don't understand, Keith. He—he never thought of—of proposing to me. I know he didn't."

"Then why—what—Dorothy, what do you mean by all this?"

"Why, it's just that—that is—I—oh, Keith, Keith, why will

you make me tell you?" she cried between hysterical little laughs and sobs. "And yet—I'd have to tell you, of course. I—I knew you were there on the porch, and—and I knew you'd hear—what I said. And so, to make you understand—oh, Keith, it was awful, but I—I pretended that—"

"You—darling!" breathed an impassioned voice in her ear. "Oh, how I love you, love you—for that!"

"Oh, but, Keith, it really was awful of me," she cried, blushing and laughing, as she emerged from his embrace. "Susan told me to defy the 'properties' and—and I did it."

"Susan!"

She nodded.

"That's how I knew—for sure—that you cared."

"And so I owe it all—even my—er—proposal of marriage, to Susan," he bantered mischievously.

"Keith, I did NOT—er—it was not a proposal of marriage."

"No? But you're going to marry me, aren't you?"

Her chin came up.

"I—I shall wait till I'm asked," she retorted with dignity.

"Hm-m; well, I reckon it's safe to say you'll be asked. And so I owe it all to Susan. Well, it isn't the first good thing I've owed to her—bless her heart! And she's equal to 'most anything. But I'll wager, in this case, that even Susan had some stunt to perform. How did she do it?"

"She told me that you—you thought your father and I cared for each other, and that—that you cared for me; but that you were very brave and were going to go away, and—leave us to our happiness. Then, when she found there was nothing to the other part of it, and that I—I cared for you, she—well, I don't know how she did it, but she said—well, I did it. That's all."

Keith chuckled.

"Exactly! You couldn't have described it better. We've always done what Susan wanted us to, and we never could tell why. We—we just did it. That's all. And, oh, I'm so glad you did this, little girl, so glad!"

"Yes, but—" She drew away from him a little, and her voice became severely accusing. "Keith Burton, you—you should have done it yourself, and you know it."

He shook his head.

"I couldn't." A swift shadow fell like a cloud over his countenance. "Darling, even now—Dorothy, do you fully realize what you are doing? All your life to be tied—"

"Hush!" Her finger was on his lips only to be kissed till she took it away. "I won't let you talk like that a minute—not a single minute! But, Keith, there is something I want you to say." Her voice was half pleading, half whimsical. Her eyes, through her tears, were studying his face, turned partly away from her. "Confession is good for the soul."

"Well? Anything more?" He smiled faintly.

"Yes; only this time it's you. YOU'VE got to do it."

"I?"

"Yes." Her voice rang with firm decision. "Keith, I want to know why—why all this time you've acted so—so that I had to find out through Susan that you—cared. And I want to know—when you stopped hating me. And—"

"Dorothy—I never, never hated you!" cut in the man passionately.

"But you acted as if you did. Why, you—you wouldn't let me come near you, and you were so—angry with me."

"Yes, I—know." The man fell back in his chair and was silent.

There was a long minute of waiting.

"Keith."

"Yes, dear."

"I confessed mine, and yours can't be any harder than—mine was."

Still he hesitated; then, with a long breath he began to speak.

"Dorothy, it—it's just that I've had so much to fight. And—it hasn't been easy. But, listen, dear. I think I've loved you from away back in the days when you wore your hair in two thick pigtails down your back. You know I was only fourteen when—when the shadows began to come. One day, away back then, I saw you shudder once at—blindness. We were talking about old Joe Harrington. And I never forgot it."

"But it was only because I pitied him."

"Yes; but I thought then that it was more aversion. You said you couldn't bear to look at them. And you see I feared, even then, that I was going to be like old Joe some time."

"Oh, Keith!"

"Well, it came. I was like old Joe—blind. And I knew that I was the object of curiosity and pity, and, I believed, aversion, wherever I went. And, oh, I so hated it! I didn't want to be stared at, and pointed out, and pitied. I didn't want to be different. And above all I didn't want to know that you were turning away from me in aversion and disgust."

"Oh, Keith, Keith, as if I ever could!" faltered the girl.

"I thought you could—and would. I used to picture you all in the dark, as I used to see you with your bright eyes and pretty hair, and I could see the look on your face as you turned away shuddering. That's when I determined at all costs to keep out of your sight—until I should be well again. I was going to be well, of course, then, you know. Well, in time I went West, and on the way I met—Miss Stewart."

"Yes." Dorothy's voice was not quite steady.

"I liked Miss Stewart. She was wonderfully good to me. At first—at the very first—she gave me quite a start. Her voice sounded so much like—Dorothy Parkman's. But very soon I forgot that, and just gave myself up to the enjoyment of her companionship. I wasn't afraid with her—that her eyes were turned away in aversion and disgust. Some way, I just knew that she wasn't like—Dorothy Parkman. You see, I hadn't forgotten Dorothy. Some day I was going back to her—seeing.

"Well, you know what happened—the operations, the

specialists, the years of waiting, the trip to London, then home, hopelessly blind. It was not easy then, Dorothy, but—I tried to be a man. Most of all I felt for—dad. He'd had so many hopes—But, never mind; and, anyhow, what Susan said the other day helped—But this has nothing to do with you, dear. To go on: I gave you up then definitely. I know that all the while I'd been having you back in my mind, young as I was—that some day I was going to be big and strong and rich and have my eyes; and that then I was going to ask you to marry me. But when I got home, hopelessly blind, that ended it. I didn't believe you would have me, anyway; but even if you would, I wasn't going to give you the chance of always having to turn away in aversion and disgust from the sight of your husband."

"Oh, Keith, how could you!"

"I couldn't. But you see how I felt. Then, one day I heard Miss Stewart's voice in the hall, and, oh, how good it sounded to me! I think I must have caught her hand very much as the drowning man grasps at the straw. SHE would never turn away from me! With her I felt safe, happy, and at peace. I don't think I exactly understood my state of mind myself. I didn't think I was in love with her, yet with her I was happy, and I was never afraid.

"But I didn't have a chance long to question. Almost at once came the day when Mazie Sanborn ran up the steps and spoke—to you. And I knew. My whole world seemed tumbling to destruction in one blinding crash. You can never know, dear, how utterly dismayed and angry and helpless I felt. All that I knew was that for months and months I had let Dorothy Parkman read to me, play with me, and talk to me—that I had been eager to take all the time she would give me; when all the while she had been doing it out of pity, of course, and I could see just how she must have been shuddering and turning away her eyes all the long, long weeks she had been with me, at different times. But even more than that, if possible, was the chagrin and dismay with which I realized that all the while I had been cheated and deceived and made a fool of, because I was blind, and could not see. I had been tricked into putting myself in such a position."

"No, no! You didn't understand," protested the girl.

"Of course, I didn't understand, dear. Nobody who is blinded with rage and hurt pride can understand—anything, rightly."

"But you wouldn't let me explain afterwards."

"No, I didn't want you to explain. I was too sore, too deeply hurt, too—well, I couldn't. That's all. Besides, I didn't want you to know—how much I was caring about it all. So, a little later, when I did see you, I tried to toss it all off lightly, as of no consequence whatever."

"Well, you—succeeded," commented Dorothy dryly.

"I had to, you see. I had found out then how much I really did care. I knew then that somehow you and Miss Stewart were hopelessly mixed up in my heart, and that I loved you, and that the world without you was going to be one big desert of loneliness and longing. You see, it had not been so hard to give you up in imagination; but when it came to the real thing—"

"But, Keith, why—why did you insist that you must?"

"Do you think I'd ask you or anybody to tie yourself to a helpless creature who would probably finally end up on a street corner with a tin cup for pennies? Besides, in your case, I had not forgotten the shudders and the averted eyes. I still was so sure—

"Then John McGuire came home blind; and after a while I found I could help him. And, Dorothy, then is when I learned that—that perhaps YOU were as happy in doing things for me as I had been in doing them for John McGuire. I sort of forgot the shudders and the averted eyes then. Besides, along about that time we had got back to almost our old friendliness—the friendliness and companionship of Miss Stewart and me. Then the money came and I knew that at least I never should have to ask you to subsist on what the tin cup of pennies could bring! And I had almost begun to—to actually plan, when all of a sudden you stopped coming, right off short."

"But I—I went away," defended the girl, a little faintly.

"Not at once. You were here in town a long time after that. I knew because I used to hear about you. I was sure then that—that you had seen I was caring for you, and so you stayed away. Besides, it came back to me again—my old fear of your pity and aversion, of your eyes turned away. You see, always, dear, that's been a sort of obsession with me, I guess. I hate to feel that any one is looking at me— watching me. To me it seems like spying on me because I—I can't look back. Yes, I know it's all very foolish and very silly; but we are all foolish and silly over something. It's because of that feeling that I—I so hate to enter a room and know that some one is there who won't speak—who tries to cheat me into thinking I am alone. I—I can't bear it, Dorothy. Just because I can't see them—"

"I know, I know," nodded the girl. "Well, in December you went away. Oh, I knew when you went. I knew a lot of things that YOU didn't know I knew. But I was trying all those days to put you quite out of my mind, and I busied myself with John McGuire and told myself that I was satisfied with my work; that I had put you entirely out of my life.

"Then you came back in February, and I knew I hadn't. I knew I loved you more than ever. Just at first, the very first, I thought you had come back to me. Then I saw—that it was dad. After that I tried—oh, you don't know how hard I tried—to kill that wicked love in my heart. Why, darling, nothing would have hired me to let you see it then. Let dad know that his loving you hurt me? Fail dad there, as I had failed him everywhere else? I guess not! This was something I COULD do. I could let him have you, and never, never let him know. So I buried myself in work and tried to—forget.

"Then to-day you came. At the first sound of your voice in there, when I realized what you were saying (to dad, I supposed), I started up and would have gone. Then I was afraid you would see me pass the window, and that it would be worse if I went than if I stayed. Besides, right away I heard words that made me so weak with joy and amazement that my knees bent under me and I had to sit down. And then—but you know the rest, dear."

"Yes, I know the rest; and I'll tell you, some time, why I—I stopped coming last fall."

"All right; but even that doesn't matter to me now; for now, in spite of my blind eyes, the way looks all rosy ahead. Why, dear, it's like the dawn—the dawn of a new day. And I used to so love the dawn! You don't know, but years ago, with dad, I'd go camping in the woods, and sometimes we'd stay all night on the mountain. I loved that, for in the morning we'd watch the sun come up and flood the world with light. And it seemed so wonderful, after the dark! And it's like that with me to-day, dear. It's my dawn—the dawn of a new day. And it's so wonderful—after the dark!"

"Oh, Keith, I'm so glad! And, listen, dear. It's not only dawn for you, but for all those blind boys down there that you are helping. You have opened their eyes to the dawn of THEIR new day. Don't you see?"

Keith drew in his breath with a little catch.

"Have I? Do you think I have? Oh, I should like to think— that. I don't know, of course, about them. But I do know about myself. And I know it's the most wonderful dawn ever was for me. And I know that with your little hand in mine I'll walk fearlessly straight on, with my chin up. And now that I know dad doesn't care, and that he isn't going to be unhappy about my loving you and your loving me, I haven't even that to fear."

"And, oh, Keith, think, think what it would have been if—if I hadn't defied the 'properties,'" she faltered mistily.

"Dear old Susan—bless her heart! And that isn't all I owe her. Something she said the other day made me hope that maybe I hadn't even quite failed—dad. And I so wanted to make good—for dad!"

"And you've done it, Keith."

"But maybe he—he doesn't think so."

"But he does. He told me."

"He TOLD you!"

"Yes—last night. He said that once he had great plans for

you, great ambitions, but that he never dreamed he could be as proud of you as he is right now—what you had done for yourself, and what you were doing for those boys down there."

"Did dad say that?"

"Yes."

"And to think of my having that, and you, too!" breathed the man, his arm tightening about her.

THE END

ABOUT THE AUTHOR

 **Eleanor Hodgman Porter** (December 19, 1868 – May 21, 1920) was an American novelist.

Born in Littleton, New Hampshire, Eleanor Hodgman trained as a singer but later turned to writing. In 1892 she married John Lyman Porter and moved to Massachusetts. Porter mainly wrote children's literature, for example three Miss Billy books, Cross currents [1928], The turn of the tide [1928] and Six Star Ranch [1916].

Her most famous novel is Pollyanna (1913), later followed by a sequel, Pollyanna Grows Up (1915). Her adult novels include The Story of Marco (1920), Just David (1915), The Road to Understanding (1916), Oh Money Money (1917), Dawn (1918), Keith's Dark Tower (1919), Mary Marie (1920), Sister Sue (1921), short stories include Money, Love and Kate (1924) and Little Pardner (1927).

She died in Cambridge, Massachusetts in 1920.

Other books by this author

Just David

Mary Marie

Miss Billy Married

Miss Billy's Decision

Oh, Money! Money!

Pollyanna

Pollyanna Grows Up

Choose from Thousands of 1stWorldLibrary Classics By

A. M. Barnard
Ada Leverson
Adolphus William Ward
Aesop
Agatha Christie
Alexander Aaronsohn
Alexander Kielland
Alexandre Dumas
Alfred Gatty
Alfred Ollivant
Alice Duer Miller
Alice Turner Curtis
Alice Dunbar
Allen Chapman
Alleyne Ireland
Ambrose Bierce
Amelia E. Barr
Amory H. Bradford
Andrew Lang
Andrew McFarland Davis
Andy Adams
Angela Brazil
Anna Alice Chapin
Anna Sewell
Annie Besant
Annie Hamilton Donnell
Annie Payson Call
Annie Roe Carr
Annonaymous
Anton Chekhov
Archibald Lee Fletcher
Arnold Bennett
Arthur C. Benson
Arthur Conan Doyle
Arthur M. Winfield
Arthur Ransome
Arthur Schnitzler
Arthur Train
Atticus
B.H. Baden-Powell
B. M. Bower
B. C. Chatterjee
Baroness Emmuska Orczy
Baroness Orczy
Basil King
Bayard Taylor
Ben Macomber
Bertha Muzzy Bower
Bjornstjerne Bjornson

Booth Tarkington
Boyd Cable
Bram Stoker
C. Collodi
C. E. Orr
C. M. Ingleby
Carolyn Wells
Catherine Parr Traill
Charles A. Eastman
Charles Amory Beach
Charles Dickens
Charles Dudley Warner
Charles Farrar Browne
Charles Ives
Charles Kingsley
Charles Klein
Charles Hanson Towne
Charles Lathrop Pack
Charles Romyn Dake
Charles Whibley
Charles Willing Beale
Charlotte M. Braeme
Charlotte M. Yonge
Charlotte Perkins Stetson
Clair W. Hayes
Clarence Day Jr.
Clarence E. Mulford
Clemence Housman
Confucius
Coningsby Dawson
Cornelis DeWitt Wilcox
Cyril Burleigh
D. H. Lawrence
Daniel Defoe
David Garnett
Dinah Craik
Don Carlos Janes
Donald Keyhoe
Dorothy Kilner
Dougan Clark
Douglas Fairbanks
E. Nesbit
E. P. Roe
E. Phillips Oppenheim
E. S. Brooks
Earl Barnes
Edgar Rice Burroughs
Edith Van Dyne
Edith Wharton

Edward Everett Hale
Edward J. O'Biren
Edward S. Ellis
Edwin L. Arnold
Eleanor Atkins
Eleanor Hallowell Abbott
Eliot Gregory
Elizabeth Gaskell
Elizabeth McCracken
Elizabeth Von Arnim
Ellem Key
Emerson Hough
Emilie F. Carlen
Emily Bronte
Emily Dickinson
Enid Bagnold
Enilor Macartney Lane
Erasmus W. Jones
Ernie Howard Pie
Ethel May Dell
Ethel Turner
Ethel Watts Mumford
Eugene Sue
Eugenie Foa
Eugene Wood
Eustace Hale Ball
Evelyn Everett-green
Everard Cotes
F. H. Cheley
F. J. Cross
F. Marion Crawford
Fannie E. Newberry
Federick Austin Ogg
Ferdinand Ossendowski
Fergus Hume
Florence A. Kilpatrick
Fremont B. Deering
Francis Bacon
Francis Darwin
Frances Hodgson Burnett
Frances Parkinson Keyes
Frank Gee Patchin
Frank Harris
Frank Jewett Mather
Frank L. Packard
Frank V. Webster
Frederic Stewart Isham
Frederick Trevor Hill
Frederick Winslow Taylor

Friedrich Kerst
Friedrich Nietzsche
Fyodor Dostoyevsky
G.A. Henty
G.K. Chesterton
Gabrielle E. Jackson
Garrett P. Serviss
Gaston Leroux
George A. Warren
George Ade
Geroge Bernard Shaw
George Cary Eggleston
George Durston
George Ebers
George Eliot
George Gissing
George MacDonald
George Meredith
George Orwell
George Sylvester Viereck
George Tucker
George W. Cable
George Wharton James
Gertrude Atherton
Gordon Casserly
Grace E. King
Grace Gallatin
Grace Greenwood
Grant Allen
Guillermo A. Sherwell
Gulielma Zollinger
Gustav Flaubert
H. A. Cody
H. B. Irving
H. C. Bailey
H. G. Wells
H. H. Munro
H. Irving Hancock
H. R. Naylor
H. Rider Haggard
H. W. C. Davis
Haldeman Julius
Hall Caine
Hamilton Wright Mabie
Hans Christian Andersen
Harold Avery
Harold McGrath
Harriet Beecher Stowe
Harry Castlemon
Harry Coghill
Harry Houidini

Hayden Carruth
Helent Hunt Jackson
Helen Nicolay
Hendrik Conscience
Hendy David Thoreau
Henri Barbusse
Henrik Ibsen
Henry Adams
Henry Ford
Henry Frost
Henry James
Henry Jones Ford
Henry Seton Merriman
Henry W Longfellow
Herbert A. Giles
Herbert Carter
Herbert N. Casson
Herman Hesse
Hildegard G. Frey
Homer
Honore De Balzac
Horace B. Day
Horace Walpole
Horatio Alger Jr.
Howard Pyle
Howard R. Garis
Hugh Lofting
Hugh Walpole
Humphry Ward
Ian Maclaren
Inez Haynes Gillmore
Irving Bacheller
Isabel Cecilia Williams
Isabel Hornibrook
Israel Abrahams
Ivan Turgenev
J. G.Austin
J. Henri Fabre
J. M. Barrie
J. M. Walsh
J. Macdonald Oxley
J. R. Miller
J. S. Fletcher
J. S. Knowles
J. Storer Clouston
J. W. Duffield
Jack London
Jacob Abbott
James Allen
James Andrews
James Baldwin

James Branch Cabell
James DeMille
James Joyce
James Lane Allen
James Lane Allen
James Oliver Curwood
James Oppenheim
James Otis
James R. Driscoll
Jane Abbott
Jane Austen
Jane L. Stewart
Janet Aldridge
Jens Peter Jacobsen
Jerome K. Jerome
Jessie Graham Flower
John Buchan
John Burroughs
John Cournos
John F. Kennedy
John Gay
John Glasworthy
John Habberton
John Joy Bell
John Kendrick Bangs
John Milton
John Philip Sousa
John Taintor Foote
Jonas Lauritz Idemil Lie
Jonathan Swift
Joseph A. Altsheler
Joseph Carey
Joseph Conrad
Joseph E. Badger Jr
Joseph Hergesheimer
Joseph Jacobs
Jules Vernes
Julian Hawthrone
Julie A Lippmann
Justin Huntly McCarthy
Kakuzo Okakura
Karle Wilson Baker
Kate Chopin
Kenneth Grahame
Kenneth McGaffey
Kate Langley Bosher
Kate Langley Bosher
Katherine Cecil Thurston
Katherine Stokes
L. A. Abbot
L. T. Meade

L. Frank Baum	Owen Johnson	Stephen Crane
Latta Griswold	P.G. Wodehouse	Stewart Edward White
Laura Dent Crane	Paul and Mabel Thorne	Stijn Streuvels
Laura Lee Hope	Paul G. Tomlinson	Swami Abhedananda
Laurence Housman	Paul Severing	Swami Parmananda
Lawrence Beasley	Percy Brebner	T. S. Ackland
Leo Tolstoy	Percy Keese Fitzhugh	T. S. Arthur
Leonid Andreyev	Peter B. Kyne	The Princess Der Ling
Lewis Carroll	Plato	Thomas A. Janvier
Lewis Sperry Chafer	Quincy Allen	Thomas A Kempis
Lilian Bell	R. Derby Holmes	Thomas Anderton
Lloyd Osbourne	R. L. Stevenson	Thomas Bailey Aldrich
Louis Hughes	R. S. Ball	Thomas Bulfinch
Louis Joseph Vance	Rabindranath Tagore	Thomas De Quincey
Louis Tracy	Rahul Alvares	Thomas Dixon
Louisa May Alcott	Ralph Bonehill	Thomas H. Huxley
Lucy Fitch Perkins	Ralph Henry Barbour	Thomas Hardy
Lucy Maud Montgomery	Ralph Victor	Thomas More
Luther Benson	Ralph Waldo Emmerson	Thornton W. Burgess
Lydia Miller Middleton	Rene Descartes	U. S. Grant
Lyndon Orr	Ray Cummings	Upton Sinclair
M. Corvus	Rex Beach	Valentine Williams
M. H. Adams	Rex E. Beach	Various Authors
Margaret E. Sangster	Richard Harding Davis	Vaughan Kester
Margret Howth	Richard Jefferies	Victor Appleton
Margaret Vandercook	Richard Le Gallienne	Victor G. Durham
Margaret W. Hungerford	Robert Barr	Victoria Cross
Margret Penrose	Robert Frost	Virginia Woolf
Maria Edgeworth	Robert Gordon Anderson	Wadsworth Camp
Maria Thompson Daviess	Robert L. Drake	Walter Camp
Mariano Azuela	Robert Lansing	Walter Scott
Marion Polk Angellotti	Robert Lynd	Washington Irving
Mark Overton	Robert Michael Ballantyne	Wilbur Lawton
Mark Twain	Robert W. Chambers	Wilkie Collins
Mary Austin	Rosa Nouchette Carey	Willa Cather
Mary Catherine Crowley	Rudyard Kipling	Willard F. Baker
Mary Cole	Saint Augustine	William Dean Howells
Mary Hastings Bradley	Samuel B. Allison	William le Queux
Mary Roberts Rinehart	Samuel Hopkins Adams	W. Makepeace Thackeray
Mary Rowlandson	Sarah Bernhardt	William W. Walter
M. Wollstonecraft Shelley	Sarah C. Hallowell	William Shakespeare
Maud Lindsay	Selma Lagerlof	Winston Churchill
Max Beerbohm	Sherwood Anderson	Yei Theodora Ozaki
Myra Kelly	Sigmund Freud	Yogi Ramacharaka
Nathaniel Hawthrone	Standish O'Grady	Young E. Allison
Nicolo Machiavelli	Stanley Weyman	Zane Grey
O. F. Walton	Stella Benson	
Oscar Wilde	Stella M. Francis